THE LIFE YOU STOLE

Playlist

"I'll Get You Home"—By The Coast

"Part of Me"—By The Coast

"Ocean"—Lady Antebellum

"Animal"—Troye Sivan

"My Blood"—Twenty One Pilots

"Outnumbered"—Dermot Kennedy

"Cringe"—Matt Maeson

"One Track Mind (feat. A$AP Rocky)"—Thirty Seconds To Mars

"Amsterdam"—Gregory Alan Isakov

"My Way"—Frank Sinatra

"Milestone"—Joey Kidney, Matt Walden

THE LIFE YOU STOLE

Book Two

Jewel E. Ann

Copyright © 2020 by Jewel E. Ann
ISBN: 978-1-7337786-8-8
Print Edition

Cover Designer: Kerry Ellis, Covered by Kerry
Formatting: BB eBooks

CHAPTER ONE

Ronin

T HE VOICE.

A light.

I waited for the end.

Hinder not the soul's intended path unto the light, lest shards of darkness shed upon thee.

When their heart stopped, I was supposed to let them be—like a walking DNR, except EMTs saved lives. We rarely pronounced someone dead in the field. We didn't deal with souls; we dealt with human bodies.

I compressed chests, shocked hearts, and breathed air into lifeless lungs. I did this knowing that less than half of CPR recipients regained a heartbeat, and only ten to twenty percent of those patients lived to be discharged from the hospital. I did it because I made the choice to be a superhero in spite of the risk of suffering eternal death.

The end came for me. My time to die. No more saving lives. An end to perpetual suffering.

Only, no light greeted me.

No voice.

The familiar ringing chimed in my ears, my connection—that energy—I shared with the soul I hindered. The life I saved. The ringing stopped when that person died. But Lila didn't die. That ringing should have stopped when I died.

The feathery pine tree branches framed the patchy, gray clouds. I blinked as those clouds spit droplets of rain onto my face. I wasn't dead.

"Lila …" I whispered, running my fingertips along my neck. It ached, tender to touch. Rolling onto my side, I groaned while climbing to my hands and knees, letting my head hang like a ten-pound bowling ball between my shoulders. I took a few labored breaths of the damp air, thick with musk and pine. And life.

Yes. I was alive.

Glancing up, I scanned the narrow trail for my phone. It taunted me, just feet out of reach. On another groan, I stretched my hand across the wet dirt to grab it and lumbered to my feet.

"Lila …" I wiped my dirty hand on my shirt and tapped her name in my contacts.

After several rings, it jumped to voicemail. Then I tried Graham.

On the second ring, he answered. "Hey, buddy. What's up?"

"Graham, where's Lila?"

"Are you okay? You don't sound so well."

I cleared my throat, trying to steady my breathing. The words flowed on a wave of panic, strained and shaky. "I just …" Closing my eyes, I pinched the bridge of my nose. "Evelyn was trying to reach Lila, but she couldn't, and she was getting worried."

Graham chuckled. "Lila's in the shower. Should I have her call Evelyn when she gets out?"

"Uh … no. It was nothing really. Is she … okay?"

"She's great. Why do you ask? Are you sure you're okay? Is Evelyn okay? The kids?"

"No … I mean, yeah. We're fine. Just, forget I called. Don't worry Lila. It was just Evie being Evie. You know."

"Yeah, I know. She worries about everything, but rightfully so since Madeline died."

"Yes." I ghosted my fingers over my neck. "Sorry to bother you."

"No problem. Give Evie and the kids big hugs from me."

"Will do."

Graham disconnected the call before I could bring the phone away from my ear. How could she be fine? What the fuck happened to me? She was it. She was the life I saved. I felt her and no one else. If that wasn't her, then what was it?

Living Lila. Constant tinnitus. The cloud of eternal death following me everywhere. Talk about un-fucking-familiar territory.

Why did my heart stop after she coded? What did that mean for her? For me? For that little thing I wanted to keep called my sanity?

I thought I knew the rules, but maybe there were no rules to a phenomenon I couldn't explain and a voice I couldn't prove. All signs pointed toward insanity, but I knew I wasn't crazy, even if everything about it felt crazy.

Did that happen? Could I truly not breathe? Or did I feel something that wasn't actually happening to me? But if I felt what Lila felt, and it *was* happening *to* her, it should have been worse for her. It made no sense that I nearly died while she was in the shower and—perfectly fine?

On wobbly legs, I trekked down the trail, the cool air nipping at my sweaty skin. By the time I pushed through the back door, the panic and discomfort subsided. Evie and the kids had already left for the library. After experiencing the scariest, most painful moment of my life, I tore off my clothes and grabbed a shower, trying to make it to my meeting on time. Wiping the condensation-covered mirror, I inspected my neck.

No redness or bruising. Nothing.

Cringing at the residual tenderness, I swallowed past the discomfort like someone had stepped on my neck and crushed my trachea.

"HOW WAS YOUR meeting?" Evie maneuvered Anya's squirmy legs through the holes of the highchair at the restaurant.

Franz crawled into the booth next to me, pulling out library books from his cloth bag and piling them onto the table to show me. I scooted the water glasses away from the books and smiled at my wide-eyed, young boy.

"It was good." I didn't remember anything from the

meeting. When called upon to speak, I had to shake myself out of a daze, and after that, I couldn't recall what incoherent words came out of my mouth.

"Are you okay?" Evie sat on the opposite side of the booth, eyes narrowed as she brought her glass of water to her lips.

"Yeah. Why?"

"You sound off. Like you're down or something. Not your usual jovial self."

"Just tired. The trail kicked my butt today."

"And you got rained on, correct?" She smirked.

"I did," I mumbled, trying to accompany my reply with a smile. She was right. I felt as off as I sounded to her. An impenetrable, invisible wall thwarted my efforts to act fine—a dozen ghosts in a room and only I could see them. They haunted me and only me.

"Well, let's stuff ourselves on pizza, get little princess and Mr. Library Boy down for the night, and then crawl into bed early too."

"I'm not tired," Franz replied, flipping through one of his books.

I forced the fakest-feeling grin, an invisible gun shoved into the back of my head. The fact that it felt forced at all kicked me in the gut. What the hell was wrong with me?

Evelyn saved me by filling the dinner conversation with hopes to drive out to California to visit her dad and sister. I nodded on cue, busying myself by helping Franz with his pizza and holding his drink so he didn't spill it. Anya kept Evelyn distracted which made my lack of engagement a little less noticeable.

After we returned home, I trudged through brushing tiny teeth, corralling wiggly bodies into jammies, and reading library books while Evelyn picked up the mess in the living room and enjoyed a hot shower. By the time she emerged from the steam-filled bathroom, my body hugged the edge of the bed, eyes closed.

"You should have been lazy with me and the kids today." She pressed her naked body to the back of mine, ghosting her lips down my spine as her hand slipped into the front of my briefs.

I swallowed, squeezing my eyes shut tighter as my body stiffened—everything except the part of it that needed to be stiff. Over five years of marriage, forty-one years of life, and *never* did I have issues getting an erection.

Degrading.

Embarrassing.

Emasculating.

Un-fucking-believable.

Forcing myself to relax didn't help. Forced plus relaxed didn't equal erection. They were oxymorons. Evelyn's hand slid back out of my briefs, leaving her body idle next to mine for several minutes—long, excruciating minutes. It felt like someone choking the life out of me all over again, only the invisible force had ahold of my dick instead of my neck, cutting off the circulation. Of course, Evelyn said nothing and did nothing. A regrettable moment that left a permanent mark, the first time her hand held my cock in a limp state. Normally, just her proximity made me hard. She could give me an erection from a smile or the slightest whiff of her flowery scent.

The sway of her hips.

The way her hair brushed along the swell of her breasts.

The purr of my name on her lips.

Literally *anything*.

Until that moment.

No explanation existed. Yet, I had to say something. It fucking killed me. I couldn't blame it on not feeling well, a logical explanation and the closest to the actual truth—or so I thought since I didn't know the true reason. My wellbeing set off all kinds of alarms in Evelyn's head, and rightfully so. That left me with an explanation as lame as my goddamn dick.

"I'm really tired. And I may have strained my groin muscle on the hike."

"Oh … sorry." She kissed my back, letting her warm lips linger between my shoulder blades. "Night."

"Night."

CHAPTER TWO

Evelyn

"The Rockies lost."

I glanced up from the register when Graham waltzed into my shop. He gave the lady sampling some lotion an easy nod. Her blush said she instantly recognized him. How could she not recognize Graham Porter, hands down the most handsome governor of all fifty states? His two guys waited for him by the door as he closed in on me.

"Where's your employee?"

I jerked my head toward the back. "Cleaning my lab."

He smirked. "I love that you call your glorified storage room a lab. It makes you sound like a real scientist."

I narrowed my eyes, imagining all kinds of bodily harm I could do to him, before retreating to the back room with Graham right behind me. "Sophie, can you watch the front while I privately insult the governor?"

Even Sophie showed her lack of immunity to Graham's enigmatic aura. She bit her bottom lip, unable to keep from looking incredibly flirty. "You got it."

After the door shut behind her, I leaned against the counter and crossed my arms over my chest, my usual position when talking to Graham, especially when he seemed to be in an overly self-assured mood. "I didn't watch the Rockies. I also didn't bet on them. Did you fly up here just to talk baseball?"

"Do you remember when I took you to New York for your twenty-seventh birthday?"

I hesitated before giving a single nod. Graham's reminiscing often ended in making me feel bad about myself, bad about him, or epically confused. I wasn't in the mood for any of that. Ronin's intimacy issue from the previous night weighed heavily on my conscience.

Rejected.

I know he didn't mean to make me feel rejected. He couldn't control his inability to get an erection. However, my mind jumped to blaming myself for not being sexy enough, as if that erection or lack thereof measured my sex appeal.

"When we passed that little soap shop in Chelsea, you told me you wanted a bath and body shop. You told me it was your dream, and you didn't care how crazy it sounded since you had a college degree. Then you said the only thing better than owning a shop of your own was not having to worry about debt like your parents worried about it for so long."

Again, I returned a cautious nod, narrowing my eyes a bit. That trip imprinted many great memories into the storybook in my head. Graham treated me like a cherished friend. We ate at the most expensive restaurants, took in a Knicks game with courtside seats, two Broadway shows, and several days of shopping.

"Well, here you go." He reached into the pocket of his light gray suit jacket, pulled out a folded piece of paper, and handed it to me.

"What's this?"

"The deed."

I unfolded it. "To what?" The tiny print of legal jargon made my head ache.

"This building."

"I … I don't understand."

He shrugged. "It's a small building, more of a nuisance than anything. You might as well just take it."

"Graham …" My jaw melted to the floor. "You can't just gift me a building worth *a lot* of money."

"Why not?"

"B—" I choked on my tongue. "Because it's insane!"

"You're my best friend. I want you to have it. Ronin is my friend too. You both deserve to have a life where you don't sweat the little things like … rent."

"Graham … this isn't a deed to my house. This is a building with other businesses paying rent. You're not simply giving me a rent-free space. You're giving me a source of revenue that extends far beyond this shop. I can't accept this." I shoved the piece of paper into his chest.

"Why not?" He took a step back, sliding his hands into his pants pockets to distance himself from the rejected gift.

"Because it's too much."

"I paid thousands of dollars in medical bills for your parents. That wasn't too much?"

I shook my head. "That was different. I would have sold my soul to the Devil to get them the treatment they needed."

He chuckled. "So, I'm the Devil?"

"If the shoe fits."

"Don't be stubborn, Evelyn. This is nothing to me, and you know it. But if anything ever happened to Ronin and you were on your own, this ease of financial burden would mean a whole helluva lot, and you know it."

"Why would you think something is going to happen to Ronin?"

"No." He rolled his eyes. "That's not what I meant. I'm just stating the facts. Things happen. Things we don't expect. Things we can't control. Do you really think I thought my wife would fall off the side of a mountain?"

I flinched, the memories burned like acid slithering up my throat.

"Exactly." He took three steps forward, resting his hands on my cheeks. "Just say 'thank you,' and let's forget about it."

"Thank you," I whispered, suffocating under the weight of his gift but losing my will to fight the senseless battle. Graham mastered manipulation, always getting his way. I knew this would drag on forever if I tried to reject his gift.

He smiled. "See … wasn't that easy?"

I didn't feed his satisfaction by agreeing with him. And he didn't let go of my face. Then it just got awkward.

"Why are you looking at me like that?" I asked with a slight nervous vibrato to my voice.

"Like what?" He rubbed his thumb over my cheek. Graham liked control. It was his favorite game. I liked taking it from him. That was my favorite game. But sometimes it didn't feel like a game.

"Like you should look at Lila … and only Lila."

"Oh, Evelyn …" He leaned down and pressed his lips to my forehead like he'd done a million times before, but it didn't feel like those other million times. "I don't give Lila a look. We communicate in a much more *physical* way."

He bent her over a chair and stuck his dick in her ass on their wedding day, an awful image *still* in my head.

I swallowed.

He smirked.

"How are my babes? Is Franz playing T-ball yet?" Graham let his hands fall from my face, returning them to his pockets.

It took a few seconds to rebound from the whiplash of envisioning Lila and him having sex to Franz playing T-ball. "If you want *babes* to play T-ball, then maybe you should have kids of your own."

He pursed his lips to the side, giving me a slight squint. "Lila is still seeing a physical therapist. I don't think knocking her up is the best idea, but thanks for your concern. We'll keep practicing."

"Why do you treat me like a locker room buddy? Do you really think I want to hear about the details of your sex life with my best friend and hear you use degrading terms like *knocking her up*?"

"Details?" A sly eyebrow quirked up his forehead, conveying too much pleasure in my misstep of words. "I haven't given you any details. Do you want details? I trust you more than anyone you're supposedly referencing as a locker room buddy."

"We love Lila more," I whispered with the reverence and true *love* she deserved.

"Yes!" Graham turned away from me, running his hands through his hair and tugging it, a very uncharacteristic move from my perfectly put-together governor friend. "We love her more. I married her, didn't I?"

I had *no* clue what he meant by that. Did he think marrying her was some sort of sacrifice? I couldn't imagine Ronin talking about me like that, even if he had trouble showing his affection for me the previous night.

That still bothered me. I was sure it ate at his ego, his manhood, but it chipped away at my ego too.

Did he no longer find me attractive?

Did he think of someone else … a perfect match like Va-ness-uh? I *still* thought about her, in weak moments, even though it was many years ago and she moved to Utah the following winter. There would always be another version of her. A good skier. Someone who liked ruffling his hair. Maybe someone who could turn him on, even after a long day and a possible pulled groin.

Fuck … I hated the insecurity. As much as I loved him beyond words, especially those actual words, I wasn't immune to feeling inferior to made-up thoughts in my head. We had the perfect life with our kids, but we didn't always have the perfect marriage.

We experienced rough times, like his opioid addiction. On a few occasions, we argued about money, and he would mention moving to somewhere more affordable, seemingly uncaring that I owned a business in Aspen and lived in the house my grandfather built.

"We would have been disastrous together, right? You wouldn't have given up your job like Lila did to take on the role of the First Lady."

I shook my head. "W-what are you talking about?"

"Had I not chosen Lila … if I would have fought for you … it would have ended in disaster, or I would have had to choose a simpler life—running the family business while you raised the kids."

"Jesus, Graham. Seriously? What the hell are you talking about? Fighting for me. Are you delusional?"

He pulled out his phone, giving his attention to the screen instead of answering me, deep concentration etched into his forehead. "I have to go. My assistant will send you copies of the deed to sign as well as all the rental agreements of the other tenants. She'll also notify them of the transfer of ownership." He grabbed the back of my head, his signature move, and kissed my forehead for a second time. "Say hi to Ronin. Tell him I'll call him about golf next week."

Ronin wasn't going to play golf with Graham, not if I told him about all the things he just said to me, and more specifically, *how* he said them. Then again, that was Graham. That had always been Graham—sweet one moment, like gifting me an entire building, and inappropriate the next moment, eluding to ridiculous what-if's when we were both happily married to other people.

My ability to make sense of it seemed impaired, at best. Lila and I joked about that night in Vancouver, how her tongue ring may or may not have been a little arousing. That didn't mean we planned to cheat on our spouses or do anything inappropriate. Right? That was because we were friends, but so was Graham. We had sex many years earlier. We joked about it. That didn't make it less of a mistake.

The ridiculous what-if road led to a disaster. Lila and I didn't discuss the what-if-we-were-lesbians scenario. We didn't sit around wondering what our lives would be like had we chosen to be together.

Graham left me with the urge to call Lila. It had been several days since I last talked to her. I needed to hear her voice—gauge her happiness.

"Evie," she answered on the third ring.

She made my name sound lifeless.

"Hi. How are you?"

"Fine."

Her "fine" showed no signs of a pulse either.

"What's wrong?" I asked.

"Nothing." She sighed so heavily I swear I could feel her breath through the phone. "Why do you ask?"

"Because you sound like someone died. Did someone die?"

"No. Just a little under the weather. Sore throat. Headache. I probably have something."

"Sorry to hear that. Can I do anything for you?"

Lila attempted a laugh, but it fell flat, more like a grunt. "You're in Aspen. I'm in Denver. I don't think it's worth the drive to bring me chicken noodle soup or something like that. Do you need something?" She got right to the point, no chit-chat.

"No. I was just …" I lost my courage, regretting the phone call. I needed to see her face to truly gauge her mood—her happiness level.

"Just what, Evie?" She sighed again. So many sighs. "Are you okay?"

The truth waited to be set free. I held it between pursed lips for a few seconds. "I'm a little overwhelmed, actually."

"Oh. Why is that?"

Pacing my lab, I ran my fingers across the stainless-steel benches, checking Sophie's thoroughness. "Graham was just here."

"He was?"

"Yes. He didn't tell you he was coming to Aspen to-day?"

"No. But that doesn't mean much. He does his thing. I do mine."

"I can track Ronin with his phone location."

"Ronin isn't governor," she murmured.

I narrowed my eyes, scratching my chin. "What does that matter?"

"Nothing, Evie. So why are you overwhelmed?"

"Graham gave me the building."

"What building?"

"This building. My shop building. He signed over the

deed to me. Did you have anything to do with this?" I knew she didn't, but I needed a way to make her feel like I might expect that generosity from *them,* not just Graham.

"No. I mean … that was really nice of him, and I would have totally agreed with him thinking it's a great thing to do. But he didn't mention it to me."

"It's … incredibly generous of you guys. I'm blown away, and Ronin will be too. I told Graham it's too much. But you know Graham, he likes to look like a hero. Always lavishly generous. You married a good man, Lila." I cringed. Why did I go overboard selling it? Oh, right, I didn't want her to think it was not only extravagant, but inappropriate—like the way he looked at me, the way he touched my face, and the way his lips lingered on my forehead a few seconds past friendship status.

The Porter curse started to catch up with me, a little dog nipping at my ankles. Feeling indebted to them— owned by them—haunted my conscience. I honestly wasn't sure I could have said no. When Graham set out to do something, he didn't stop until he found success. Lila marrying him was the perfect example.

"I think it's great." Her somber tone didn't sell the word *great.* "You're family to us. A true sister to him. Family takes care of each other."

If only he looked at me like a sister, but he didn't. I felt ninety percent sure of that. The ten percent doubt kept me from confronting him or telling Ronin.

No amount of certainty would convince me to tell Lila. It would forever change our friendship. I couldn't take that risk. I'd let their marriage fall apart before I'd let anything touch our friendship.

"Yes. We are family." *That* was the truth. Lila and I were family. I no longer knew where Graham fit on the family tree. "And family takes care of each other." I needed to remember that. I needed to take care of Lila. "Let's do lunch. I can drive down on Wednesday. Ronin has the afternoon off, so he can watch the kiddos."

"Um … sure. Let me check with Graham."

"He's your husband, not your guardian. Why would you need to check with him?"

"Sometimes he makes plans for us."

"Without *checking* with you first?"

"Yes, Evie. If you have a problem with it, you'll have to take it up with Graham. I'm sure it will go over real well given the fact that he just gifted you an entire building."

Closing my eyes, I let out a long breath. I knew why I felt eternally indebted to Graham. I just didn't know why Lila did. Scores weren't supposed to be kept in marriages. Husbands weren't supposed to reign over their wives.

CHAPTER THREE

A MILE OF windy road away from home, my Jeep
veered off onto an empty gravel trailhead. Before
turning off the ignition, a couple and their dog walked
past my door, the lady tossing me a smile as she tightened
her ponytail. Then the trees swallowed them up, leaving
me alone. I cradled my phone in my hands, letting my
thumb hover over my mom's name in my contacts.

Graham crossed a line. Lila wasn't herself. And Ronin
felt a million miles away after the previous night. I needed
someone.

If Ronin could speak of voices in his head, I could call
my dead mother. The sound of her voice on the recorded
message burned my eyes with hot tears. My hand
clenched the phone tighter, as if I could hold her words
and pull her back into my life. All this time I had a piece
of her lingering in my life. How did I not think to
question if my father had disconnected their phone?

*You've reached Corey and Madeline. We're too lazy to
answer your call. Please leave a message.*

Just before it clicked over to record the message, she
giggled. My dad must have made her laugh before she

ended the recording. I'd never know if he loved Mom like he loved his first love. Their house in Denver sat idle and untouched with the exception of his single bag of clothes that he took to California. That meant something. It meant he wasn't ready to say goodbye. That kind of denial only existed in the depths of a shattered heart.

"Hey, Mom ..."

I blinked, unleashing months of pain. Who was I to judge denial? I hadn't been to their house since the day of her funeral. Mom lived in those walls—every picture on the mantel, every fringed pillow on the navy crushed velvet sofa, and the baskets filled with quilts stitched by her hands, petite and perfectly suited to thread needles, decorate birthday cakes, and wipe tears. I missed those loving hands.

"You left quite the void." I laughed, swiping my fingers across my wet cheeks. "Franz still asks about you. I told him you had to leave this life for something new, but part of you lives in the things you loved most, like the birds that gathered at the feeders in your backyard. Now, whenever he sees a bird, he says, 'There's grandma.' It's beautiful ... and completely heartbreaking."

The fragility of my existence vibrated through every cell in my body. The perfect life existed on a narrow ledge with a sea of tragedy awaiting ten stories down on the other side. It was surprising how much strength the human body possessed, yet a single misstep left you free falling to unforgiving waves of despair ready to crush your existence.

A few too many cancer cells.

The slip off the edge of a mountain.

A tiny finger reaching for an exposed wire.

"That says so much, doesn't it? I guess we can only hope our lives mean enough to leave an un-fillable void, proof that we're part of something greater than a singular entity. Did you know that your love was my happiness, your strength was my success, but your willingness to let go … well, it's become my greatest hope. Hope that this isn't everything."

Leaning my head back against the headrest, I closed my eyes where Mom resided in my memory. The smile she gave me when my dad rolled his eyes at my decision to open a bath shop.

Evelyn, I'm proud of you … always.

I knew I would always love Franz and Anya that way. Everyone needed someone in their life who was just so damn happy to be part of their existence that absolutely nothing else mattered. A mother's love should be every-thing—*always*. A love that transcends time. Still, I felt her love. *Always*, I would feel her love.

"Uncle Josh moved grandma to Florida last week. She's been quiet and a little confused since you died. I'm glad she'll be closer to family since I don't get to Denver that much, especially come winter."

I missed her so much. The pain felt like a new organ in my body with its own pulse. Or maybe that part of my heart broke free and would forever throb, reminding me of what I lost. Disconnecting the call, I dialed the number again, just to hear her voice. Before it went to voicemail, I pressed *End* and called her another time.

Repeat.

Repeat.

Repeat.

You've reached Corey and Madeline. We're too lazy to answer your call. Please leave a message.

"I miss you, Mom."

"HEY, SUE." I toed off my shoes as Anya ran toward me. "I'm sorry. I made a quick stop, but I assumed Ronin would have been here." Anya stretched her arms up to me and I picked her up. "Hey, sweetie." She smelled like lavender, just like Sue.

"Ronin called and said he was meeting some friends for dinner. He said he messaged you."

I frowned, releasing squirmy Anya to her feet again while fishing my phone from my pocket. Sure enough, Ronin left a message. I must have missed it while repeatedly calling my mom's phone.

Ronin: Having dinner with Noah.

"Huh. I missed his message. Again, I'm sorry. I should have come straight home."

"Don't apologize." Sue waved me off as she tiptoed down the hallway. "Boo!" Peeking her head around the corner to Franz's room, she grinned. "Your mom is home. I'll see you tomorrow."

"Bye," he said.

Anya rolled around on the floor, wrapping herself up

in a small blanket like a burrito. Toys littered the floor, books covered the sofa, and dishes awaited washing. Just how I liked it. That meant Sue spent the day playing with the kids. Usually, Ronin and I would work together to make dinner and piece back together the house.

Not that night.

"You've been crying." She tilted her head to the side, eyes squinted as she threaded her arms through her cardigan. Sue always wore a cardigan, even in the summer.

On a shrug, I returned a half smile.

Sue reached for my hand, giving it a squeeze. "It's a lot—raising a family, working full-time, nourishing a marriage, and trying to deal with grief when it feels eternal."

Trapping my lower lip between my teeth, I nodded. Her words could have been my words. More than that, they could have been my mom's words. We guard ourselves from negativity and hate, yet kindness and empathy pack the biggest punch because they expose our vulnerability.

"Is there anything I can do?"

"No—" I cleared the frog from my throat. "No. Thank you, though. Your words helped."

Sue released my hand and chuckled. "I'm not sure about that. But if you say so." She slipped on her shoes.

"They reminded me that it's okay to *feel*. Since feelings get in the way sometimes, it's easy to suppress them as a means to get through the day. Go to work. Be a mom. I was late getting home because I pulled off along the side of the road and let myself feel for a few minutes."

Another sad expression stole Sue's face. How could it not? I had to pull off the road to cry and miss my mom without wearing that stupid I'm-okay mask. Even if I didn't degrade myself and call it pathetic, it was, at the very least, really sad.

"I'm good now." I smiled at Franz waltzing toward me, holding a new Lego creation, a shark of some sort.

"Okay. Goodnight, then."

Sue left me in the middle of a mess with my two favorite people on Earth. "That's an amazing shark." I squatted next to him.

"It's a swordfish, Mommy. Not a shark." He handed it to me, wearing a contagious grin.

"Silly me." After inspecting it, I handed it back to him.

He ran back to his room, and I crawled toward Anya. She giggled as I nuzzled my face into the top of the blanket to find her, kissing her cheeks and neck.

"What do you say…" I eased onto my side and hugged her to me "…we go get pizza since Daddy is having dinner with Noah."

"Yes!" Franz yelled from his room as Anya gave me her own version of excitement with a "Yes!" She mastered mimicking her big brother.

Turning a blind eye to the messy house, we piled into the Jeep and drove to our favorite pizza joint. The waitress ushered us to a booth toward the back corner of the restaurant.

"Daddy!" Franz made a beeline to the opposite side of

the restaurant to a booth by a window next to the outdoor patio.

My heart stopped. As sure as Lila's heart stopped that day on the mountain and Ronin's did too, my heart stopped when I watched Franz crawl into the booth next to Ronin because Noah was not the person on the opposite side. Noah didn't have chin-length black hair, and he didn't wear red lipstick. He didn't have a petite body with ample cleavage.

"I'll set your menus at the far booth," the waitress said. "I'll get your drink orders when you're ready."

I didn't respond. I couldn't respond. My body remained still, like my heart and my lungs, in the middle of the restaurant. As Anya tried to wriggle out of my arms, I blinked and my heart restarted with a faint beat. Ronin kissed Franz's head, wearing a pensive expression—a guilty expression.

No one ever imagines their life ending on a Monday night in the middle of a pizza joint, yet there I was, watching my life fall apart with my kids oblivious to the destruction. To keep from dropping Anya in her attempt to follow her brother, I tightened my grip and forced my numb body to cross the restaurant.

Did he see it?

The betrayal.

The anger.

The complete destruction.

I never … ever imagined Ronin having an affair. And I certainly never imagined finding out in a restaurant with our two kids.

"You should have told me you were thinking pizza tonight," Ronin said, eyeing me like a cop eyed a criminal holding a gun.

"I made a swordfish, Daddy!" Franz had no clue.

I couldn't look at Ronin, not for one more second. My gaze shifted to the woman in the seat across from him.

"Adrianne, this is my wife, Evelyn." His voice shook.

It. Fucking. Shook.

"Evelyn, this is Adrianne. She's a friend from, um …"

A slight wrinkle formed along Adrianne's forehead as her brown eyes flitted to my bumbling husband. God! She looked twenty-five.

"Nice to meet—"

"Franz," I cut off Adrianne, "the waitress is waiting to take our order. Let's go." I fought Anya's efforts to escape from my hold while grabbing Franz's hand.

"Noah just left. He'll be disappointed he missed seeing you guys," Ronin's lies fell on deaf ears as I dragged my kids to the booth.

"I want to sit by Daddy."

"Franz, Daddy is done eating. You can see him later."

Two glasses. There were two glasses at his table.

Two.

Two glasses.

Two plates.

One empty pizza pan.

Noah would have made three.

On some sort of super mommy autopilot, I ordered our pizza and drinks. I stiffened, as Ronin approached our

26

table in my peripheral vision.

He bent over and kissed Anya's head as she played in the highchair with crayons and a coloring sheet. "Listen, before you guys arrived, I offered to give Adrianne a ride home. She lives about two miles from here, and it's dark. But I can tell her I can't if—"

"You should give her a ride home." I stared at my water, jaw set. If I looked at him, he would know how much he just destroyed my world. And I didn't want him to see that in front of the kids.

Without another word, he weaved his way toward the exit.

I didn't eat a bite of pizza or take a single sip of water. Mommy super autopilot fed my kids, wiped faces, and paid the bill.

"Daddy!" Franz broke free from my hand the second he saw Ronin leaning against the front of the Jeep.

I unlocked the doors as if he wasn't there. When he tried to take Anya from me, I jerked my torso.

"Evie ..."

I fastened her into her seat while Ronin made sure Franz was secured in his seat.

"Move," I said, staring at his black boots. His jeans and T-shirt-clad body rested against the driver's door, hands tucked into his front pockets.

"I'm driving you home."

I didn't give a shit to the whereabouts of his car. All I knew was I didn't want him driving me home. Looking at me. Talking to me. Anything ... I didn't want anything he had to offer at that moment.

"Evie ... don't let your mind go there. It's not what you think."

"What I think is I need to get the kids to bed. I have a messy house to pick up. I need a shower. Get the fuck out of my way!"

I hoped Franz couldn't hear us. My barely restrained anger threw out the F-bomb, and I instantly regretted it. Ronin grabbed my wrist and pried the key from my hand. Had the kids not been there, I would have walked home or taken a cab.

We drove home in silence. The late dinner put the kids to sleep before we pulled into the garage. Ronin shut off the ignition and reached for my hand. I jerked it away from him and climbed out of the Jeep.

Everything felt numb except my heart. It hurt.

This happened to other people not me. Ronin loved me. Was love no longer enough?

We carried the kids into the house where we pushed their half-awake little bodies through an abbreviated nighttime routine. After we closed their doors most of the way, I took three steps toward the messy kitchen before pivoting on my heels. Ronin stopped the second I turned toward him.

"How could you?" I whispered on a breath that felt like my very last one.

Ronin deflated with a wince, slowly shaking his head. "Evie ..."

"Last night ..." I couldn't even say it. In my heart, I knew it wasn't me the previous night. Even if I felt a little rejected. But seeing him with that woman left me without any words to express my true feelings.

"Evie, it wasn't you."

"It felt like—"

He pressed his finger to his lips as my words gained strength. Before I could risk another word waking the kids, Ronin brushed past me, right out the front door. I followed him. We didn't fight often, but when we did, it was outside while the kids slept.

"You're not this stupid." The second I shut the door behind me, he had my face cradled in his hands. His words sharp. His grip tight. "I'm not cheating on you."

I clawed at him, trying to free myself. "Let go of me!"

He released me, planting his hands on his hips, head down.

"You said Noah. Dinner with Noah." I crossed my arms over my chest to protect my heart, but it was too late. Ronin already stabbed it with a guilty look and a dinner date ready to suck his dick.

"I *did* have dinner with Noah. Just as we finished eating, Adrianne walked past the booth. Noah had to get home. Adrianne sat down, and we just got to talking. Then you showed up with the kids. That's it."

I paused my tapping foot. On a laugh I shook my head. "No. That's not it because you haven't told me who the hell Adrianne is. All I know is when you looked at me in the restaurant all I could see was this pale, guilt-ridden expression on your face. Then you introduced me to this *young,* beautiful woman. And I swear … I swear to god, Ronin, she had the same look on her face. You both looked like you got caught! Caught by your wife. Caught

29

by your kids!"

"This is about last night. There's no way you would jump to cheating had I not had … *issues* last night. You're taking it personally. And it wasn't personal."

"Stop deflecting! You had the opportunity in the restaurant. You had that opportunity in the car. In the house. And the second we stepped outside here … and you still haven't told me who the hell that woman was!"

"Evie—"

"Nope." I returned a sharp headshake before he could say another word. "Try again."

He sighed. So much pain radiated from every inch of him. Too bad. I hurt more.

"Did you fuck her?"

"I'm not even justifying that with an answer."

Yes. The answer was yes. I wasn't sure what hurt the most—the betrayal or his inability to say the words.

"I …" Everything died in my chest.

I love you.

It was too late. I wouldn't beg.

Wiping the tears that showed up in place of those three words, I shrugged. "You're wrong. I *am* stupid. And I'm tired. I'm hurt beyond words. So if you can't answer me, then five years of marriage and two children clearly don't mean anything to you." I reached for the door handle.

"Everything," he whispered. "Five years with you and our two children mean *everything* to me."

I rested my forehead against the door and closed my eyes.

"Yesterday, on my hike, something happened. It felt like someone was strangling me. I couldn't breathe. My life played before me like this farewell reel. You ... Franz and Anya. It just seemed like my luck had ended. Then I realized it must have been Lila. Someone was strangling Lila. But then it just ... stopped. And I could breathe again. I called Lila, but she didn't answer. So I called Graham. He said she was taking a shower. He confirmed she was fine."

"Why didn't you tell me?" I whispered beneath the heavy weight of his confession. My forehead remained pressed to the door. Something in my heart wouldn't let me turn to look at him. Not yet. Not with the image of that woman still in my head.

"Because it really fucking scared me, which meant I couldn't tell you with any sort of certainty that everything would be fine. And I refused to put that on you ... not when I know damn well you're still grieving the loss of your mom, when you *still* look at me with a glitch of distrust in your eyes because I tried to blow up our marriage with a bottle of pills."

I just ... I wanted my mom. I *needed* my mom.

"The woman in the restaurant." I squeezed my eyes shut tighter, but her guilty face looking at his guilty face still haunted me. "If you don't tell me about her, I will go insane thinking only one thing. *She* is the reason you didn't want me last night."

"No!" He grabbed my arms and forced me to face him. "You don't get to say that. Not *ever*. It's not that I didn't want you. I just couldn't have you in that way because something happened yesterday, and I don't know why. I felt broken. *Broken.* Like nothing in my body worked right. Feelings of despair and hopelessness enveloped me, and I couldn't shake it. I couldn't will it away. And it scared me."

I understood broken. I understood despair and hopelessness. Ronin telling me everything but the one thing I needed to know continued to feed my despair and hopelessness … it continued to break me, break *us*.

"The woman," I whispered.

He closed his eyes for a few seconds. "I had dinner with Noah. He had to leave. She walked by my booth and sat down to talk. She is in my support group. Yesterday, I wasn't myself after the incident on my hike. Adrianne noticed. So when she saw me tonight, she took the opportunity to ask me if I was okay. The guilt you thought you saw on our faces wasn't guilt. It was nerves. We were nervous you would recognize her."

"Why would I recognize her?"

"Because she's Adrianne Craig."

Blinking several times, I let her name swirl around in my head, looking for recognition. When the switch flipped, I felt no relief, just more despair.

Adrianne Craig was a home-wrecker for hire. She destroyed many marriages by secretly videotaping sex acts with wealthy men. Sometimes angry wives hired her. Sometimes other wealthy men hired her to bring down their business competition. I wouldn't have recognized her because she consistently changed her appearance to keep her "business" thriving. Supposedly she quit for unknown reasons. Graham told me she tried and failed to scheme his father. He also told me she didn't just do the job for the money; she did it to prove a point—no man was perfect. She enjoyed ruining marriages the way Graham and I enjoyed betting on sports.

"That's …" I inched my head side to side, wiping my tear-stained cheeks. "That's fantastic. I thought you were cheating on me. Instead, you've simply befriended a woman who seduces men just to prove she can. I feel much better. What is her addiction? Sex? Sadism?"

"Heroine. And befriending someone isn't the same as having sex with them."

"Does *she* know that?"

"Evelyn …" He frowned.

"Ronin, what are we if you can't tell me that you had something happen to you that was so frightening you thought you were dying … that you thought Lila was dying? What are we if you allow a woman with a reputation like Adrianne's to sit next to you in public where people you know, people I know, could see you?"

What are we if Graham touches me inappropriately and gifts me something like a whole damn building and I don't tell my husband?

"I can't always protect you with the truth." He slid his hand behind my head and brushed his lips along my cheek.

"You can't always save me with a lie," I whispered. "Save *us* …"

"We don't have to be perfect to be forever." His other hand slid up my neck, the pad of his thumb tracing the line of my jaw.

"Roe, I'm scared."

His lips brushed mine. "Me too, Evie. Me too …"

I wasn't sure why Ronin's vulnerability made me feel safe. Maybe in our imperfect world, where the truth sometimes felt like a weapon and a well-intended lie served as the strongest shield, vulnerability was the unspoken promise that *together* we would survive the war.

"I need to pick up the toys," I breathed the words against his lips.

"Yes," he whispered back to me.

The hand behind my head moved to my breast, cupping it so gently it elicited a painful ache.

"And clean the kitchen …" My breaths shortened, filling the air between us with unspoken needs that didn't involve the kids' toys and dirty dishes.

"Yes," he repeated. Our lips touching, but not kissing.

His hand fell from my breast, tracing the contour of my stomach and the curve of my hip before sliding down the front of my shorts. I drank his breaths and he drank mine, my eyes fluttering shut as he slowly … gently … dragged his fingers across the delicate fabric of my panties—every touch wordlessly asking for permission, as if he hadn't ever touched me there before.

After a few seconds, I swallowed my fear and let my fingers brush the soft denim, inch by inch making their way to his erection, pressed hard to the zipper of his jeans. My thumb outlined it, circling its head several times. Ronin's chest expanded with a deep breath.

We weren't a troubled married couple with two

young kids on the other side of that door. There was no room for more truths or lies.

Not a breath for words.

Not an inch to move.

Not a thought to consider.

Just a bubble encasing a man and a woman.

Just one touch chasing another.

Just a single need.

Our mouths fused together, sending each hard breath through our noses. The kiss demanding, but our hands remained gentle, patiently waiting. It hurt too much to sort through the rubble of thoughts in my head, so I just kissed Ronin.

And he kissed me.

He slid his hand from my pants, and I tugged open the button to his jeans as the momentum—the need—spread from our kiss, down our bodies, like relentless waves thrashing in a storm. Ronin's gaze met mine as he lowered his body, peeling my shorts and panties down my legs.

I love you.

I love you too.

The words were there, swirling like the invisible wind. They were *always* there.

For every night of kids in our bed, pain-driven wedges between us, sickness, and sadness ... we claimed one moment for ourselves again. A moment that didn't care about the flash of headlights from the road beyond the curtain of trees. A moment that didn't care about the chill of the door at my back. An imperfect moment in our forever.

With half of my clothes discarded on the porch's wood floor and Ronin's jeans and briefs slid partway down his thighs, we fucked.

We laid down our weapons.

We made love.

And I knew in that moment that it wasn't just Franz and Anya that I would protect with my life. It was Ronin too. He didn't share my DNA, but he shared my soul.

I would fight for him.

And he would fight for me.

There would be truths.

There would be lies.

Never perfect—always forever.

CHAPTER FOUR

"**Y**OU LOOK GOOD." Lila hugged me.
I smiled.

Thoughts of Ronin over the previous twenty-four hours spread like warm rays of sunshine across my chest. I married a great man. A wonderful father. A faithful friend. After we made up on the porch in the wake of our near falling-out, he helped me clean the kitchen and living room. We showered together. And I fell asleep, hugging his chest, while he read a book under the soft glow of his reading light. By morning we were four in bed. Crowded, yet happily content.

"You look too formal for lunch with me in my jeans and a tee." I laughed as she released me.

"I have a meeting after lunch with teachers from the NEA." She strutted in her high heels toward the formal dining room, showing off her full recovery from the accident.

"Well, your little business suit and silk neck scarf make you look like a flight attendant for British Airways." My flip-flop-clad feet followed the click of her Manolo Blahniks.

"Graham bought it for me."

"Graham bought you something that's not lingerie?"

"Yes. What were the chances, right?" She took a seat at the long table that accommodated twenty.

I sat across from her, feeling way too underdressed for lunch—a lunch I imagined being a simple sandwich and iced tea.

"Are you good? I mean … for real good? I know you have stress with the whole politics part of your life, and there's nothing you can do to change that as long as he's governor. But beyond that, are things good?"

Lila sipped her water, gently setting the crystal stemmed glass back on the table. "I don't like you worrying about me. It hasn't been that long since your mom died."

"Yes. But I do worry about you, even if … to be completely honest, I need a break from worrying about you, my dad, Ronin …"

Her eyebrows furrowed. The thick eyeliner and heavy fake lashes made her eyes look completely black. "Why do you worry about Ronin?"

My husband was right: sometimes we hid the truth to save people from pain. Was it right? I didn't know that answer. Very few things in life held black and white absolution. I never told Lila about Ronin—not his connection to her since the accident and not his opioid addiction. It killed me to hide some of the darkest times of my life from my best friend. I did it to protect her.

What would she have been able to do with that information? Knowing he shared her pain would have only made her pain worse. Knowing that her pain caused his addiction—*especially* after losing someone she loved to addiction—would have destroyed her. I did the only thing I could … I raised my shield of lies to protect her from the truth.

But she was better. Her pain was gone. Maybe I could let go … let her be a friend to me again like I had been to her for so many months.

"Before I say anything, I need to know—and I need you to be honest—are you okay?"

Lila remained stone still for several seconds, completely unblinking. Then she straightened her back and made a slight adjustment to the silk scarf around her neck while clearing her throat. "Yes. I'm okay, Evie. I am your friend. I am here for you."

I looked for the truth in her eyes, but all that gray hid the truth. After so much tragedy, I couldn't see what was right in front of me. Grief and pain left me blind to everything I thought I knew. Ronin was right. Relationships could be perfect, or they could be forever, but they couldn't be both.

"I would never share this with Graham. I never told my mom. And I'm only telling you because I trust you with my life."

Lila nodded slowly. The unspoken reminder of her loose tongue at my fortieth birthday party passed between us. I saw it on her face, that flinch of regret, and I hoped she saw the sincere forgiveness in my eyes.

"The accident Ronin had when he was a child, the electrocution?"

She nodded. We'd spoken of it only briefly.

"He had a near-death experience …"

I proceeded to tell her everything—the trips to the hospital, the inability of doctors to figure it out, his visit with a parapsychologist, even the opioid addiction.

She gasped, flinched, reached for my hand, and cried. I reassured her nothing was her fault. Everything was an accident. A very misfortunate string of circumstances.

"You believe him?" she asked. Her blank stare fixed on the partially eaten plate of food in front of her.

I poked with a fork at the remnants on my own plate. "Yes. He just … he knew too much about your pain. But then …" I shook my head.

"Then what?"

Setting my fork aside, I dabbed my mouth with the white cloth napkin. "Over the weekend, he went for a hike and this feeling of being strangled stopped him in his tracks. He thought he was dying. I think he even started to black out. I'm not entirely sure. But then it stopped. He tried calling you. Did you know that?"

Lila pulled up her sleeve and glanced at her watch. "I'm so sorry." Her voice shook a bit—or so I thought. Again, another shade of gray I couldn't decipher. "I'm out of time. I have to leave in a few minutes to get to the meeting. Can I walk you out?"

I twisted my wrist to check the time. "Shit. I'm sorry." We had talked for over two hours. "I need to head back home too. Sue has a class tonight. She teaches painting at one of those wine and art places groups of friends drink and paint." I stood as Lila stood. "Thank you. I can't even begin to tell you how badly I needed to share all of this with you. I just hope you know it's not your fault in any way, and Ronin is fine."

Well, he was sort of fine. I hadn't totally wrapped my head around the strangling sensation he had over the weekend. Adrianne Craig distracted me from that. I didn't tell Lila about Adrianne. Too much truth for one day.

"Thank you for opening up to me." She hugged me. "I really wish you would have told me this a long time ago."

"You know why I didn't." I stepped back, taking both of her hands and giving them a firm squeeze.

She returned a sad smile and several tiny nods.

"Let's do a couples' thing sometime. I'm anxious to put all of this behind us." That was true. I was also anxious to see how Graham and Lila interacted. It had been a while since I'd seen them together. I also needed Lila to prove to me that she could keep everything I told her a secret.

"A couples' thing." Her lips pulled into a firm smile as she gave the tails to her scarf a little tug to tighten the knot. "I'll mention it to Graham when he gets home."

"Will he be gone long?" I asked, making my way to the foyer.

"No. Actually, he returns tonight. It was just a one-day trip."

"Perfect. Let me know what he says." I opened the door. "Love you, Lila."

"I love you too." She stepped just outside the door

and watched me until I got into my Jeep. Then she lifted her hand in a tiny wave before I pulled out of the circle drive toward the gated entrance to the estate.

I felt like the world had been lifted from my shoulders ... or at least five of the continents and an ocean or two.

Lila

TEN SECONDS AFTER Evelyn headed back to Aspen, a car picked me up to take me to my afternoon meeting. Following the meeting, the car returned me to the Porter estate, where I shared one of three sprawling mansions on the million acres of land. It *felt* like a million acres. A million acres of freedom that turned into a million acres of prison.

What happened to my life? My marriage? My husband? As much as I loved Graham, I hated our new life and the duties it bestowed upon us. I hated Governor Porter, but I still loved the man who swept me off my feet. In spite of everything, I found myself searching for the tiniest of reasons to excuse his behavior—his cold demeanor that he blamed on the stress of the job mixed with the expectations of his family.

Some days I felt the pressure of the vise wrapped around his life. Those were the easy days, the days I bent over backward to please him ... to make his life a little easier. Other days ... well, I didn't even know that man who wore the platinum band I slid onto his finger five years earlier. Life changed us. It weathered us. It tested our resilience and our humanity.

I was due for my annual physical, but I couldn't go. Not yet. Instead, I settled into my oversized leather chair in the corner of the bedroom—my bedroom—and opened my laptop in search of explanations.

Conditions that cause bruising.
Unexplained bruising.
Blood disorders.
Clotting disorders.

I searched and searched until I found the only logical answer. Tears filled my eyes. I hoped I would never have to tell Evelyn, but I knew I might. So I had to be prepared, armed with knowledge and the ability to give her hope that I would be okay.

"I have leukemia," I whispered to myself, wiping away my tears. Then I proceeded to learn all I could about this cancer, a cancer that was rarer in forty-somethings, but not impossible.

Easy bleeding.
Bruising.
Weight loss.
Persistent fatigue.
Fever and chills.

"You're not ready for bed."

I jumped, shutting my computer, and glanced up at Graham paused at the threshold to my room, loosening his red tie. He always looked handsome in a suit and that red tie I gave him for his birthday. I didn't expect to see him. My assistant said he was at the Governor's Mansion. I rarely stayed there, but he used it as an occasional "getaway." Probably from me. So when she told me he was there, I made the assumption (actually hoped) he'd decided to stay the night and get some work done.

"It's not even seven." I tucked my bare feet beneath me, still wearing my navy skirt suit and silk scarf—my long hair in loose curls down my back and around my shoulders just like Graham liked it.

He took calculated steps toward me, completely untying his tie, letting it drop to the floor before working the buttons to his starchy white shirt. I tried to forget my internet search, not that it mattered because I couldn't hide anything from my husband. He elicited a warring of emotions from me. An icy tingle slithered along my spine, making every muscle rigid, while the warmth in my heart fed on the way my pulse reacted to his proximity, the way it always had done. That never changed. It was how I knew we weren't broken.

"Did you miss me?" He smirked, shrugging off his shirt, revealing his defined torso—abs for days beneath a thin smattering of dark hair on his chest.

I was the envy of so many women. Every day I reminded myself of that.

"Nice scarf." He knelt in front of the chair.

I returned a nervous smile, hoping the man before me was the man I loved. Graham untied the scarf, sliding it from my neck as slowly as he'd slid off his tie just seconds earlier. The scarf floated to the floor. Gentle fingers swept my hair off my shoulders, exposing my neck.

With the same feather's touch, he traced the bruises. "It's nothing ..." His lips replaced his fingers, kissing my neck. "You're fine. Right?"

I wanted to believe him. Could denial become truth if we just believed hard enough?

"I'm fine," I murmured, closing my eyes.

"Want me to show you how much I missed you?" he whispered next to my ear.

Was he asking me for permission? Governor Graham demanded me. Pre-marriage, pre-Governor Graham asked ... begged me to surrender to him. I no longer cared about the bruises. I wanted that Graham. Maybe it was naive of me to think the bruises were an accident, an isolated incident, but I needed to cling to even the tiniest shred of hope.

"Yes." I threaded my fingers through his dark hair, ridding it of its orderly confines. I wanted messy, desperate Graham.

He removed my jacket and blouse. A low growl rattled his chest when he saw my light pink lace bra. His favorite.

"Take it off," he ordered.

I swallowed my fear, convinced that I held a bit of control in that moment. I *needed* to know I still had some control. "You take it off."

Graham arched a single eyebrow, but I couldn't tell if it was playful or scornful. That had become a hard read for me. A hard line of sorts. When he didn't say anything, that icy feeling along my spine overtook the warmth in my chest.

"I …" I cleared the nerves from my voice with a tiny cough. "I had lunch with Evelyn." There was no good reason for me to say that to Graham, except he seemed to relax whenever we talked about Evelyn.

His arched eyebrow disappeared as I'd hoped it would. "How is Evelyn?" He reached behind me and yanked the straps to my bra. I knew the hooks had to be broken or bent.

I swallowed hard. "Good," I whispered, trying to keep from showing my concern.

"I like good." He didn't touch my breasts. He just … inspected them with a tiny frown before lifting his dark eyes to meet mine. "On your knees, facing the back of the chair."

I rubbed my lips together, the lower one quivered a bit, so I bit it, shrinking under his scrutinizing gaze. Shifting my body, I knelt on the chair, pressing my breasts against the soft leather as my hands gripped the back of the chair.

Graham worked my tight skirt up my hips. "What was Evelyn wearing today?"

I narrowed my eyes, not daring a glance back at him. "W-why are you asking me that?"

He fisted the back of my thong and ripped it into two pieces. I flinched; it wasn't the first time he'd destroyed my panties. It was just the first time he did it while asking me about Evelyn.

"She's always wearing shitty clothes that barely match. I just wondered how terrible she looked compared to my beautiful wife today."

"Ung!" I bit the back of the chair as he shoved three fingers, which felt like his whole damn hand, into my vagina.

"Jeans?"

"Uh-huh …" I pinched my eyes shut.

"Figures." He chuckled, working his fingers deep inside of me. "Worn T-shirt?"

I returned a barely detectable nod, desperate for him to touch me in a way that made me wet, in a way that softened the slide of his fingers inside of me. Talking about Evelyn's clothes didn't do it for me.

"Was the tee tight? Did it show off her little tits and those diamond nipples of hers?"

"Graham … please …"

Please stop talking about Evelyn. Please touch me like you love me. Please …

"You, baby…" he withdrew his fingers "…you sucking Evelyn's puckered little nipples is still my favorite memory. It gets me so … fucking … hard …" He spread my cheeks and planted his mouth between my legs, bringing me to a quick orgasm as tears spilled down my face. I knew he wasn't thinking of me as his tongue teased me, as he used the product of my pleasure to lube my backside, as he unzipped his pants, as he fucked me where there was zero chance of me getting pregnant.

I closed my eyes, disappearing to a different mind space, and I wondered who would submit to him in that way after I took my last breath.

CHAPTER FIVE

Ronín

"**I** FEEL GUILTY." I teed up on the eighth hole of the Aspen Golf Club. "Evie has the day off. She's been begging me to take some time off, maybe take a vacation. Yet here I am, playing hooky this morning for eighteen holes with you. These four hours will cost my bank account a solid week in Orlando, wearing Mickey ears and shopping for princess dresses."

"You're living the fucking dream, man." Graham pulled out his driver after I landed one straight down the fairway. "I've made so many mistakes. Missed so many opportunities." He took a practice swing. "I became the man I said I'd never become—my father." Graham out drove me, as usual. But I out skied him. That shouldn't have mattered, but it did to me.

"Your dad was never in politics, was he?" I asked.

"No."

We returned our clubs to our bags and hopped into the golf cart, followed by two of his security detail in the golf cart behind us.

"But he sold his soul to live up to the family name. He married a woman who didn't know the first thing about raising a family, so they hired other people to do it. He fucked around on her, and she turned a blind eye to it." Spinning the tires at first, we sped off down the fairway. Graham ignored the cart path and the club rules to stay on it.

"Please tell me you're not fucking around on Lila."

He shot me a side glance and a smirk. "No. She's much too accommodating for me to feel the need to wander."

His answer soured my expression, so I turned away to hide it. I knew all about guys being guys. Talking the talk in front of other guys, then going home to a wife who pussy whipped them. I wasn't sure if Graham was one of those guys. For some reason, I doubted it.

"Evie thinks Lila will be a great mom. So even if you think you've turned into your father, Lila is definitely not your mother."

"Yeah, well, just between us, I think Lila has some health issues in that department. I can't seem to knock her up. And trust me, it's not for lack of trying, and it has nothing to do with my swimmers. But don't say anything to Evelyn. Lila's still in denial. Until she comes around on her own, it's best to not broach the subject."

I climbed out and plucked my iron from my bag. "I won't say a word. Knowing Evie, she'd offer to be a surrogate."

"Wouldn't my screwing your wife make things awkward between us?"

I stopped, halfway to my ball, and glanced over my shoulder.

Graham grinned. "I'm just fucking with you. We don't need a surrogate. The politically correct thing to do would be adoption. People love that shit."

If I bought into Evelyn's belief in parallel universes and their connection to lies, then in some other universe Graham was fucking my wife. I wasn't stupid. He looked at her like he owned a piece of her. I wasn't sure if it stemmed from their close friendship, all the things his family had done for her and her family, or that nauseating fact that he managed to get into her pants in college.

"Fuck …" My ball landed in the sand trap.

"Lila mentioned Evelyn's desire to take a trip or do something together. I can take some time off around the Fourth. Have you ever been to the Hamptons? The kids would love playing on the beach and swimming in the pool. There's golf, tennis, ATVs … and shopping for the women."

I returned my iron and waited for Graham to take his next stroke, a good twenty yards ahead of me.

After another perfect placement, he sauntered toward me, not gloating one bit. An interesting thing about Graham Porter … he could play golf with anyone, but he liked playing with me. Why? I didn't know. I was an average golfer on my very best day. Graham played like he could have walked onto the PGA tour but chose politics instead. However, he never gloated about his game. In fact, he often offered helpful tips with my swing or my grip on the club.

"Evie mentioned doing something together. I guess I assumed she meant dinner sometime, not a family vacation."

"Four to five days at the most. The kids will love the fireworks there. Won't cost you a dime. We fly out on my jet. No hotels to pay for. Plenty of food and entertainment. How can you say no?"

Easily. N-O. Probably not so easily said, once I ran it by Evie, unless Lila already told her. I didn't want to be rich like the Porters. Our three-bedroom, two-bathroom log cabin filled with two kids, my beautiful wife, and five years of memories left me content. Not wanting for anything. Yet, I always wondered if Evie envied the fancy stuff. The posh party Graham threw her for her birthday, the private jets, the all-expenses-paid trips with her two best friends ... my ski patrol salary didn't come close to giving her that life. When I chose to be a paramedic and then work for ski patrol, it never occurred to me that I would have any great need to make a lot of money. Simplicity suited me just fine.

"It's a generous offer, Graham. I appreciate it. I'll talk with Evie tonight."

He slammed the accelerator and veered off to the right, again ... nowhere near the cart path. "I can call her if you need me to sell it."

"I don't need you to sell anything to my wife."

Graham grinned. "True. I don't sell her things; I just give them to her. Like the building. I know she thought I overstepped some boundary, that it was too much, but it wasn't. We're friends ... family really. And family takes care of each other."

Scratching my cheek, I asked the question I hated to have to ask, but I had no clue. "What building? What are you talking about?"

"Whoa!" He stopped so quickly, I had to brace my hand against the dash. "She didn't tell you I signed over the deed to her building so she wouldn't have to worry about rent or anyone else making the decisions about the building?"

My anger started to boil. I wasn't even sure who was feeding it at that point. Graham? Evie? Myself?

"She didn't mention that yet. How kind of you. I'd have to agree, it's a bit too kind. She can't accept it."

"Oh …" He hopped out and handed me my pitching wedge. "I didn't give her a choice. It's ridiculous and completely ego-driven to not accept it. I don't need the building, the rent, the hassle. I know, if the tables were turned, she'd do the same thing for me." He nodded to the sand trap. "You're going to have to get some air on it or it will roll back into the bunker." Again, without sounding judgmental or condescending, he coached me on my golf game like a friend or brother.

I understood Evie's frustration with his personality. One minute you wanted to break his nose, the next minute you found yourself begrudgingly mumbling the words "thank you." Still, she should have told me. I didn't appreciate feeling like the uninformed husband. It gave Graham the appearance that we kept secrets from each other. That thought made me cringe. I had kept my fair share of secrets from Evie, but I did it to protect her.

Biting my tongue and unclenching my fist to take the club from him, I walked the fucking thin line between embracing Graham as a friend (that he most likely was not) and the enemy I feared most. Whatever the saying was about keeping your friends close and your enemies closer definitely applied to Graham Porter and his obsession with my wife.

I SQUEEZED IN a few hours of actual work after golfing and picked up bread, bananas, a jar of pasta sauce, and toilet paper on my way home. Three sets of eyes and accompanying smiles greeted me before I shifted my Subaru into park a few feet from the toy-scattered driveway. Franz and Anya abandoned their plasma cars, charging at me as I climbed out of my vehicle. I barely got the door shut before they tackled me. Giving into their play, I stumbled back, folding to the ground to be their new jungle gym.

"Da-ee!" Anya straddled my neck, planting her hands on my cheeks and showering my face with kisses while Franz shoved my knees toward my chest to hop onto my legs for me to teeter-totter him.

"Oof! What did I do to deserve this? And what's Mommy doing?"

"Sweeping," Evie called from the two-stall garage, all legs in her frayed-edge denim shorts, tight pink tee, and old, not-so-white Chucks. "Some of us had to work the whole day *and* clean out the garage."

"I love that we share our locations with each other. But you know ... those aren't always accurate, especially at this altitude."

"Pfft ..." She pushed the broom behind a pile of debris to the middle of the garage floor.

I lumbered back to standing, shedding two kids like a mama dog calling it quits on mealtime for her pups. They wandered back to the driveway clogged with way too many toys, and I retrieved the sack of groceries from the backseat.

"What can I say?" I sauntered into the garage as her dirt-smudged face gave me the stink eye. "Graham wouldn't take no for an answer. You know how that is ... like when he gifts you an entire building."

Her scowl dropped from her face in less than a single breath, instantly replaced with a cringe. I continued toward the back door without giving her a second glance.

"It slipped my mind."

I opened the door. "Like winning the lottery slips someone's mind." The door slammed shut behind me.

Two seconds later, she opened the door, straddling the threshold to keep an eye on the kids while I prepared for her shitty excuse. "It was the day I saw you sharing a booth with the notorious home-wrecker. The building slipped my mind in the midst of feeling like my marriage was over."

"The building and the income from rent is worth millions, yet you let Adrianne distract you from sharing that with me?" I folded the sack and turned toward her.

Evie glanced out at the kids before returning her attention to me. "Yeah, because my marriage is priceless."

Game over.

"You're not playing fairly."

"It's not a game. It's my life. The one where I have two young kids, a business, a husband with a connection to the afterlife and a new acquaintance with a terrible reputation for sleeping with anything that moves. Oh! And did I mention my best friends are rich and give me elaborate gifts whether I want them to or not? Wait! One more fun fact—I call my dead mother's phone just to hear her voice and leave her messages."

I drew in a long breath through my nose and let it out slowly as my feet took me to my wife. After giving another quick glance to Anya and Franz, she tipped her head back, eyeing me with all five-and-a-half feet one hundred and twenty pounds of attitude, daring me to speak another word on the matter. My guy brain took a three-second time-out to imagine what I might have done to her if we hadn't had the spawn squad for an audience.

"Graham and Lila invited us to their place in the Hamptons for the Fourth of July. I think we should take the kids and your bikini and go."

After a few narrow-eyed blinks, her expression relaxed. "Really?" She squeaked with a jolt of excitement.

Lila's her best friend. Lila's her best friend.

In spite of my cautious Graham vibes, Lila would always be a part of our life, which meant Graham would be too.

"Really." I tugged on her braided ponytails, her hair nearly white from the summer's sun.

Evie threw her arms around my neck. "Roe, you're the best!"

I liked being the best. Maybe not the best golfer. Maybe not the best bank account balance. Maybe not the best at spewing off baseball stats. But the best husband would do ... that and best skier, best lumberjack, best dad, and best lover.

Fuck you, Porter ... this woman is mine.

CHAPTER SIX

Evelyn

"NICE LIFE," I murmured to Lila as the driver pulled into yet another Porter estate—or compound. What did you call it when someone owned half of the Hamptons? Okay, not half, but enough to build a small neighborhood if the houses weren't all fifteen thousand square feet with pools, tennis courts, and putting greens.

The guys, including Franz, rode in one vehicle while Lila, Anya, and I rode in another vehicle. Four adults, security detail, two kids with car seats, and luggage required a caravan of vehicles and space.

"It's so insignificant. Isn't that why Graham is my husband and not yours?" Lila stared straight ahead through black sunglasses covering half of her face.

I chuckled from the backseat with Anya. "What's that supposed to mean?"

"While I was traveling abroad and you and Graham were attached at the hip, eating at expensive restaurants, driving fancy cars, traveling to New York, shopping for designer clothing ... remember I said those same two words to you on the phone? You had just returned from New York, and I was in Germany. I said you were living a *nice life*, and you told me it was *so insignificant*. Remember? The grass is greener on the other side scenario. You said it was all just *things*, and they lose their appeal when you have them so readily at your disposal."

"Coveting is half the fun." I nodded as Lila glanced over her shoulder at me.

"Yes." Her lips twisted into a sad smile. "So it's okay; you can covet my life and I'll covet yours."

"My small log cabin and Jeep with a gazillion miles on it?"

"Your kids who think you're a queen and your husband who kisses your feet."

The vehicle pulled to a stop. I started to formulate my rebuttal, the simple fact that she could start her own family and that Graham worshipped her too, but I didn't know if those were still facts or not.

We spilled out of the two vehicles into the warm July sun and salty ocean breeze, sandwiched between acres of private land leading to the water and a twelve-bedroom, fourteen-bathroom mansion, fully staffed, and all ours for the next four days. Everything reeked of privilege. Ronin rushed our two kids into the house for a much-needed potty break, followed by Lila in her skinny denim capris, heels, and a blazer too warm for July.

"Impressed?" Graham slid his aviators down his nose and winked at me as I gawked at my surroundings. He shone in his casual jeans and white polo. The wind made quick work of messing up his hair, which was a better look for him anyway.

"Why? Are you trying to impress me?" I flung my purse over my shoulder and made my way toward the house.

"Always." He chuckled, right on my heels.

But it wasn't funny because I felt the truth behind that one word. I used to think Graham's efforts to impress me were his way of hoping I'd run to Lila and gush about his amazing life, to gush about *him*. And sometimes I did. Maybe that was why they ended up together. However, they were in fact together. There was no need to impress anyone any longer—least of all me.

I turned around so quickly he had to grab my shoulders to keep from knocking me over. "Why?" My head canted.

His eyebrows furrowed. "Why what?"

"Why try to impress me?"

He rubbed his full lips together, but it didn't hide his smirk. "It's the challenge, Evelyn. It's always been the challenge with you."

"So if I confess that I'm impressed, will the challenge be over?"

"Oh, Evie, Evie, Evie ..." He bopped the tip of my nose with his finger, pushed his glasses up his face, and brushed past me. "It will never be over."

By that point, it was hard to recall the exact moment I sold my soul to the Devil. Was it when Dad's kidneys failed? Or was it before that? Was it that day in a bar off campus where a handsome guy everyone simply referred to as "G" bought me a beer and bet me two more that

USC would kick Stanford's ass? If it wasn't that day—because I bet on Stanford and they made the most incredible comeback in the fourth quarter—then it was six months later when I lost a bet and didn't have the money to pay up. Graham agreed to take payment in the form of my misery. Three shots of tequila.

One.

Two.

Three.

I honestly don't remember how we got from the bar to his condo. I just remember him suggesting we do something stupid "just for the fuck of it." Not hell of it; I really think he said fuck of it. It made me giggle. He later blamed my "adorable" giggle on his hands pulling off my shirt and groping my breasts over my bra. I remember thinking it was a bad idea, but I couldn't recall saying the actual words because I apparently giggled again, which made him want to pull down my jeans. I for sure knew *that* was a terrible idea. As I started to express my opinion, he yanked the crotch of my panties aside and let his tongue assault me. Well, *I* let his tongue assault me because three shots of tequila and a warm tongue sliding between my legs, teasing my clit, felt pretty damn good that night.

Sloppy. That was what I remembered about that night. Everything was sloppy—his groping hands, his face with *me* on it, the way he fumbled for a condom after giving me an orgasm.

The awkward, drunk probing for the right place to stick his dick.

The quest for my breasts when he couldn't unlatch my bra.

The condom slipping off three thrusts in because he only rolled it halfway on.

The debacle of the second condom attempt when he couldn't get the packet opened.

The begging for me to let him go bareback and pull out.

A horrid, embarrassing, awkward, drunk night of the worst sex ever between two friends.

The next morning, we woke up on the floor—yeah, because we were too drunk to make it to the bedroom— half clothed and sulking in the silent embarrassment of the line we crossed.

On a sigh, I shook my head to rid those memories from the forefront of my brain before scraping my flip-flops along the stone drive to the front door, the gates of a new kind of hell.

"We have rooms for the kids next to yours." Lila nodded toward the left.

I followed her through room after luxurious room, basically eight houses the size of mine, before we reached the "wing" of the house that would be ours for the next few days.

"Graham and I had Laura, the estate manager, get a few toys for the kids to make them feel at home."

"Lila, you didn't have to do that. We brought some toys, and there's a beach and a pool," I replied.

"Franz can sleep in here." She grabbed the handle to a door on our right.

"No. That's Anya's room." We turned toward Graham's voice as he, Ronin, and the kids caught up to us.

"Whatever." Lila shrugged. "It doesn't matter."

"But it does." Graham plucked Anya from the floor, tearing her hand from Ronin's hand. "This is a room for a princess."

Lila opened the bedroom door. When Graham pushed past her, entering first with Anya, Lila stumbled back a few feet, eyes flared, lips parted. My face morphed into similar shock at the room painted in soft shades of pink, a plethora of little girl dolls and toys, and a wood chariot toddler bed in the middle of the room.

"Graham …" Lila whispered.

He set Anya in her bed and kissed her cheek. "Do you like your room, Princess Anya?"

She giggled and nodded.

"So cool!" Franz raced into the room and jumped onto the bed with Anya.

Ronin's possessive hand slid around my waist, resting on my belly while he pulled my back to his chest. I didn't miss the stiffness of his entire body.

"Did I exceed your expectations?" Graham lifted Lila's chin with his finger. He kept a playful smile on his face, but it did nothing to erase the tension in her brow or the overall vibe of discomfort between all of us.

"It's …" She managed a nervous smile. "It's a bit more than a few toys."

"Yes." He kissed her forehead and tucked her under his arm, shooting us a triumphant grin. "Lila thinks of Franz and Anya like her own kids. And so do I. So … this is what we would do for our own kids. Right, babe?" He tightened his grip on her waist.

Lila swallowed, erasing the concern from her face. "Of course."

I wanted to yank her away from Graham and hug her. Anyone could see how blindsided she felt by his gesture— how guilty she felt for showing any sort of shock. Of course, she loved Franz and Anya like her own. But they were, in fact, not her children. Why did Graham do that? A complete slap in the face to my best friend who wanted children of her own.

"Come on, buddy. We have a surprise for you too." Graham beckoned Franz with a wave of his hand.

When we stepped into the bedroom across the hallway, it felt like stepping into the ocean. Blue walls with hand-painted sea creatures, just as many toys as Anya's room, and a submarine bed.

"Is this mine?" Franz's wide-eyed gaze landed on Ronin and me.

"No. It's not yours. Not our house. But it's where you'll stay while we're here." I narrowed my eyes at Graham.

Of course, Graham returned a smirk at my displeasure, like he'd won. But it wasn't a game.

He released Lila's waist and hunched down behind Franz, resting his hands on Franz's shoulders while his lips settled next to my son's ear. "It's yours, buddy," he whispered.

Franz raced to the bed and bounced on it for a few seconds before frantically checking out the cool and really expensive toys.

"Da-eee!"

Ronin released me and crossed the hallway to see the doll Anya held while rocking in the little pink and white striped chair that fit her petite body perfectly.

"You're overstepping boundaries," I said, knowing the only people who could hear me were Graham and Lila. She needed to know I was on her side, that I recognized how over-the-top and way out of bounds Graham stepped with his expensive gesture, gift, bribe or whatever the fuck he thought of it.

"It's money, Evie," Graham said with a hint of exasperation as he turned his back on Franz and slid his hands into the front pockets of his jeans.

My gaze shifted to Lila, looking for help or more signs that I had every right to be upset about his gifts.

Her eyes shifted to her feet for a few seconds. "Graham has more money than he'll spend in a hundred lifetimes."

"*We,* Lila. Not just me."

Her head snapped up, and she eyed him for a few seconds before nodding. I had no idea what he so often said to her with a single look, but she always seemed to fall in line with him. And I hated it. I hated myself for throwing her into his arms years earlier.

"It's a packaged deal with us. *We* like to give elaborate gifts … because we can. And those who can, should." She gave me a resolute nod.

Who was that woman saying that shit? What did Graham do to my best friend? Rewire her brain?

A satisfied grin spread across Graham's face. He took a step forward, keeping his hands in his pockets, and leaned down to whisper something in Lila's ear. Her cheeks turned red as she nodded. He stood back to full height and gave her a subtle nod toward the door.

Lila shot me a quick glance and a half smile, nibbling her lower lip. "I'm going to take a nap. Let's plan on heading to the beach in an hour."

My head canted as I squinted at her. "A nap?" I laughed a little. "Are you serious? It's one o'clock. Are you not feeling well?"

"I'm fine. Flying makes me drowsy. A quick nap will make it so I'm less cranky later."

"Are you a two-year-old?" I coughed another laugh of disbelief. "Less cranky? Seriously?"

"Nap is code, Evie. Do you want her to say what she really means in front of the kids?"

My nose wrinkled at Graham, and when I slid my attention to Lila for confirmation, she kept her rather dead gaze on Franz. Where did the life go from my friend?

"No, I don't." I grabbed her hand, giving it a squeeze. Still, she didn't look at me, but she squeezed back. "I'm going to unpack a few things and get the kids snacks. The beach in an hour sounds perfect."

"Thank you, Evie." She released my hand and disappeared down the hallway toward the opposite end of the house.

"In case you're still keeping score…" I said in a soft voice so only Graham could hear me "…I'm not *impressed* with the way you treat your wife."

He studied me with an unreadable expression, shoving his hands farther into his pockets, sending his shoulders toward his ears. Graham pulled off the boyish look on very rare occasions. I called them glimpses of the young man who befriended me years earlier.

"I'm sorry."

"Sorry for the way you treat Lila? Sorry for the things you do to manipulate me? Sorry for buying my children's affection? What exactly are you sorry about?"

Twisting his lips, he dropped his focus to the floor between us, watching his feet as he stepped closer to me. "Yes."

Why?

Why was Graham intertwined, glued, stitched, and cemented into my life? He acted like an errant child—my errant child. I didn't know how to handle his bad behavior because he seemed to stay one step ahead of me. And on the worst days, the days he said and did the most hurtful things, I didn't know how to un-love him. That was how he hurt me.

"Franz, I'm going to unpack a few things. We'll have snacks soon."

He ignored me. Why wouldn't he? His new BFF, aka Uncle Graham, dropped a pretty penny on a roomful of toys. I questioned if we'd be able to coerce him out of the house to play on the beach.

When Ronin saw me step into the hallway, he picked up Anya and the white teddy bear she hugged to her chest and followed me. I peeked right and left, stopping when I found the room with our luggage at the end of the king bed.

"This is Lila's handbag, not mine." I picked up the white leather shoulder bag.

Anya reached for me.

"Trade. I'll take the bag to Lila. You get Squirmy ready for the beach."

We made the trade, our gazes locking. I frowned, hugging her to me.

"It's fine." Ronin held Lila's bag in one hand and cupped my face with his other hand, leaning forward to brush his lips over mine, pecking at them playfully. "I don't like it either. But our kids adore our friends right now. We'll take Graham out back and beat him up later," he whispered.

I grinned. "I four-letter-word you so much."

He bit my lower lip, giving it a playful tug before releasing it. "Watch it ... if you open up that can of worms, you'll regret it when we need it the most."

On my death bed ... or his. That was when I wanted to share those three words with him. I didn't want rainy days, final straws, or the end of a rope. I wanted those words to be a final breath after a long life of *showing* everything. I wanted to prove to ourselves and the whole world that words were empty without the true actions to back them up.

"Go. You might have to leave it outside her door. She's getting ready to ... nap or something."

"Okay." He left a solid kiss on my lips and sauntered off.

My king.

CHAPTER SEVEN

Ronín

I PLAYED IT cool, walking that stupid line, when Graham unveiled his surprise for our kids. He ruined Christmas for the rest of their childhood. What could we possibly get them after he bought them one of everything from Santa's workshop?

Stopping at the door to Franz's room, I debated saying something to him, knocking out a few teeth, or simply breaking a rib or two. But his back was to me. He and Franz were on the floor building something with Legos.

"I loved building with Legos when I was young like you, Franz. I used to build little Lego people to be my friends because ..." He paused his hands and sighed. "Well, I didn't have a lot of friends when I was your age."

"You didn't have friends?" Franz murmured, keeping his hands busy with the Legos.

"No. But you're much cooler than I was, so you don't need to build friends or buy them. You have cool parents."

Franz nodded slowly, probably not getting Graham's point. Again, Graham made it hard to completely despise him. As much as I didn't want to be affected by the "poor" little rich kid's story, it made enough of an impact to keep me from saying anything, so I continued toward the other side of the house to find Lila.

All the doors were shut, so I gently knocked on each one. Evie said to just leave it outside the room, but I wanted to make sure Lila was okay. I'd had this clawing need for weeks to make sure she was fine.

"Come in."

I received a soft response after knocking on the last door. Opening it slowly, I opened my mouth to tell her I had her bag, but I choked on the words. Lila stood at the window, her back to the door, gazing out the shutters tilted just enough to see out without letting anyone see inside the room. I should have backed out of the room as quickly as possible because she wasn't wearing anything but a black thong—and a smattering of bruises along her back and along the curve of her ass, her winged tattoo hard to make out in the mess of bruises.

All the moments over the previous weeks of feeling jolts of pain, the skin along my back burning at times, and a general tenderness when the kids jumped on me or Evie curled her fingers into my flesh when we made love … it all made sense. Yet, at the same time it made no sense whatsoever.

"Lila …" I whispered.

She startled, whipping around with one arm covering her breasts as she reached for a blanket on the bed with her other hand. "Ronin!" She gasped, eyes wide and feral as she wrapped the blanket around her body.

My hand released her bag to the floor by my feet and I clenched my fists. "Did he do that to you?"

Her head jerked back, eyes blinking in rapid succession. "What?"

I took a few slow steps toward her. "The bruises."

"No." Her head whipped side to side in several hard shakes.

I wanted to demand she show me her bruises as I didn't get a close look to inspect them, but I saw them. They were there and unmistakable.

Her fear felt tangible in that moment as clearly as our connection rang endlessly in my ears, reminding me of the rules I broke and the price I'd forever pay.

I saw them ...

I couldn't ignore the truth. As much as I wanted to welcome all kinds of doubt, it had yet to make a case.

"Lila—"

"No! It's not what you think. It's not what you think you *feel.*"

I winced. "She told you."

Biting her lips together, she nodded.

Secrets ...

They haunted me at every turn—mine, Evie's, and I feared Lila's might too.

"Is it true?" Pain plagued her face.

I didn't want her to feel bad or any sort of pain for something she didn't do ... something she couldn't control.

"Yes. But I'm fine. You're not. The bruises, Lila. You can tell me. I can help you." I would help her. If that meant ending Graham's life, I would do that for her because she was my wife's best friend. And I sure as fuck didn't save her on that mountain only to let her husband hurt her.

Tears filled her eyes, and she blinked them away before a single one broke free. "You can't help me." Drawing in a shaky breath, she tightened her hold on the blanket and tipped her chin up. "It's not Graham. And … Evie can't know. Not ever."

"No." I rubbed the back of my neck. "There's nothing you can't tell her. She's your friend. And so am I. Let us help."

After a swallow, she eased her head side to side, jaw clenched, eyes hard on me. "She can't *ever* know. And I'm sorry. If this…" she narrowed her eyes "…this thing you feel from me is real, I'm sorry you have to feel it. If I could prevent it, I would."

"Prevent what?"

Her face morphed into a mask—a numb, emotionless mask. Not a wrinkle of anything to read into her thoughts, her feelings. "I have leukemia."

Cancer.

It took me several seconds to make sense of her confession. Bruising? Maybe. Like that? It seemed unlikely.

"That's a lot of bruising for—"

"I slipped on our marble stairs at home. Honestly, I grabbed the railing. I landed on my butt and the edges of the stairs scraped along my back. It didn't even hurt that badly at the time. But … I swear even a firm hug can leave bruises at this point. I try to be careful."

Cancer.

Evie *just* buried her mom.

"It will destroy her," Lila whispered.

I blinked several times as Lila's words echoed my thoughts. It would absolutely destroy Evie.

"Lila … I'm … Fuck … I don't know what to say." I deflated. If those were bruises from leukemia and I tried to accuse her husband of abusing her, that would have made me a total asshole.

"Say you won't tell Evie."

"Jesus …" I parked my hands on my hips and turned my back to her, glancing up at the ceiling. "If I tell her, it *will* destroy her. But if I don't tell her … will it destroy us?"

"I'm sorry," she whispered.

My chin dropped to my chest, and I shook my head slowly. "You're sorry? For having leukemia? That's so fucked-up, Lila."

"It's manageable. Maybe there's nothing to tell. She never needs to know that you know. Not if I live … not if I die."

If she dies … I could die with her.

I almost did after her accident.

"Graham should be finding the very best doctors." I turned back to her. "Right?"

"Of course." She returned an easy nod that didn't match her pensive expression. "I'm doing some alternative treatment. Less pain for me, less pain for—"

"What's going on?"

I turned to Graham, stepping into the room with wide eyes flitting between me and his naked wife wrapped in a blanket.

"Ronin brought me my bag," Lila spoke in a rush.

Graham's uneasy gaze locked with mine, asking me questions without saying a word.

Did I see Lila's bruises?

Would I tell Evie?

What did I know?

"He's not going to tell Evie about the cancer."

His head and gaze inched from me to Lila like a million things chased around his brain, expression blank, lips parted.

"The cancer …" he whispered.

"I'm sorry," Lila murmured. "He walked in. I thought it was you. He saw the bruises from the leukemia. He's not going to tell Evie."

I didn't promise that.

Without taking his attention away from Lila, Graham brushed past me to embrace his wife, kissing her softly on her head while she buried her face into his neck. I took it as my cue to leave. What would I say to Evie? I … I didn't know.

"If you suffer, she will know. I won't be able to hide it." I didn't know if Graham knew about my connection to Lila. I wasn't talking to him anyway. Without another look back, I exited the room, shutting the door behind me.

A sob broke from Lila as I stood there, listening for a

few more seconds.

"How did this happen?" she sobbed.

"Shh … nothing has happened. I told you, baby, you're fine. *We're* fine. Okay? You believe me, right? There's nothing to tell. He won't tell her. Everything is fine. I promise."

I couldn't walk away. Graham's assessment didn't help my situation. They were both in denial. And I was in the middle.

As I started to take a step away from the door, Graham's tone changed into something less sympathetic. "He saw you naked?"

I couldn't hear her response, maybe she didn't have one or maybe it was a simple nod. Had he walked in and seen Evie like that, I would have been upset too … not at Evie, just the situation.

"Did that turn you on?"

However, I would not have asked her that, even if the thought crossed my mind. Lila wasn't turned on by me seeing her; she was horrified. I *felt* her horrific fear and embarrassment.

"Are you sure?"

Again, I didn't hear her answer. And I should have walked away, but I couldn't. My trust in Graham was complicated, to put it mildly. I didn't trust him to do right by his wife, and I hated the feeling that settled in my gut, but I couldn't help it. He coveted my wife too much. Where did that leave Lila? Well, that was what I wanted to know. So, I listened.

She grunted.

He shushed her.

"When I fuck you, do you think of him?" he asked in a strained voice as the unmistakable sound of flesh slapping together crawled through the cracks around the door, a whisper ... an erotic echo.

I didn't want to know that answer. Running a rough hand through my hair, I took slow steps away from the door, giving myself time to pull my shit together before Evie looked at me. Even if I thought of telling her the truth, it wasn't going to be on a holiday trip with the kids.

With each step, I focused on the ringing in my ears—Lila.

I felt a mix of sadness and an overall dull, numbing pain. Was it the news?

Did I feel *her*?

Did her emotional pain seep into my existence? Was it what they were doing in the bedroom?

Did she not enjoy it?

I just wanted to rid her from my body, but I couldn't. I took a part of Lila or maybe she took a part of me that day on the mountain. It fucking sucked not having complete control, a broken autonomy like someone else was pulling the strings. I was nothing but a puppet, a voodoo doll.

CHAPTER EIGHT

Graham

I FUCKED MY wife and thought about my best friend. I hated the bruises on her back; it made it more difficult to picture Evelyn because she didn't have bruises on her back. No … Evelyn's back was perfect.

Everything about Evelyn was perfect, except she married the wrong man. She let him crawl between her legs and put babies in her belly. That didn't please me. But I would eventually forgive her, and we would raise Franz and Anya as our own.

Franz … who the fuck names their kid that?

"Graham … it … it hurts …" Lila whined.

It hurt because we didn't fit like I fit with Evelyn. I stopped. The last thing I needed was Lila sulking like a victim after Ronin saw her situation. I could barely touch her without her skin blooming in shades of reds and blues. She collapsed forward, burying her face in the pillow, leaving her marred back staring at me and a raging hard-on pulsing for Evelyn. I closed my eyes where the only thing I could see was Evelyn. Then I jerked off onto

Lila's back.

Did I hate myself for allowing the four of us to get into such a pickle? Of course. I thought my pursuit of Lila would make Evelyn jealous. Did I develop misplaced feelings for Lila in the process? Naturally. She wasn't a terrible person, just not the person for me. Lila was regrettable collateral damage.

But it went too far. I didn't see the signs, and I let it go too far.

A husband and two kids. How did I let that happen? How did Evelyn let that happen? I married Lila, but I didn't put a fucking baby in her. I wanted Evelyn to pay for everything, but not as much as I just wanted her. So I'd take her baggage. I just needed to wait for Ronin to fuck up their marriage and for Lila to … well, I wasn't sure yet.

Sometimes tragic things happened, like her cancer. If anything happened to Lila, Evelyn would feel destroyed, broken beyond repair.

Lucky for her, I would be there like I was *always* there to pick up the pieces … to save the day.

CHAPTER NINE

Evelyn

I PUT ON my bikini while Ronin unpacked his clothes, Franz played in his room, and Anya jumped on our bed. "I'm going to get the kids snacks while you finish getting ready for the beach. Don't let Miss Wild Thing fall off the bed."

"Okay," he mumbled.

"Is something wrong?" I canted my head, adjusting the ties on my bikini bottoms.

Ronin glanced over at me from the dresser where he tucked a few pairs of shorts into the top drawer. "No. Nothing is wrong." He smiled.

I didn't completely buy it because he could fake his smile, but he couldn't fake the look in his eyes. On a slow nod, I mirrored his smile, and if he could read me as well as I could read him, then he would have seen the doubt in my eyes. But if he did, he didn't say anything.

"Okay. I'll be in the kitchen. Grab the sunscreen and bag of towels when you come out."

"Will do."

I shuffled my bare feet down the hallway, curling my toes into the plush rug with each step before poking my head into Franz's room. He didn't even look up from his Lego creation. When I stepped into the kitchen designed for royalty, I stopped and shook my head. The kitchen alone had to be worth twice as much as the value of my house.

Green granite counters, warm woods mixed with stainless steel appliances, two islands, one as big as a continent. An impressive fireplace anchored one end of the room by a large dining table. A flat screen TV. Multiple sinks.

"Who lives like this?" I whispered to myself, shuffling toward a long section of cabinets, hoping I could find something along the lines of a box of crackers.

"Fuck me …" Graham's voice behind me sent a chill along my spine, erecting the hairs along my neck. Why did just the sound of his voice feel so … violating?

I swallowed and kept walking like he didn't affect me. "Watch your language, please. There are kids in the house. And I'm certain the only person who will F you is Lila because for whatever reason, she finds you attractive." I started opening cabinet doors.

Complete bullshit. Graham had sex appeal, the rich guy kind. I preferred the ski patrol kind. But there was no way I would ever feed his ego by admitting that he always looked like a model walking off the cover of a fashion magazine. Women made fawning over him their favorite pastime.

But not me.

"I can't swear because there are children in the house, but you can walk around in that pathetic excuse for a bikini? Is your husband really going to let you out of the house wearing that?"

"Yes," I replied with as much confidence as I could muster. As I raised onto my toes to grab a box of round crackers from the top shelf, Graham pressed his body to my back, pinning me to the counter. I sucked in a sharp breath not expecting him to do that, not expecting to feel him *hard* against my backside.

Graham reached for the crackers, caging me with his body. "Well, then he's fucking stupid," he whispered, retrieving the crackers.

I slowly exhaled as he set them on the counter in front of me and took a step back so I could turn around.

I wanted to scream ... really *scream* at him for crossing a line that should never ever have been crossed.

For every touch.

For every look.

For every word whispered—as if not saying it aloud or in front of Lila and Ronin made it okay. How did I tie myself to the Devil? How did I feed my best friend to the most dangerous wolf?

Always ... the score was *always* the Porters: everything. Needy, broke, desperate, manipulated Evelyn: nothing.

"What is wrong with you?" I clenched my teeth, gritting out the words as quietly as possible.

He crossed his arms over his white T-shirt-clad chest, lips twisted. "I'm not following."

I shot a million daggers at him, sliding my gaze to the erection tenting his swim trunks and giving a tiny nod toward it.

He didn't follow my gaze. Why would he? He knew damn well what I was referring to. "I just left the bathroom where my wife was showering. But if you keep staring at it, you might have to take part of the blame … or credit. However you want to look at it."

My gaze shot to his. I didn't want to *look* at it in any way, shape, or form. Nor did I want it pressed to my back. I cleared my throat, hating the flushed feeling in my cheeks that Graham could see, that fed his ego. "Why is she showering *before* the beach?"

Graham wet his lips, rubbing them together for a few seconds. "She got into a … *sticky* situation." He winked.

I cringed, fighting the bile working its way up my throat.

"Listen…" he adjusted himself "…all kidding aside …"

Kidding? *That* was his idea of kidding? Had Ronin seen him pinning me to the counter with his erection, it would have turned into a bloody fiasco, ruining friendships, and terrorizing the minds of my young kids.

Graham continued, "I'm glad you suggested this. Lila and I love spending time with you guys. You really are family, more so than my own family." He shook his head, rubbing the back of his neck. "I need to do a better job of finding balance. Once my term is up, I'm going to get out of politics. As much as I don't love the family business with my dad still having his hand in everything, it's a good job. It would allow me to be home with my family more often."

Family.

There he went again. Whiplash. He manipulated me in a way I couldn't prove without taking the risk of ruining not only my relationship with him, but with my best friend. Graham played in the gray area, stepping out of bounds just long enough to say or do something inappropriate then falling back in line before anyone else noticed.

"So you're planning on having a family?"

Again … AGAIN he did it—raking his gaze along my body like he had the right to do it. "I don't know what the future holds." He ogled my breasts, the breasts he liked to poke fun at. "But at the very least, I want to spend more time with Franz and Anya. Skiing, golfing … attending their plays and sporting events. You're my best friend, Evie. I love your kids like my own."

"Mommy, I'm hungry." Franz ambled into the kitchen, holding a Lego boat. His blue eyes alight with pride and his hair messy like mine. Thankfully, he inherited some color to his skin so he didn't have to go through life looking like his White Walker mom. It was my completely unbiased opinion—we made really beautiful children.

"You're hungry? Hungry!" Graham scooped Franz up into his arms, buried his face into Franz's neck like gobbling him right up.

Franz giggled.

It was endearing, as I'm sure was Graham's intention.

Befriend me.

Make me indebted to him.

Marry my best friend.

Befriend my husband.

Spoil my children.

Remind me on a daily basis why I loved him.

Then … remind me on a daily basis why I had grown to resent and even hate that same friendship.

There were reasons why people said some gestures were too grand, making it impossible to ever be repaid. People like Graham and all the other Porters thrived on the eternal indebtedness of everyone else around them.

Graham set Franz on the counter. "I've got you covered, little man." He retrieved a plate and proceeded to fill it with crackers, cheese cubes (that someone had piled neatly onto a tray in the fridge), grapes, strawberries, pumpkin seeds, and a few chocolate squares. "My nanny used to hide two little squares of chocolate beneath the healthy stuff on all of my snack plates." He winked at Franz.

A nanny raised Graham. I wasn't sure if that explained why he was such an asshole ninety percent of the time or if the nanny was actually the reason why ten percent of the time he wasn't an asshole—a true friend to me, a kind husband to Lila, and the fun uncle who spoiled my kids.

"Mommy hides chocolate in her closet." Franz outed me. Traitor.

Graham slid his gaze to me, quirking an eyebrow accompanied by a knowing smirk. "You *still* hide chocolate?"

"Yes, in her sock drawer," Ronin piped up, carrying Anya into the kitchen.

"How do you know that? Are you snooping in my drawers?" I glared at Ronin.

He set Anya on the counter next to Franz and grabbed my face. "It's called putting away laundry, babe."

Before I could respond, he planted a solid kiss on my mouth, something our kids saw on a regular basis. But Graham didn't get to see it very often. And I wanted—needed—him to see it. So when Ronin started to pull away, I grabbed his shirt and jerked him back to me. No tongue or anything inappropriate in front of the kids. Just a good, solid, I-love-this-man-and-he-loves-me kiss.

"Get a room."

I grinned against Ronin's mouth for a second before releasing him and turning toward Lila's voice.

"We could." I laughed. "Or ten. You have enough of them."

She fetched a plate and put food on it for Anya. Our friends would be good parents. Maybe having their own kids would force Graham to fall in line and embrace the blessings in his life, treat me in an appropriate way, and fix all the pieces that felt broken at that moment.

Maybe.

"Now I feel underdressed." I frowned at Lila, who usually showcased her perfect curvy body in a chic bikini. Not that day. She wore board shorts and a swim top. "Where's your bikini?"

She shrugged, cutting up grapes for Anya. "I had several moles removed from my back last week, and I'm not supposed to expose the area to the sun."

"Bandage them," I suggested, stealing a grape and popping it into my mouth while Graham set out more plates of food, mumbling something to Ronin like "eat up."

"I have to lather sunscreen on my back, and then the bandages don't stick. I know you like how I look in a bikini, but you'll just have to wait until my back has healed."

Graham laughed. Ronin seemed to ignore the whole conversation. And Lila cracked a tiny smile, giving me a quick glance.

I held onto my frown in spite of my desire to smile back at my friend cracking a joke. Lila had a knack for covering the truth, no matter how grim it was, with her own brand of humor. Much like myself, she could cover tragedy and sadness with a wicked smile and a dose of untimely humor. Ever since the accident, I felt like something broke Lila's spirit. On my birthday, she came to life again, but that was just the alcohol or maybe it was just a cover-up. Fake happiness.

However, we were in the Hamptons to have fun, so I put a lid on the scrutinizing and decided to make the most of our time there.

"I do like you in a bikini, but I'm good with you covering up for a few days. Less competition for attention on the beach. This forty-year-old mom needs all the catcalls she can get. Enjoy your thirties while they last … for the next six months."

"No. You don't need the attention." Ronin glanced

up from his plate of food, leaned against the counter, giving GQ Graham a run for his money. There was a lot of sexiness in the kitchen that day.

I stuck my tongue out at him.

"Mommy!" Franz giggled, sticking his tongue out at Ronin as well.

My husband rolled his eyes at me. "Nice role modeling, babe."

"I try."

"Margo can make us lunch. She should be back soon." Graham pulled the barstool out from under the island and sat beside Franz's dangling legs, giving the bottom of his bare foot a tickle until Franz jerked on a giggle.

"I think this spread is plenty." I laughed, gesturing to the buffet of food Graham arranged on the island.

"Do you paddle board?" Graham asked Ronin.

"Yes," he answered without elaboration or much enthusiasm in his voice.

Something was up with him. I just didn't know what it could be.

"Lila is amazing at it." Graham winked at her.

She returned a small smile.

"I bet Franz will be a natural too, unlike his mom."

"Baiting me in front of my kids where I can't properly defend myself is not fair, Graham Cracker." It just came out. I hadn't called him that in a while. And it felt good.

"Graham Cracker?" Franz laughed.

"Sorry." I smirked. "Franz, we're supposed to call him Governor Graham Cracker."

More giggles ensued.

Lila kept herself occupied, helping Anya eat her snacks while Ronin pulled out a stool and took a seat as well. I wedged my way between Ronin's body and the counter, perching my ass on his shorts-clad leg.

He pressed his left hand to my bare abdomen and fed me a strawberry with his right hand. After I chewed a bite, I twisted toward him, giving him a narrow-eyed inspection. "Are you sure you're okay?" I whispered.

His gaze shot over my shoulder to everyone else, studying them for several seconds before relinquishing a tiny nod.

We left the food out for Margo, Graham's and Lila's cook, to put away so we could soak up some sun. I offered to stay on the beach and play with Anya while everyone else paddle boarded. Graham was right. Franz stood right up and kept his balance, although he seemed to enjoy sitting on it, letting Ronin paddle him around.

Lila meandered around on her board for a while before returning to the beach to hang out with Anya and me under the blue sun umbrella. We played with the bucket of beach toys supplied by our overly generous friends.

"I love watching you and Graham with the kids."

"Well…" she pulled a cloth out of her bag and wiped her sunglasses "…we love being with them."

"Yet … you don't have your own kids. I'm not trying to harp on you, but did you hear me mention you'll be forty before long? I feel like if you don't have children soon, you won't have them at all. And I *know* you've always wanted to have children of your own." I listened to the string of words tumbling from my lips, internally scolding myself for having that conversation with her when the talk I should have had with her involved my blessing for her to leave him.

Leave the politics.

Leave the spotlight.

Leave the man who said and did inappropriate things to her best friend.

I *so* badly wanted her to leave him, but on her own accord. My indebtedness to Graham left little room for me to be the instigator of their breakup. But if Lila decided to leave him without any interference or encouragement from me, then he couldn't hold that against me and my family.

Instead of saying any of that to her, out of fear of how Graham would react, out of fear of how *she* would react (since she always defended him), I encouraged her to make herself even more connected to him. The insane part? I thought a child might bring them closer together. I thought it would bring happiness to Lila's life and reset Graham's priorities—maybe fix his moral compass. How was it possible to want them together and apart at the same time? I didn't know. It had to be Lila. Her happiness meant as much as my own. I wanted to share mom stories. Pregnancy cravings. I wanted to see her dreams come to fruition like mine had.

"I'm sure we'll have them sometime." Fake smile.

I recognized it because I invented it.

Equal parts fright and elation filled my chest. *That* was a yes. Even fake answers held a spark of truth. What I saw inside earlier, the two of them interacting with Franz and Anya, was real. At least, it felt real. Lila would be a great mom, and Graham would pull his head out of his ass and be a great dad. The thing with Graham was his competitive spirit wouldn't allow for anything less than greatness. I knew he'd feel the need to be as great of a dad as Ronin and far superior to his own father.

My nose wrinkled. "I know this sounds terrible, but I needed to hear you say that. I needed to know things would be okay between you and Graham. It's your life, but I've never been able to fully separate your lives from mine, and when you're not doing well, I'm not doing well. Not in the sense of Ronin *feeling* you, but just because I still feel responsible for the success or failure of your relationship."

"I'm glad." Lila tipped her head back in the beach chair. "I feel responsible for your happiness too."

Ouch …

That felt wrong. A gut punch of reality. Was that how it sounded when I said it to her?

"Wow …" I exhaled a breath of reality. "That's not good. How did I not see it until you said it back to me? Being responsible for someone else's happiness is a lot of pressure."

Lila rolled her head to the side. I couldn't see her eyes behind her glasses, but I imagined them filled with deep thoughts. "Thank you," she whispered.

"For what?"

"For finally seeing that." She straightened her head again.

Ouch ... just ... ouch ...

A few minutes later, the rest of the paddle boarding crew trudged up the beach with their boards in tow.

"Mommy! Mommy! That was so much fun!" Franz tried to run toward me, getting tripped up in the sand.

"That's great, babe. I knew you'd like it."

"Where's my hat?" He stabbed his little hand into the bag, coming up empty.

"Did you leave it on the counter?" I frowned at him, knowing that was exactly where he left it.

"I'll run and get it." Ronin slipped his feet into his flip-flops.

"I'll go with you." Lila stood. "I need to use the restroom."

They took one of the two golf carts parked at the end of the path that connected the house to the beach. Franz plopped down in the sand, sorting through the beach toys.

"Will you put more sunscreen on my back, Franz? I think I'm burning." To leave plenty of room in the shade for Anya to play, I sat halfway in the sun, my back taking the brunt of its rays.

"Okay," he mumbled as I slid the lotion from the side pocket of the bag.

"I've got it." Graham plucked it from my hand and dropped to his knees in the sand behind me.

"I see people with serious zoom lenses on their cameras, just over the hill. I don't think you should lay a hand on me. It won't look good in the tabloids tomorrow," And ... I didn't want him spreading lotion on my back.

Not since he'd made it clear that making me uncomfortable was his favorite game.

"It's a well-known fact that you're my best friend. The kids are right here. Our spouses were just here too. I'm not worried about the tabloids."

That was bullshit and he knew it. The photos wouldn't have the kids in them, and the gossip articles wouldn't mention Lila's and Ronin's presence either.

I stiffened when his hands, slathered with lotion, moved along my back. "It doesn't have to be a lot, just get some on my shoulders really quick and that will be good," I squeaked before clearing the trembling frog from my throat.

"It won't. Your whole back is pink." He made the slowest fucking strokes along my back. Thoroughly covering every inch of it.

Slipping his hand under the straps to my top, then sliding lower until his fingertips just barely breached the inside of my bikini bottoms. Every move so very slow as I held my breath and smiled at my kids. Smiled for the cameras.

"Graham!" I seethed as his hands slid around to my abdomen. "I can reach that area just fine." My hands covered his hands to stop his motion.

"Sorry, I just had some extra lotion on my hands." He chuckled, climbing to his feet and brushing off his knees before claiming Lila's chair and tossing his hat over the front of his board shorts.

He had an erection. I didn't see it, and thank god, I didn't have to feel it that time, but I knew it. And I *hated* it.

CHAPTER TEN

Ronin

"I'M NOT GOING to say anything to Evie … yet." I broke the silence after a wordless ride to the house.

Lila opened the front door and glanced over her shoulder, giving me a slow inspection followed by a single nod. "Thank you."

"Some people live a long time with leukemia if treated promptly and managed properly."

"True," she slipped off her sandals and padded toward her bedroom.

I kicked off my flip-flops and headed to the kitchen to find Franz's hat.

"Hello." A brunette, maybe in her fifties, glanced over her shoulder as she poured some sort of batter into a pan.

"Hi. I'm Ronin." I grabbed Franz's hat.

"I'm Margo. It's nice to meet you. Are you enjoying your stay in the Hamptons?"

"Yes. So far it's been good."

"Can I get you anything?"

I smiled. If I needed something, I'd get it myself.

They lived a much different life than I had ever experienced. It wasn't that my family was ever poor. My parents did well, but there was a huge difference between "well" and the top one percent.

"I'm good but thank you." I headed back to the foyer to wait for Lila.

I waited.

And waited.

Concerned, I ventured toward her bedroom, tapping the door several times. "Lila?"

She opened the door. Again, she gave my whole body a long inspection. So much sadness resided in her eyes. Nothing like the Lila I met in Vancouver. "Right now, can you feel me?"

"I don't know. Some days it's hard to separate my own feelings, my own aches and pains, from yours. I attribute the inexplicable to you."

"So you feel what I *physically* feel?"

Twisting my lips, I thought about the right answer. I wasn't sure I possessed it. "Well, I thought my connection to you was purely physical but now I think it's more than that."

"More how? You know what I'm thinking?"

I chuckled. "I can't read your mind, if that's what you're asking. It's still just a feeling, but I think it's emotional. So if you're depressed right now, then yes, I feel you. I think I feel you when you're so …" I shook my head. I didn't need to go there. This part of me felt a strong need to crawl into her head to know how much of her I really felt.

"When I'm so what?" Her head canted to the side.

"Nothing."

"Finish it, Ronin." She sounded just like Evie.

After blowing a quick breath out of my nose, I continued, "I think I feel your ... *libido*. Or maybe lack thereof. Maybe you're sort of turned off by Graham. I feel like I've felt your lack of desire to be intimate with him. I've felt that toward Evie, and I don't have a damn clue why that would be ... unless it's you."

She tipped her chin to her chest. "I'm sorry."

"It's ... it's fine." I couldn't muster more than a lame *it's fine.* That in and of itself proved just how much her depression had taken ahold of me. She didn't want to be in the Hamptons any more than I did. She wanted to be at home, shutting the blinds and crawling into bed, giving life the middle finger.

I tried again, hoping I could at least act like I wasn't walking under a constant cloud of gloom. "It's not your fault. Please don't ever think that." I rested my hand on her shoulder, and something happened. A feeling.

She tipped her head, leaning into my touch, closing her eyes. My pulse increased a bit, each beat in my chest gaining strength. And I felt ... good.

A different good.

Normal.

The ringing in my ears stopped.

But she wasn't dead.

I pulled my hand away. She opened her eyes, appearing a little startled by my quick retreat.

It took a few seconds, but eventually the good feeling

disappeared.

The ringing in my ears returned.

I second-guessed what I thought happened while we shared a long silent moment.

Did she feel something?

I had to know, so I inched my hand toward her again, pressing my palm to her cheek.

No more ringing.

No more pain.

No more emotional fatigue.

She drew in a shaky breath, pressing her hand over mine, again closing her eyes. My hand was on her cheek, but it felt like a gentle hand on my own cheek. It felt … good.

My hand slid from Lila's face to the back of her neck, spreading warmth along my own skin. The silence—the true silence—made it hard to let go of her. I just wanted to stand there and feel good for a little bit longer. A ray of light squeezing through an opening in the clouds on a cold day.

Before I could force myself to let go, she took a step forward, sliding her hands up my chest and around my neck, leaving a trail of warmth. I pressed her head to my shoulder, wrapping my other arm around her. We didn't say a single word. We just stood there, embracing each other.

What could we possibly have said?

Of course, it was weird and probably wrong to hug Lila for so long, but it didn't feel wrong in that moment. It felt good. Not necessarily right, just good. And when you wander through long days not feeling happy, not feeling alive, not taking full breaths or giving your all to those who love you ... well, a moment of normalcy, bliss ... *good* is pretty fucking amazing.

We held each other for at least five minutes that felt like five seconds when I forced myself to let her go. Before I could say anything—not that I had a clue how to explain what just happened between us—a voice echoed from the foyer.

I took two huge steps backward, blinking several times as I realized I still felt good, the ringing in my ears no longer there. Guilt swirled around us, but I didn't let it touch me.

"Ronin?" Evie called.

"We're coming!" Lila smiled, a real one, while picking up Franz's hat that I'd let drop to the floor and sliding out the doorway past me. "I was just showing Ronin the rest of the house."

I followed Lila.

"I pinched my finger in the umbrella when we moved everything so the kids could start digging in a new area of smooth sand. It's not that bad, but I should wash it and put on a Band-Aid because it broke the skin and doesn't want to stop bleeding."

"I have a first aid kit in the bedroom," I inspected her finger.

"Of course, you do." Evie mocked at my always pre-paredness.

"I'll meet you guys down at the beach." Lila held up Franz's hat. "Someone will be wondering where his hat is at."

"Thank you, Lila. We'll be out in a few minutes." Evie headed toward the bedroom.

I gave Lila one last look. I wasn't sure what it said. Maybe, W*hat the fuck just happened?* Maybe the look held no actual words at all.

She gave me one last glance too. It was kind. It held hope without regret. Neither one of us would ever intentionally hurt Evelyn. Lila's lack of guilt told me it was okay. The moment between us meant something different than intimacy, like someone getting a massage. It felt good in a way that wasn't sexual. It was one person physically doing something for another person. An exchange.

That was it.

Period.

Lila pivoted and waltzed out the door, and I made my way to the bedroom. Evie was in the bathroom, washing her finger. I fetched a Band-Aid and ointment from the kit.

"Does it hurt?" I dabbed the ointment onto the cut and covered it with the Band-Aid.

"No."

"That's good." I grabbed her head and kissed her, and it built like igniting an explosive. It wasn't my intention, and I didn't expect it. But the second my lips touched hers I *needed* her. Plunging my tongue into her mouth, I devoured her, feeding on all the lost moments from the previous weeks.

Evie stiffened at first, clearly caught off guard by my

sudden need to kiss her. Hell, I couldn't explain it either. The ringing was gone. I felt good. A kind of good I hadn't felt in many months. And all I wanted to do was show my wife how good I felt and share that amazing feeling with her.

Without demanding an explanation, her fingers claimed my hair, her tongue warring with mine. I knew what my needs were and why they demanded attention right that very minute, but I didn't know why she clawed at me with equal need. Had it simply been too long since I showed her that level of affection?

Whatever it was took on a life of its own. I untied her top, letting it fall to the floor. We broke our kiss just long enough for me to shrug off my tee. Then our mouths crashed together again. Her breasts pressed flush to my chest. I managed to untie one side of her bikini bottoms before she shoved down the front of my swim trunks and stroked my dick several times.

I couldn't remember the last time I felt such urgency, maybe never. But why was her touch just as desperate? She pressed her hands to the vanity counter and hopped up. We kissed again as I fisted my dick and guided it between her legs as she wrapped those sexy legs around my waist.

"Roe …" She moaned as I slid into her in one hard thrust.

"Fuck … Evie …" I murmured over her lips. "I need this so badly." I palmed her ass, trying not to leave marks on it, but it was hard to harness any kind of control while I held her from sliding back as I moved inside of her like I needed it to breathe.

Harder.

Faster.

Deeper.

Evie cried out when she orgasmed, biting my shoulder, clawing my back. A few thrusts later, I stilled, feeling myself release for an eternity. I couldn't ever remember having such an intense orgasm. My whole body shook, and I nearly collapsed to my knees.

I touched Lila and it made me want to fuck my wife into another dimension. Something was messed-up. And I knew it when I came down from my high, eased out of Evie, and the ringing in my ears returned.

"Thank you." She grinned. "I needed that more than you can imagine." Evie hopped off the vanity and shuffled to the toilet.

Wrong.

I didn't have to imagine how much she needed that because I needed it more.

CHAPTER ELEVEN

"**H**AS LILA STARTED treatment?" I asked Graham as we enjoyed cold drinks in the clubhouse before teeing off. Evelyn and Lila stayed at the house to play by the pool with the kids.

He chewed a cube of ice, each crunch accentuating the tense muscles in his jaw as he stared out the window at the well-dressed elite in their golf carts cruising around the course. "She's looking into options. I'm encouraging her to get more opinions."

"How's the alternative treatment working? I mean, she doesn't seem too bad. Is she tired a lot?"

I was depressed most of the time, but I wasn't exhausted. People with leukemia suffered severe exhaustion.

Graham bit his lips together, his eyes slightly narrowed at me. After several seconds of just … looking at me, he nodded slowly and hummed. "Yes, the alternative treatment seems to be helping, at least with the symptoms."

"What kind of alternative treatment is she doing?"

He glanced at his watch. "We're up." He stood. "I'm feeling good today, buddy. Hope you brought your best game."

Lila had cancer. I couldn't give two fucks about a golf game.

After we made our way through eighteen holes, talking about random shit as if his wife wasn't possibly dying, we made it back to the house in time for dinner.

"Mrs. Porter." Graham kissed Lila's head as we passed through the great room.

She looked up from her book and smiled at me. The rest of her body seemed to stiffen beneath Graham hovering over her.

"How was golfing?" She closed her book, letting it rest in her lap.

"Perfect. I should have joined the PGA instead of running for governor," he mumbled, sauntering out of the room toward the bedroom. "I'm going to grab a quick shower. Feel free to join me."

Lila's cheeks turned pink as her smile faded into a grimace.

I averted my gaze to avoid making her feel any more uncomfortable. "Are Evie and the kids here or at the beach?"

"The bedroom." Lila pushed the ottoman away and sat up straight, depositing the book on the table next to the Tiffany lamp. "The sun zapped the energy from the kids. They both fell asleep after she gave them a bath. I peeked in on them ten minutes ago. She's asleep too."

I jutted my chin toward the book. "What are you reading?"

She flipped it over to show me the cover.

"Paranormal?"

She nodded, wrinkling her nose. "Don't judge me for loving vampires."

I laughed. "No judgment. I went through a big vampire phase in my early twenties."

"So before you devoured mystery novels, you were intrigued by blood and fangs?"

Pulling the ottoman out another foot or so, I sat on it facing her. "Before my near-death experience, I was obsessed with superheroes. Still am." I smirked and that brought a fantastic grin to Lila's face. "Then I became obsessed with all things paranormal. Now I don't have to read about it because I swear I'm living it."

Her smile left her face, replaced with knitted eyebrows and wrinkles etched into her forehead. "I'm not going to let my pain burden you."

I felt her on too many levels for her to be able to say that to me with any certainty or true conviction. The elephant in the room squeezed between us, staring us both in the face until the awkwardness reached a suffocating level.

"About yesterday …"

"No." Her head shook on repeat. "That was on me. I needed someone to embrace me without expecting something in return. And I didn't let go because I let myself believe that you needed something from me too. Which is ridiculous because—"

"It's …" I sighed, squeezing my eyes shut for a few seconds. "It's not ridiculous, Lila. When we touched, I felt …"

Good?

How could I say that? That sounded creepy. Her best friend's husband feeling good in the arms of a woman who wasn't his wife.

How messed-up was that? Saying it aloud wasn't going to make it sound any better.

"You felt what?" she whispered.

"Nothing." I glanced up at her. Lila resembled Evie in so many ways, including the innocence in her blue eyes that screamed for the world to just be kind … just be fair. It shouldn't have been me keeping her secret. It should have been Evie comforting her lifelong friend. "I felt no pain. I felt no connection to you. I felt normal. But I only felt that way *because* we were touching. When I released you the first time, that peace lingered for a little while. When I released you the second time, it lasted even longer."

Lila hugged herself, shoulders turned inward.

"It's okay." I rested my hands on my knees, drumming my fingers. "You don't have to believe me. If it weren't happening to me, I sure wouldn't believe me. And I'm not trying to make you uncomfortable."

Her eyes glossed over into a blank stare, aimed in the vicinity of my shoulder. I stood, opting to stop talking before I said anymore. Lila didn't need my problems. Turning toward the hallway, I took two steps and stopped. Lila's hand rested on my shoulder with my back to her. My eyes closed …

The ringing stopped.

The sorrow melted.

The pain vanished.

I drew in a shaky breath as her arms snaked around my torso, her warm cheek against my back. It felt like God himself embracing me. The good God. Not the one who cursed me. My hands inched up to cover hers. Once again, we stood idle, giving in to the unexplainable, feeding an undefinable need. With each touch, we crossed a barrier into a world that didn't feel real because Evie and our kids were my life, the only reality I ever wanted. Yet, touching Lila felt right and good.

Not painkiller good.

Not sexually good.

Not even Evie good.

Touching Lila felt good like my legs carrying my body, my heart circulating blood, my lungs claiming air. When we touched, I didn't feel her. I felt me.

Only me.

Truth? I wanted Lila to give me back what she took or take back what she gave me. I didn't know. I just knew that something *fit* when we touched.

It's wrong.

I knew it was at the very least, a little wrong, yet I didn't want her to let me go. The longer she held me, the longer I would feel normal for Evie and the kids.

"Lila?" Graham called.

Without a word or glance at each other, Lila released me and I walked toward the bedroom.

"Yes?" Her voice echoed as she padded down the hallway in the opposite direction toward their bedroom.

"Did you move my hair gel?"

She replied with a barely audible, "No."

The kids were on the king bed, still sleeping in spite of Evie running the hairdryer in the bathroom. I slid open the paneled door, glancing over my shoulder to see if the kids stirred.

They didn't.

My beautiful wife shot me a sideways glance and a blinding smile to go with it. "I fell asleep with a wet head," she said while turning off the blow-dryer.

I locked the door and grinned at her.

No ringing in my ears.

No feelings of depression.

No pain.

Her gaze flitted to my hand that turned the lock. "They'll wake up any second, Mr. Alexander." The way her eyebrow quirked into a crooked peak did nothing to help her case. It reminded me of all the *things* I loved about Evelyn Alexander.

In some ways it broke a tiny part of my heart too. Just minutes earlier, her best friend touched me … took away my pain. But it didn't make me want Lila. It made me want my wife. That had to mean something. That had to be what mattered most.

"You won't let me say what I want to say …" I took two steps in her direction. She looked like an angel booted out of Heaven—a wicked grin, nearly white messy hair, and a mischievous twinkle in her eyes. "So I have to *show* you." I grabbed her waist and jerked her into my body. The brush from her hand fell to the tile.

She cringed. "Oops …"

"Mom?" Franz's sleepy voice called from the bedroom.

"Ma," Anya mumbled.

Lifting onto her toes, she planted a kiss at the corner of my mouth with her full, upturned lips. "You've been a little *frisky* on this trip. Why is that?"

Why? Well, because it was pretty damn incredible to make love to my wife without feeling her best friend's emotional and physical distress.

Just *so* many words I couldn't say to her.

"I took time off work, but my dick never takes a vacation. He's always *hard* at work."

"I see. Dick is quite the competitor. I'm not going to lie … I like good, *stiff* competition." She grabbed Dick. (Yes, his official name was born in that moment. A fitting name without pretense or too much pomp and circumstance.)

I narrowed my eyes. "And I like it when you give me the world's biggest boner as our spawns climb out of bed to make their way to—"

Knock. Knock. Knock.

"Us." I sighed.

"I'd better go. Sorry. Hate to leave you hanging." She released me and winked.

"Bobbing," I grumbled. "You're leaving me bobbing. I'd prefer it to hang. But it won't at the moment."

Evie giggled, unlocking the door and shooting me her evil angel smirk. "He's such a dick."

"The biggest one ever." I, too, had an evil smirk.

"Fact." She opened the door. "How was your nap,

babies?"

"I not a baby." Franz rubbed his eyes, his blond hair unruly like his mom's hair.

Anya bypassed Evie's outstretched arms in pursuit of me. I told Dick to chill the fuck out. My daughter didn't need to see him showing off for her mom. Mini Me with her jet-black hair and dark eyes nuzzled into my neck as I carried her out of the bedroom. Her tiny hands patted my back. Anya always patted my back when I hugged her. She didn't do it to Evie, just me. I swear she knew I needed it. I needed that nonverbal "You're okay, Daddy."

CHAPTER TWELVE

Lila

EVELYN AND GRAHAM had sex—in college.
I didn't have sex with Ronin. I just let him hold me. It damn near brought me to tears. For those silent minutes in his arms, I didn't think about dying. I didn't feel any pain. I simply felt *needed*.

The rest of our holiday in the Hamptons went well. With the exception of feeling Ronin's eyes on me more often than usual, I think we met and exceeded Evelyn's expectations. Graham removed his political hat and spent our time in the Hamptons playing with the kids, golfing with Ronin, and pinning me to every surface of the bedroom to have sex.

It was rough, but that was just him. The fact that he could have found another bed to sleep in at night yet chose to sleep next to me, gave me a spark of hope that we would be fine. In spite of all the issues with my health over the previous year, I thought we might be able to salvage something and make the most of it for as long as possible. I didn't believe anyone was truly unredeemable.

"Do you think treatment will cure your cancer?" Graham asked as we entered the foyer after arriving home from the airport.

Without a pause in my stride, I climbed up the right side of the dual grand stairway. "I hope so," I murmured.

He followed me. The warm bubble from our time away popped, and I felt the cold shiver of reality again.

"You researched this? Leukemia and bruising?"

"Yes." I continued to my bedroom.

"Who else have you told?"

I grunted a laugh. "No one. Don't worry, you won't have to deal with my *illness* in the news."

"Lila." Graham grabbed my arm.

I flinched.

He loosened his grip. "I'm sorry this happened to us. But I'm going to do everything in my power to fix it."

I tugged my arm from his hold and turned toward him, tears in my eyes. "This didn't *happen* to us like a kitchen fire. You get that, right? You get how scared I am. Right? You get that every time you look at Evelyn the way you do, it hurts as much as my *cancer diagnosis*."

Maybe. Just maybe if he saw just how much he hurt me on so many levels, he would stop. Something would click in his brain.

He blew a breath out of his nose, taking a step back and crossing his arms over his chest while taunting me with his ridiculous smirk. "And how exactly do I look at Evelyn? Because from my vantage point, I've chased you for years. I've voiced all the things about you that I find far superior to Evelyn."

"She's your friend. You shouldn't degrade her in any way. You shouldn't compare her to anyone else. You should respect her. Her life choices. Her husband. Her children." I swatted at a tear that escaped. "And I am your wife. You shouldn't degrade me emotionally or physically. You shouldn't compliment me by putting down someone you feel has inferior qualities to me. Over the past few days, I got a glimpse of who you used to be—kind, fun, and loving. I fell in love with the man who took care of my best friend while I traveled the world. I fell in love with the way you cared for *Evelyn*—not me … Evelyn. Kindness is attractive. I *miss* the kind man I married. But I had the opportunity to see him again, and it gave me hope. Don't rip it away. Fix. You. Graham. And I'll be fine. We'll be fine."

The muscles in his jaw pulsed as he drew in a slow breath, hands fisted. Regret knocked at my conscience, scolding me for saying those things to him, but I didn't let it in. I stood brave and strong, willing to accept his reaction. The days of regretting my feelings were over.

"You're right." His forehead wrinkled as he nodded slowly, gaze dropping to his feet. "I can do better. When my term is over, I will make more time for family, especially the kids."

Hope.

There it was. I craved that hope.

"I want that." I salvaged a smile from that tiny spark of hope. "I'd started to give up hope that we would have children."

"Oh …" Graham lifted his gaze to me. "I mean Franz

and Anya." He reached for my face and my whole body hardened like a statue. "People with leukemia don't have babies." On a shrug, he brushed his thumb over my lips. "You can't wait forever to start treatment because you told Ronin. The clock has started. Even if he doesn't tell Evie, he's going to expect you to fight this. So if you weren't prepared to be sick and unable to participate in future plans with the rest of us, if you weren't prepared to spend your days in bed resting, if you weren't prepared to lose your hair, then you shouldn't have told him."

Pulling his hand from my face, I grimaced. "Ronin saw the bruises. What was I supposed to tell him? His mind immediately went to the idea that you're abusing me, Graham." Anger escalated my voice. "How does that make you feel? Because he sure as hell wasn't going to keep that a secret from Evelyn. So do you have a better idea to explain what he saw? Had you been in my shoes, what would have been your explanation?"

"I'm not upset with you for telling him. I'm simply stating the facts."

"I *hate* the facts," I seethed, but my anger didn't stop the tears. "Don't you hate them too? Don't you ask yourself how we got here? How our big dreams turned into this? When you see this…" I twisted my back to him, lifting my shirt to show him my colorful skin "…does it make you cringe? Does it break your heart? Do you seriously not ask yourself, *how did we get here?*" I dropped my shirt and faced him again. "Because this isn't fair." All my emotions rushed out into a wet, blubbering mess. "I didn't ask for this life! I don't want this life! So stop acting like this is my fault. Like I made my bed and now I have to lie in it."

With quick steps, he backed me into the wall just outside of my bedroom. His arms stretched over my head, pressed to the wall to cage me in with his body. I held my breath as I'd come to do quite often in his presence.

"Look at me."

I stared at his chest for a few more seconds before lifting my gaze to his cold eyes.

"I was in a good mood. I'd like to stay in a good mood. Can we forget about your *issues* for the night?" He sucked in a long breath and blew it out slowly. "Now, I'm going to get caught up on some work downstairs. Why don't you take a bath and I'll be up later and make everything better."

I wouldn't have sex with him. He couldn't make everything okay by sticking his dick inside of me after using the term *issues*. He liked to ride the line. Blame me for things that weren't my fault.

Twist reality.

Cast doubt.

Flaunt hope.

And slay dreams.

After he let me out of his body cage, I took a bath behind a locked bathroom door and settled into bed. I retrieved my journal from under my mattress and transcribed the events from the previous days. Graham liked to make me think everything that wasn't perfect in his life was somehow my fault. So I put the words we said to each other in writing to reread them again and again, thinking that if I somehow had done something wrong, I might see it more clearly after my mind had a chance to settle. By the time I finished writing page after page of my miserable life, my eyes hurt and so did my hand. After securing the journal in its hiding place and double-checking the lock on the bedroom door, I shut off the light and prayed for dreams of a better life.

But the thing about dreams that really sucked was they were often interrupted by real life—a king who kept keys to all the rooms in his castle.

In spite of my intentions to hold strong, I didn't say no—not aloud. In my head, I screamed it. In my head, I packed my bags and left. In my head, I never came back from Germany during my wanderer days after college. Evelyn never had the opportunity to convince me to give Graham a chance. In my head, I held on to a piece of dignity.

The next morning, I woke just after five in desperate need to pee. I eased out of bed, praying I didn't wake the monster beside me. He rarely stayed the night in my room. He called the rare gift of his presence all-night *love*. I called it control. I wasn't even sure when we split into two rooms. It started with him being up late and not wanting to wake me. We still shared the massive closet and bathroom—for a while. Then he took clothes and toiletries to his new room, again so he didn't wake me early in the mornings.

I was always to blame, and Graham was the martyr.

Everything ached, right down to my bones. *Leukemia* had that effect. When I tiptoed back into the room to grab my robe and cover my naked body before escaping to another room, Graham switched on the sconce by his side of the bed.

The light burned my eyes. He twisted from side to side, stretching his back. When he noticed me, he paused. Weeks earlier, I would have called that same look apologetic and regretful. Not anymore.

He wasn't my husband anymore. I didn't care what vows we exchanged. I shared my bed with a stranger.

"Have you ever considered boxing? It's a wonderful form of exercise." He yawned.

Boxing.

I hadn't turned on the light in the bathroom, but I suspected his reasoning for suggesting boxing had little to do with my need to get a good workout and a lot to do with the colorful shapes along my skin. Tying the sash to my robe, I padded to the door, turning at the last second.

"Do you like this? The way I look? Because I'll let go if you will. I won't have to unintentionally ruin your day anymore. You won't have to call me Evelyn when you're fucking me in the most impersonal way imaginable."

"I'm sorry." He ran both hands through his hair. "I was tired."

Tired.

Tired people didn't want sex. Tired people didn't get erections. Tired people *didn't* call their wives the wrong name.

"Did you ever really love me?" I whispered.

He glanced up, blinking slowly. Had he shown any sort of grimace, any sign at all that my question was absurd, I might have felt a flicker of regret, maybe even a spark of hope. "I loved you then. I love you now."

Lies.

He couldn't have said what he said and did what he did and still claim to love me. If that was love, then I hated love.

"I'm not giving up or letting go. 'Til death do us part. And no one's dying today."

CHAPTER THIRTEEN

Ronin

L
ILA WAS DEPRESSED.

I was depressed.

Depression didn't care about the awesomeness of your life. Two spunky kids. And a wife who took up singing in the shower.

"That was my song." I sipped my coffee while scrolling through the newsfeed on my phone—that was depressing too.

Embarrassing politics.

School shootings.

Reality TV updates.

"Well, if you're not going to sing it, then someone should." Evie kissed Franz on the head as he thumbed through a book.

My boy.

"Anya must be growing. She slept through my amazing concert." Evie smirked, pouring a cup of coffee before dishing up a bowl of oatmeal.

"Why not sleep in? She doesn't have preschool like

big stuff over there." I jerked my head toward Franz.

"Ugh … I can't believe he's starting preschool." Evie leaned down to kiss me before sitting in the chair next to me. "Franz, did you brush your teeth?"

"Uh-huh."

"Breakfast. Teeth. Lunch packed." I shot her a smile.

It felt forced.

Everything felt forced.

Fucking depression.

Since July, I'd talked to Lila twice. I didn't understand how she was going to go through cancer treatment and keeping it a secret from Evie. I didn't understand how her mere touch in the Hamptons temporarily took away my pain.

Our two conversations did nothing to reassure me that the secret I kept from Evie wouldn't destroy my marriage or their friendship. Lila said, "I'm taking care of it." That was it. No elaboration. No time to talk. Each call ended in under two minutes with a quick, "I have to go. Give Evie and the kids a kiss from me."

"What's your angle?" Evie narrowed her eyes at me. "Did you do something wrong? Will I be mad? Did you break something?"

I lied to you.

You'll be pissed off.

I broke your trust.

"Can't I be a good dad and get my son ready for school just because? Do my intentions have to be driven by guilt?"

"No." Her lips pursed to the side. "But I'm worried.

All joking aside, you haven't been yourself. You seem down, but like you're trying to hide it. Maybe I'm the one who did something wrong."

"Evelyn, you've done nothing wrong. I'm fine. Really. There's been a lot going on at work. Noah's considering retirement, and I know they're going to offer me his job. I haven't decided if I want it."

"Why wouldn't you want it?"

That was just it … I did want the job but discussing it with Evelyn distracted her from my other issues.

Your friend has cancer.

I feel her depression.

If she suffers … I will suffer too.

If you find out I lied to you, it will be worse than any amount of physical pain.

"It's a lot more responsibility."

That was true.

"So you might have to work more hours?" she asked, sipping her coffee.

No. Same number of hours, just more things to do in those hours. And less time on the slopes. That sucked … unless I had to deal with symptoms of leukemia.

"I'm not sure yet, but that's a possibility." I finished my coffee and took my cup to the sink.

"Well, I'm good with whatever you decide. Since rent isn't an issue, I can see about Sophie working more hours or hiring another employee so I can be here for the kids more often."

I grabbed my water bottle and my keys. "I appreciate that, babe." Before slipping on my shoes, I leaned over the back of the sofa and nuzzled Franz's neck. "I love you, big stuff. Have a great first day of school. I can't wait to hear all about it."

He giggled and wiggled away from my overly aggressive affection. "Okay … I will."

While slipping on my shoes, I crooked a finger at my wife. She pushed back in her chair and granted my request.

"I'm sorry." I wrapped my arms around her waist, bringing her flush to my body, stealing her heat, and inhaling her flowery soap scent. "Tomorrow I'll put on the concert. And I won't worry about this job. They haven't even offered it to me yet." Ignoring the ringing in my ears and the headache pulsing my left eye, I presented a happy face to my wife because she deserved it. On my worst day, she deserved my best smile.

"Don't ever apologize for feeling stressed." Evie kissed along my jaw and up my chin to rest her lips against mine. "Have a wonderful day." When she kissed me, I tried to focus only on the kiss, not the clawing discontent and unavoidable feeling of hopelessness.

"You too."

AFTER WORK, I attended a meeting, choosing to sit a few rows behind Adrianne Craig. I didn't know all the details of her sordid past, just that many women, including my wife, thought she was the Devil. People changed. I hated judging the Adrianne I knew based on her past. After all, everyone in that room had a less-than-perfect past or else we wouldn't have been there supporting each other through recovery and sobriety.

"Wait up, Ronin!" Adrianne jogged behind me as I fished the keys from my pocket on the way to my Subaru.

"Hey." I turned just as she caught up to me. "What's up?"

"I have a friend who's looking for a ski patrol position. You wouldn't happen to know if there will be any spots available where you work, would you?" She curled her black hair behind her ears and wrinkled her nose.

"Maybe. I'll look into it and let you know."

"I'd really appreciate that. Give me your phone, and I'll add my number to your contacts."

I slid my phone out of my pocket, unlocked the screen, and handed it to her. She stared at the home screen for a few seconds. It was a picture of Evie and the kids at the kitchen table making cookies. "How did you meet your wife?" She opened my contacts and typed in her information.

"We met at a cafe in Vancouver the day before I moved here. She was traveling with her friends."

"Fate, huh?"

I shrugged. "I'd like to think so."

She handed my phone back to me. "Lucky lady." She wet her lips before giving me a flirty grin. At least it looked flirty. I wasn't sure. Evelyn sharing Adrianne's past had tainted my mind. Maybe it wasn't anything more than a friendly smile.

"I'm the lucky one."

"Funny …" She crossed her arms over her chest, lifting and exposing more of her cleavage in the deep V-neck of her tight white tee. "I never would have taken you for the guy who settled down and started a family. When you've spoken of your past—your love of adventure, a true wanderer—I would have taken you for the eternal playboy. A repeat offender in the heartbreak department."

"Yeah, well, that was the case before Evie."

She took a step closer, twisting her lips while plucking an invisible hair from the shoulder of my shirt. "My theory is: once a heartbreaker, always a heartbreaker. She may have tamed you for a while, but your instinct to break free and seek a new adventure will surface, and you won't be able to suppress it. You'll resent the one thing you never thought possible to resent."

"What's that?" I furrowed my brow, taking a step backward.

"Love. In all its good intentions and time-tested appeal, love is nothing more than deadweight on our hearts. It's the strongest drug of all, yet no one shows up to these meetings to discuss the damage love did to their life. But the truth is, most addicts became addicts because they stopped feeling loved, or loved too much, or lost their focus—probably because they chose to love the wrong person or they felt they weren't good enough or strong enough because no one had ever loved them enough to make them feel worthy … *love*. Stupid. Fucking. Love."

Adrianne lost her flirtatious expression. Some sort of embarrassment or pain replaced it. Someone broke her heart. That was why she wanted to prove that no man was above the moral standard line. And what could I say? I hadn't cheated on my wife, but to say I wasn't secretly looking for an excuse to visit Lila would have been a lie.

"I'm sorry."

Her gaze shot up to mine. "For what?"

"For your pain."

After a brief pause, she nodded slowly. "Are you apologizing on behalf of all men?"

"Well," I chuckled. "I'm not sure I've been granted that sort of authority, to speak on behalf of *all* men. But on behalf of good men—at least those who try to be good—I can say we're sorry you've been treated badly, unfairly, or whatever that person or people did to cause you pain that might have contributed to why you have to attend these meetings."

She grunted, narrowing her dark eyes a bit. "Good men are the worst. They're blind to their infallibility. They think they're *good,* which makes them incapable of seeing their faults. They unknowingly put themselves in harm's way because they're overconfident. They buy a coworker a drink, claiming innocence and friendship, then they blame their spontaneous moment of infidelity on whiskey or tequila. They slither home and try to hide from the guilt, but eventually it pours out when their wife says something as simple as, 'Thanks for taking out the trash, Bob. You're the best.' Then he falls to his knees, sobbing like a baby who lost his binky."

I grinned, trying to dismiss her generalizations about good men. "You don't think that's a bit cynical? Are you saying bad men are better?"

"Bad men are my favorite. They unapologetically take what they want without excuses. They fuck you once in the bathroom of the bar, again in the car, and against the outside of your apartment door. They don't think about getting caught because they made up their minds before ever sticking their dick in you that *you* were worth the risk. I've never had a *bad man* make me feel like I was a bad decision. And I've never had a bad man cheat on me and ask for a second chance or forgiveness."

Again, she grunted a laugh. "Maybe bad people are perceived as being bad when in actuality they're brutally honest. And good people are in fact the liars we can't truly trust. They claim those lies are their attempt to save us from feeling too much pain. Nope. Give me the bad guy who doesn't even take off his wedding band over the guy who nervously rubs his thumb over his naked ring finger while staring at my cleavage."

I jabbed my thumb over my shoulder. "I'd love to hear more about your stereotypes for men, but today was Franz's first day of school, and I want to be home in time to hear all about it over dinner."

"Sorry. I'm sure you're in a bit of a conundrum. That wasn't fair of me."

"What conundrum is that?" I turned and continued toward my car.

"You can't win. If you stick with the good-guy stereotype, you know I think you're a coward who doesn't have the gumption to take what he wants whenever he wants it. On the other hand, if you go with the bad-guy image, it's basically an invitation to pursue you."

"What the hell?" I stuttered as her words become nothing but background chatter when my flat tires came into view.

"Oh … that's not good." Adrianne squatted, inspecting the tire, one of two flat tires.

One tire would have passed as a bad tire or a nail. Two tires raised suspicion. I lived in an uppity ski town. Vandalism was rare. Anyway, who slashed two random tires? No one. So that meant I had pissed someone off. But who? I had no known enemies.

"Not how I wanted this day to end." I retrieved my phone again to call Evie.

Adrianne stood and rested her hand on my arm. "Don't bother anyone, especially your wife since it's your kid's big day. I'll give you a ride home."

She was right. Evie planned on making lasagna, Franz's favorite, and probably cookies—snickerdoodles. She was likely in the middle of meal prep. "I can call my friend Noah or a taxi."

"Don't be ridiculous." She tugged on my arm until I stumbled a few steps toward her. "I'm right here. I have no family. No plans. I won't take no for an answer. Let's go."

Bad ideas usually came with good reasons. Maybe she'd drop me off at the end of my drive.

"Oh, sorry." She laughed, reaching over the console as I opened the passenger door to her red BMW. "Casper is *my* baby. His toys end up spread throughout my house and my car." She tossed several dog toys into the backseat. "But I can't complain. He's the best dog."

I slid into the seat and shut the door. "What breed of dog?"

"Bernese Mountain Dog."

"That's a large dog."

She laughed. "Yes. He's huge. A gentle giant." Backing out of the parking spot, she shot me a playful wink.

"I'd love to get a dog for the kids."

"Oh! You should get one from the breeder where I got Casper. She only has one litter a year. It's not a business, just a passion. They are well cared for and very healthy."

"I'll think about it. It's been a while since I suggested it to Evelyn. I brought it up before her mom died, but we decided to wait. And we just haven't talked about it again."

"I didn't know her mom died. I'm sorry."

I nodded several times. "Thank you."

"My mother has been battling cancer for the last year, so I've been slowly preparing for the possibility of losing her."

"Oh, I … I didn't know."

She shrugged. "I don't tell that many people, probably because I don't have any friends."

What was I supposed to say? Before I had a chance to think of something, she said it herself.

"It's hard to make and keep friends when people think I'm after their husbands. You don't know how much it means to me that Evelyn isn't that way. Clearly, she feels secure in your marriage. I hope you never do anything to break her trust in you."

I glanced at her, but she kept her head forward, both hands white-knuckled on the steering wheel. Someone broke Adrianne, which sent her down a path of destruction, obliterating the lives of innocent and some probably not-so-innocent victims. She never shared specific details in the group, but resentment dripped from her words—the grinding of her teeth, the sharp release of her breath.

"Trust is hard. It comes in many forms. We trust the people we love to be honest, but we also trust them to protect us. What happens when the two are at odds?"

"Depends." Adrianne's deep red lips twisted to the side. "You have to be sure your intentions are true ... pure. If you lie to someone you love to protect them, it better be completely for them."

"Have you ever lied to selflessly protect someone?"

"No." She smirked. "I did it for money and revenge, but I never disguised it as love."

I shook my head, glancing out the window as we approached the road to my house. Before I had a chance to say anything, she turned right.

Taking a thick swallow, I scraped my teeth along my bottom lip. "Should I be worried that you know where I live?" Inching my gaze back to her, I waited for a response. *Anything* to explain how she knew where to go.

Her expression fell flat as if she didn't hear me. I didn't mumble or whisper. The radio was off. The road had been smooth. She heard me.

"Toby's story irritated me tonight. I didn't buy a word he said. I can't believe Mike didn't call him out on it. Seriously ... who blames their addiction on their fifteen-year-old daughter?"

Toby's fifteen-year-old daughter ran him over *on purpose* with an ATV. He got addicted to opioids. Adrianne must have caught something in the story that I didn't. The guy had half a leg amputated, and his wife left him because she just couldn't handle being married to a "cripple." And his daughter got off scot-free because Toby told the police it was an accident.

I loved my kids right down to my soul, but I wondered if even that kind of eternal love could be severed if one of them chased me down for nearly a mile, weaving in and out of trees until I tripped, allowing them to run over me multiple times like roadkill.

So, while I didn't completely understand Toby lying for his daughter, I also didn't understand Adrianne being so critical of his moment of honesty earlier. I mean … he broke down in tears, feeling like a failure, wondering what he did wrong. Apparently, taking away a child's cellphone after catching her with two naked guys in the back of the family minivan was what old Toby did wrong.

Note to self: Don't give Franz and Anya cellphones— ever.

But really, screw Toby, his psycho daughter, and his heartless wife … I had bigger issues. Adrianne made it to my driveway without asking me for my address or assistance in navigating. And when I asked her about it … she brought up TOBY!

"I should come inside and say hi to Evelyn. I feel like we didn't get to say much to each other at the restaurant when we met." She put her BMW in *Park*.

"How did you know where I live?" I unbuckled my seat belt and opened the door, staying in the seat until she answered me.

Adrianne gave me a soft smile. "Calm down. It's not near as interesting or suspicious as what you're clearly thinking." She rolled her eyes. "I was behind you a few weeks back." She jerked her head toward the main road. "You pulled into your driveway. I assumed you lived here. I guess this could have been really embarrassing had it not been your home." On a wink, she lowered her voice, "Like … had it been your mistress's house."

"I don't have a mistress."

Her mouth quirked into a half smile as she lifted a single shoulder. "Well, that's why I figured this had to be your house. Sorry. I wasn't trying to spook you. Just an honest coincidence."

Had Adrianne not shared part of her story, had Evelyn not told me about her home-wrecking past, would I have been so distrusting? Probably not.

As I started to climb out of the seat, my wife, peeking through the kitchen window, snagged my attention.

"I'm sure Evelyn would love to say hello to you."

One hundred percent not true.

"Please, come inside for a few minutes."

My options were all terrible. Not inviting her inside would have made my innocent plea to Evie much harder. Who invites their mistress into the house? Adrianne was *not* my mistress, but perception meant everything at that point. Evelyn could be upset that I let Adrianne give me a ride home. But if I invited her into the house, she couldn't accuse me of anything more. Right?

Fingers crossed.

"Sounds great!"

It didn't. It sounded like a horrible idea. All the good ideas vanished when I agreed to let her give me a ride home.

"Hey," I peeked my head in the back door, laying it on the chopping block for my wife. "I had two flat tires, so Adrianne gave me a ride home." Adrianne followed me as I stepped into the house.

"Hello again." Adrianne waved at Evelyn.

Evie wiped her hands on a dishtowel, more like strangled the towel. I predicted my neck would be next. "Hi," she replied through clenched teeth and a forced smile.

"We didn't get to talk much the night we met. I just wanted to tell you how much I appreciate you loaning me your husband when I need an ear. I don't have that many friends."

I stood on the sideline between the two women with my hands shoved into the pockets of my jeans.

Evie didn't offer Adrianne anything more than a slow nod and an unblinking inspection like a fighter sizing up her competition.

"Well, thanks again for the ride." I took a step toward Adrianne, herding her toward the door. But she didn't budge one inch.

"Anytime. It was quite…" she bit her lip and fluttered her eyelashes "… fun."

Fun? No, it wasn't fun. It was a ride. A ten-minute ride. I had no idea why she insisted on giving me a flirty grin while doing weird things with her eyes.

"I wouldn't call having two flat tires *fun*. Still ... thanks for the ride." When she *still* didn't budge, I stepped around her and opened the door. What could I say? See you later? The voice of reason in my head whispered *not* to say that. The last thing Evelyn would want to hear was that.

"I'd love to have coffee sometime." Adrianne ignored the open door behind her as she addressed my wife again.

Evie shrugged. "You don't need my permission to have coffee."

I loved that woman, even if she refused to let me say the actual words.

Adrianne chuckled. "I meant, I'd love to have coffee with you sometime."

"I don't drink coffee."

Lie.

"Oh. Well, how about tea?"

Evie returned a tightlipped smile and shook her head.

"Wine."

"I don't drink alcohol."

Another lie.

"Water?" Adrianne curled her hair behind her ears.

"Yes, I drink water. But who gets together over water? Thank you for returning *my* husband to me. Goodnight." Evie turned, resuming her cooking.

Adrianne pivoted, shooting me a sad smile. "I guess friends are overrated," she mumbled like a rejected child on a playground as she stepped out the door.

"Goodnight." I refrained from saying anything else

because I couldn't read Adrianne, but I could read my wife.

"I could have picked you up," Evie said with her back to me as I shut the door. "Noah probably would have picked you up. They also have these people called cab drivers or Lyft drivers that will drive you home for a small fee."

On a sigh, I toed off my shoes. "She was insistent. I just wanted to get home. I didn't want to stand in the parking lot arguing with her over a ten-minute drive." Before she could say another word, my arms slid around her waist and my chin rested on her shoulder. "Are Franz and Anya playing in their rooms?"

She nodded to her phone on the nanny cam app and the split screen video footage of their rooms.

"Did Franz have a good first day?"

Another nod.

"Are you going to speak to me tonight? I need to call and get my car towed, but I need to know we're good first."

Evie dropped the bread knife on the cutting board and wiggled out of my arms to turn toward me. "Fun. She called the ride fun. What happened in her car that was so fun? Because she bit her lip like she wanted to eat you."

"Evie … I don't know." My hands fell to my sides. I had to work in the morning. And two flat tires weren't going to get me there. But I didn't want to miss eating with my family. I just wanted to have a nice dinner and skip the third degree. More than that … I wanted to not feel so damn depressed, and I wanted my head to stop hurting. My left eye still felt like it was going to explode. "I'm going to go see the kids."

As I started to turn, Evie grabbed my wrist. "That's it? That's the best you have?"

Yes. That was the best I had. Not feeling the urge to plead my case—to beg for her to tell me she wasn't mad, that she understood—was proof that something was seriously messed-up in my head. "What do you want from me?"

"I want you to kiss me like you missed me. I want you to back me into the nearest wall and put your hands in places that would confuse the kids if they caught us. I want you to whisper in my ear all the incredibly dirty things you can't wait to do to me when the kids go to sleep."

I wanted to *want* to do all of those things. I just … didn't. Not with Evie. Not with Adrianne. Not with anyone. It was like someone reached into my body and ripped my sex drive right out of me, leaving behind a pathetic, limp man with the world's sexiest wife.

"Maybe another night when I don't have to figure out how I'm going to get my car fixed and back in the garage by morning. I'll check on the kids while you finish up, unless you need me to do something else."

She deflated.

I was unexplainably damaged, but not completely broken. Framing her face in my hands, I bent forward and brushed my nose against hers. "This raincheck has *nothing* to do with what's-her-name."

Evie placed her hands over my hands and lifted onto

132

her toes a fraction to kiss me. I didn't deny her. I liked kissing my wife, even if it didn't ignite me the way it did before Lila got sick.

She fought me when I tried to end the kiss. The fingernails of one hand clawed into my hand while her other hand moved along my abs and below my waist. Her body turned to stone. We stopped.

My eyes closed as my forehead rested against her forehead.

"I thought it would take longer than five years for us to get to this point," she whispered, releasing my limp dick and turning away from me to resume cutting the bread.

"Evie—"

"The kids are waiting for you. Just go."

CHAPTER FOURTEEN

Evelyn

"I'M CO-PARENTING," I said as soon as Lila answered her phone. After weeks of not talking about Adrianne's attempt to befriend me, weeks of not having sex, weeks of not discussing Ronin's inability to get an erection with my hand stroking his junk, I decided I needed my best friend.

"Hi," she sounded groggy.

"Sorry. Were you sleeping?" I glanced at my watch, cutting a new batch of soap.

"No. But I'm a little tired." She cleared her throat, coming back with a little more strength in her voice. "What do you mean you're co-parenting?"

"I'm living with the father of my children. We cook meals, clean, play with the kids, and share a bed—never crossing the invisible line in the middle. Sometimes, like before he leaves for work or right when he gets home, he gives me a hug and kiss on the top of my head, but that's it. It's the affection you'd give your mother or a sister, maybe even a friend."

I thought of all the times Graham gave me the same kind of attention. At that point, I would have given anything for Ronin to look at me the way Graham looked at me. Why was the wrong person giving me the "more-than-friends" look?

"Has he told you why he's not showing more affection?"

I sighed. "No. Well, sort of. He blames it on stress with work. But we've been through a lot of stress in our nearly six years of marriage, and it's never had this effect on us. The problem is, on the outside we seem fine. He's going to work, engaging with the kids, he even asks me about things at my shop and does his fair share of helping out around the house. Like I said, he's a roommate, a co-parent. I miss my *husband*. My lover. But I'm afraid to say anything because …"

"Because why?"

I wiped my hands on a towel and picked up my phone, bringing it closer to my face in the unlikely chance Sophie could hear me from the front of the shop. "I don't think he can get an erection. And I don't want to embarrass him by asking about it."

Silence.

I waited.

And waited.

She had licked my nipples. Why did erectile dysfunction silence her?

"Lila?"

"I'm … I'm here. Just thinking."

"Do you think I should say something? And if so,

what? How do I make him not feel bad?"

"It's probably stress."

"Or an affair." I didn't really believe it, but I wasn't immune to insecurity.

"Evelyn, you know better than that."

"Remember Adrianne Craig?"

"The woman who took down so many prominent men with nothing more than her reckless cunt? Yes."

"She's in Ronin's support group. I caught them having dinner one night." Caught was a strong word. I wasn't sure they were trying to hide anything. "And she drove him home a few weeks ago because he had flat tires. She asked me out for coffee."

"You're not serious."

I paced my lab, feeling on edge again. Why did Adrianne make me so uneasy? I *knew* Ronin would never cheat on me. And he certainly wouldn't bring his mistress to the house if he did cheat on me.

"I'm serious."

"Tell him to find a different group."

I laughed, rubbing the back of my neck. "Then he'll think I don't trust him."

"Tell him it's her you don't trust."

"I don't trust her to what? Not rape him. He's twice her size. Clearly, he'll see that I don't trust him to resist her if she makes advances toward him."

"She's a professional home-wrecker. The thing is … she doesn't even have to fuck a guy to ruin his life. All she has to do is cast doubt by—"

"Driving him home and flaunting herself in front of

his wife," I finished.

Lila sighed. "Yeah. That."

"If he's not sleeping with her, it still doesn't explain his lack of sexual desire for me. It sucks. It totally sucks to feel like your husband doesn't want you like that."

"Tell me about it," Lila said in a soft voice.

I cringed. "How are things between you and Graham?"

"Fine. Why do you ask?" Her words came sharp and defensive.

"A while back, you told me he basically scheduled time to have sex with you in his office. Things didn't seem so fine then."

She sighed slowly, like she needed to exhale but didn't really want me to hear it. "Nothing to worry about. We're having sex, still in his office and in bed too."

I chuckled. "Don't sound so enthused."

Lila said it like a description of chores she begrudgingly had to do.

"It's just …"

"Just what?" I asked.

"Nothing."

"Maybe I should talk to him."

"Don't. Him thinking I'm telling you things doesn't make them better. It makes them worse. Would you want me telling Ronin that you're confiding in me about his issues?"

"No." I frowned. "I hate that we can't help each other. Remember when we used to be able to solve each other's issues?"

"Yeah," Lila whispered with such a solemn breath. "I miss those days."

"Me too."

"Just be patient with Ronin. You've both been through a lot over the past couple of years. He was a pillar for you after your mom died, while still dealing with his own addiction recovery. Marriages go through unexplainable rough patches. This is just one. It will pass."

"Is that what's happening with you and Graham? A rough patch?"

"No. I think him becoming governor fundamentally changed him. He's not the same man I married, so either I can accept it or …"

"Leave?"

"Sure. Listen, I have to go, but keep me informed on things between you and Ronin. I'm always here for you."

"Thanks, Lila. That goes both ways. Please don't ever forget that."

I ended the call, feeling a little better in some ways and a little worse in other ways. There was no comfort in knowing that my life wasn't perfect and neither was Lila's life. My kind of misery didn't love company. Her unhappiness compounded my own. It sucked.

Before I could wrap the bars of soap, my phone rang and my sister's face popped up on the screen. "Hey, Katie."

"Guess who had IVF this morning?" she practically squealed.

"I'm thinking you, but last month you said you weren't even close to having the money to try it again."

"Until Graham gave me the money. He said I was like his little sister and he wanted to see me start a family. Evie, he's the best! I love Ronin, but how did you not end up married to Graham? He saved Dad's life, he helped prolong mom's life, and now this."

A painful knot formed in the pit of my stomach, another thing forever tying me to Graham Porter, another thing I would never be able to repay—an eternity of indebtedness.

The score: Porters—everything. Evelyn—nothing.

If only I could have saved Graham from a burning building, shielded his body from a gunshot wound, or donated an organ he needed, I might have been able to work my way out of the hole.

"Evie? Did you hear me?"

I cleared my throat and stumbled over my words. "Y-yeah. I … that's … great. I'm happy for you." That was on me. Graham asked me about my dad and Katie, and I casually mentioned how they were saving up for IVF. It just slipped …

"I need you to visit Graham and give him a big hug from me. Promise me you'll do that?"

"Sure." I cringed. "How's Dad? I haven't talked with him since last week."

"He's good. Grandpa and Grandma have been going through a bunch of stuff in their attic, and I think it's been tough to see so many photos and memories of Mom."

"We need to go through her stuff."

"I know." Katie sighed. "Just not now. I'm not ready

and neither is Dad."

I didn't argue. My plate had reached capacity. The last thing I needed was a stroll down memory lane at a time when I so desperately needed my mom.

"Keep me up to date. Love you, Katie."

"Will do. Kiss Franz and Anya for me."

I hummed a mm-hmm before pressing *End.*

CHAPTER FIFTEEN

"**Y**OU CAN'T JUST close down a whole restaurant for me." I frowned at Graham as he stood from the table in the far corner of the posh downtown Denver sushi bar. I called him the day before, requesting lunch in the next few weeks. He made it happen the very next day.

Private jet transportation.

Car waiting for me at the airport.

And a closed down restaurant.

"I can and I did." He pulled me in for a hug.

A little too tight.

A little too long.

His hands a little too low on my back.

Lips that lingered too long next to my ear when he whispered, "Anything for you, Evelyn."

Graham Porter, the boy in college, befriended me. Governor Porter, the man with more money and power than one person deserved, manipulated my feelings, my family, my job, my whole damn world. Hence the reason for requesting lunch.

After I wiggled for him to release me, he let me go and slipped off his black suit jacket. My friend was unquestionably a very handsome man in a three-piece suit—very David Gandy.

"A soup and sandwich lunch, Graham. This is all very unnecessary." I sat down as a waiter rushed to lay a crisp white napkin on my lap and scoot my chair in a fraction.

"If you want soup and a sandwich, I'll have it brought here."

I rolled my eyes. "I'm sure the owners of a sushi restaurant would love for you to have food from another restaurant delivered here."

"Fuck them. If they don't like it, I'll buy the restaurant and turn it into a soup and sandwich joint."

"You're insane." I brushed off his comment, even though I knew he would do something that crazy without thinking twice. "Katie called me."

"Oh, yeah." He took a sip of his water. "How's she doing?"

"Well, she could be pregnant. But you know this because you gave her money for IVF."

He shrugged that same stupid I-do-whatever-I-want shrug. "And?"

"You have to stop buying my family."

"Buying?" He chuckled, leaning back and crossing his arms over his chest, eyes dancing with mischief. "I'm pretty sure everything that I've done for you and your family is considered helping, not buying. I've never asked for anything in return. Not so much as your vote when I've ran for office. But I'm dying to know … did you vote for me, Evelyn?"

"Why pay for Katie's IVF? You've been in the same

room as her maybe five times, counting Mom's funeral. It doesn't make sense."

The waiter filled the table with plates of food that Graham must have ordered before I arrived.

When he left us alone, Graham shifted his gaze to me. "I did it for you."

"I don't think friends pay for things like this. Maybe if Katie were your friend, but she's not your friend."

"You're my friend." He placed several pieces of sushi onto my plate.

"That's not enough."

"It's everything." He paused, dark eyes lifting to me again. "Lila can be *your* best friend, but you are mine."

My gaze averted to the chopsticks by my hand. I picked them up and rolled them between my thumb and index finger as I weighed my words. "You make me uncomfortable."

"Why?"

I couldn't look at him, but I felt every ounce of his gaze on me. "Because the things you say, the looks, the way you touch me … it feels inappropriate."

"Inappropriate or wrong?"

Risking a glance, I narrowed my eyes. "Is there a difference?"

He took a bite and chewed slowly, studying me with a cocked head. "Wrong is when it feels wrong because it is wrong. Inappropriate is when something is wrong, but a need or desire whispers to our conscience that it doesn't completely feel wrong. An affair is inappropriate."

"An affair is wrong." I bit out the words so quickly it

made his head jerk backward.

"Rape is wrong. An affair is inappropriate. Robbing a bank is wrong. Fingering your wife under the table during the annual Governors' Dinner at the White House is inappropriate."

I clenched my jaw, priming my comeback. "Tell me you love Lila."

He smirked bringing another bite to his mouth.

"I love Lila."

"We love Lila more."

He chewed, inspecting me through eyes formed into slits.

"Tell me *you* love *Lila* more," I said.

Graham dabbed his mouth with his napkin. "More than what or whom?"

"More than everything and everyone."

Rubbing his lips together, his gaze fell to his plate. My heart fell into my stomach, heavy and pulsing. Painful and terrified.

"More than me," I whispered. "Tell me you love Lila more than you love me."

His Adam's apple dipped when he swallowed. "I married her," he murmured.

Tears burned my eyes. "Tell me you love *her* more than you love *me*."

The man I loved right down to the deepest parts of my soul couldn't look me in the eye or face me at night when we slept. He held my heart hostage, each breath captive … waiting for a look, a smile, the tiniest touch.

The man I vetted, molded, groomed, and campaigned

for my best friend to marry … *he* gave me everything money could buy. Sometimes he gave me a look, a smile, a touch … but it wasn't *the* look, smile, or touch. My heart didn't belong to him. And while I loved him for many reasons, none of those reasons came close to the one reason I loved Ronin Alexander—that one completely wordless reason.

My heart just knew. One feeling. One force. One moment in Vancouver that told me I had arrived.

"Why …" Graham sighed, shaking his head. "Why did we bring so many people into this? Why were you so stubborn? This could have all been avoided."

I squinted. "Wh-what are you talking about?"

Rubbing his temples, he closed his eyes. "We married the wrong people."

No. No, no, no!

My jaw unhinged as I stared at him without blinking, waiting for him to open his eyes and see that he was so very wrong. But he didn't open his eyes, and I couldn't find a single word. I could barely find my next breath. Tossing my napkin on the table, I shoved my chair back and ran toward the restroom.

Before the door completely closed behind me, I felt his presence looming over me like a storm cloud. I rested my hands on the edge of the sink and squeezed my eyes shut, erratic breaths congesting in my throat as they tried to make their way past the boulder of emotion.

I stiffened when he pulled my hair off my shoulders, letting it slowly fall from his fingers, down my back. "*You* regretted our night together. I never did. *You* put words in my mouth like I surely regretted it too. *You* were the one who said we could be friends or nothing, but if we were more than friends it would end badly. *You* made the best night of my life sound like a clumsy fucking mistake. Yet, we'd agreed to officially start dating weeks earlier. Sex is part of dating. Why did you end it just when we were getting to the good part? Do you have any idea how that made me feel?"

With tears trailing down my cheeks and my heart slowly cracking, I glanced up in the mirror to his red-eyed reflection. My mouth opened to speak, but nothing came out. What could I say?

I'm sorry?

I never knew. I *honestly* never knew he really wanted that.

"Y-you made fun of me—my twiggy figure, tiny boobs, and bleached hair. You said I fit in with the guys because I looked like a guy."

His head moved side to side in tiny increments as pain etched his whole face. "It was my stupid, childish way of flirting with you. I could have had any girl, a million friends, a nicer place farther from campus, but I chose you. How could you not see it?"

My brain felt like a ten-car pileup in the middle of a snowstorm.

I couldn't see through my blurred vision.

I couldn't hear past the blood rushing through my ears.

And the iciest of chills crawled from the bottom of my spine to my head, intensifying the ache.

"You wanted Lila," I whispered.

"I wanted to make you jealous."

I shook my head over and over. "You chased her."

"You said she'd never give me a chance. I wanted to prove you wrong. I wanted to prove to you that I was worthy. I thought if I could make Lila love me that you'd see me differently too. You'd see me through her eyes. And I liked a challenge." He pressed the heels of his hands against his eyes, making a tight fist with his fingers. "And you did too. You. Did. Too." His hands fell to his sides, and he blew out a quick breath as his shoulders folded inward.

I turned to face him, drawing in a long, angry breath. Why? Why did he have to ruin everything? "You don't make someone jealous by using their best friend as a pawn!"

"You don't make love to someone and call it a fucking mistake less than twenty-four hours later!" He planted his hands on his hips and leaned in toward me a fraction.

He looked … hurt. The anguish on his face. The unshed tears in his eyes. The way his angry tone broke when he said the words "make love."

Sixteen years.

Our friendship spanned sixteen years. Nearly ten years longer than I'd known my husband. Graham wanted for nothing. And even if he had, I didn't have a single thing to offer him. I had never been more than a science geek with a bath shop and sick parents. I wasn't the prettiest. I loved sports, but I couldn't stand up on skis, make a basket, catch a football, or hit a golf ball.

Graham's parents didn't care for me.

Yet, there I stood in a bathroom with the Governor of Colorado, wondering why he looked at me like I crushed every single dream he'd ever dared to imagine.

He swallowed hard, but refused to blink, refused to release a single tear. "You married the wrong guy."

Oh, Graham, Graham, Graham …

"No. I didn't. You fell in love with the wrong girl." I didn't hold back a single tear. My hand reached for his chest, and I placed my palm against his heart. "But you married the right one. And she loves you. And I *know* you love her too. Maybe …" I bit my lips together for a few seconds, finding the courage to say what I needed to say to my friend. "Maybe what you and Lila have is not the same kind of love I have with Ronin. But that's okay. My father lost his first, and maybe his most powerful love, many years ago. It didn't keep him from loving my mom. If you love me, Graham, you will love Lila as your wife and me as your friend. And we will not speak of this again."

We wouldn't speak about it, but I would never forget it.

I would never forget the day Graham destroyed the four of us.

I would never forget the day he took away my plausible deniability.

"I'm a patient man." He lowered his mouth to my forehead, resting his lips there while I stood stone still, scared of his touch, devastated by his confession. "I'll wait for you." When he stood tall again, taking a step back, his signature cocky smile slid up his face. All signs of the broken man just seconds earlier vanished. "Let me know when Katie gets a positive pregnancy test. She promised to name it Porter if it's a boy."

My stomach churned, pushing bile up my throat. He made her promise to brand my nephew like a reminder, once again, that he owned my whole family.

"Don't give me that frown, Evelyn." He tugged on the cuff of his shirt, and his cufflink fell to the floor with a *clink*. I gripped the edge of the counter as he hunched to retrieve his gold cufflink that landed right between my hot pink tennis shoes. After he plucked it from the ground, he leaned forward, putting his nose a half inch from my crotch without touching me.

My stomach churned more, and I could taste the acid on my tongue. He made me feel trapped, responsible, like a terrible friend to Lila and wife to Ronin. Graham had to give me one last reminder that I became friends with the Devil and my life would always reside in a special kind of hell.

Taking a long, embarrassing, nerve-grating, bone-chilling sniff, he lifted his gaze to mine. "I've never forgotten the way you smell." He blinked slowly like my scent intoxicated him. "The taste of you on my tongue."

My jaw stung from clenching my teeth so tightly. My skin burned with anger. My pulse drummed out of control as I internally screamed, but only a whisper escaped from my trembling lips. "I hate you."

Graham stood, resting his hands beside mine on the counter, trapping me in the cage of his body. His playful smile vanished, the lust in his eyes drowning in the black pool of his evil soul. I didn't know if it was the money, power, or truly my unwillingness to see how much he wanted me sixteen years earlier, but the Graham Porter I used to love was no longer alive. "You don't hate me, Evelyn. You hate that I own you. You hate that I *do* know what you taste like because you came in my mouth over and over again that night. You hate that you can't block those memories from seeping into your head when Ronin fails to give you everything you need. You hate that your debt to me will never be paid. But more than anything … you hate that you will never stop needing me. Needing me to be the perfect husband to your best friend. Needing me to play the charade with Ronin so you don't have to tell him the truth and watch your world fall apart. Needing me to rescue your sick family because we know your dad's kidney won't last forever. And there's nothing…" he lowered his face closer to mine, his warm breath poisoning my skin "…and I mean *nothing* that gives me greater pleasure than knowing the woman I love *needs* me."

He held me hostage, and it didn't matter that his body was pressed to mine in the bathroom of a sushi restaurant because his hold on me reached everywhere, inches or miles. It was invisible and it felt inescapable.

"But the day will come, my sweet Evelyn," he whispered while dragging his lips from my cheek to my ear, "that I will expect something in return."

"W-what?" The stuttered word squeaked past the tiny airway in my throat.

Graham kissed my earlobe. "You."

I blinked a new round of tears as Graham pushed off the counter and sauntered to the door. Before he opened it, he paused, keeping his back to me. "Let's all do dinner soon. And Evelyn? I agree ... we don't need to discuss this again. Not with each other, not with anyone else. For everyone's *safety*, this needs to stay between us."

CHAPTER SIXTEEN

Ronin

THE GOOD NEWS?
After a trip to visit my doctor, he agreed I was suffering from depression. Validation soothed my need to feel sane.

The bad news?

Antidepressants didn't work because I wasn't actually depressed. The chemical imbalance wasn't actually mine. I was feeling Lila's depression. Lila's leukemia. Lila's aches and pains. Lila's nonexistent libido. Lila's everything.

Opioids worked. They took away all the pain. But I knew I could have the opioids or I could have Evelyn and the kids, but I couldn't have both. I chose my family.

However, I started to wonder if my depression (Lila's depression) was contagious. Evelyn stopped pressuring me to tell her what was wrong with me. She stopped snuggling into my back at night, which had been a painful reminder that I'd become a terrible husband who had no desire to have sex. She even stopped stealing my job of singing in the shower, yet *another* painful reminder that our life revolved around work and the kids.

Nobody sang in the shower.

Nobody made love in our bed.

Nobody sent me flirty pictures during the day with a blowing-kiss emoji and a "Can't wait to see you!"

I missed feeling good. I missed getting a hard-on just thinking about Evelyn. I missed busting my ass to get the kids in bed so I could have their mom all to myself. The list of things I missed became too long to remember. That was the worst part—I started to forget what it felt like to have a life with my own feelings, a sense of control over myself.

"Hey." Lila answered her door, greeting me with a sad smile.

My desperation led me to her. When I called to see if she could see me, Lila agreed without question.

"Hey." I looked around as I stepped into the foyer.

"It's just us." She shot me a reassuring smile. "I gave the staff the day off, and Graham is out of town."

"Your face." I grimaced.

She ghosted her fingertips along her jaw, along the yellowed brown bruise marks that were still visible.

"I'm taking a martial arts class. It was Graham's idea. He said I can never be too safe. And we both agreed exercise is good. Unfortunately, I bruise easily. But so far, I've been able to cover it up with makeup when I'm in the public eye."

"Swimming. Walking. Pilates. Yoga ... *not* any sort of contact sport. What were you thinking? What was Graham thinking?" I pressed my finger under her chin to tip her head up a little more to see the extent of the bruising, but it was nearly gone.

What hadn't disappeared, not even a little, was the instant physical transformation I felt the instant I touched her.

No more pain.

No more ringing in my ears.

No more depression.

I didn't know what she felt when I touched her. It didn't make sense for Lila to feel anything at all from me. But that didn't stop her from leaning into my touch.

Dropping my hand from her chin, I waited for her to look up at me.

"You're miserable," she whispered.

It wasn't my intention to make Lila feel guilty for anything. She didn't make a deal with God ... or whatever greater force cursed my life so many years earlier. The leukemia wasn't her fault. *Nothing* was her fault.

"Are you?" I asked instead of admitting or denying my own misery.

"Yes."

"Are you getting treatment?"

She nodded slowly.

"Chemo? Radiation?"

Tears filled her eyes as she relinquished another single nod. "I started last week." She pivoted, wiping her eyes while heading up the stairs. "I want to show you something."

Lila had lost weight. Her tailored light gray pants hung loosely on her, so did her white long-sleeved blouse that would've usually flowed perfectly over her curves. That day it looked two sizes too big, hiding all the parts of her that Evie used to envy—her breasts, the perfect curve of her hips, and the lines of her backside.

"How will you explain this to Evie?" I asked, following her down the long hallway. "The weight loss? The hair loss if you have it? Nausea? Lethargy? You won't be able to hide from Evie. Or the public. You're in front of cameras all the time."

"I'm not worried about the cameras. They truly add ten pounds. And as I said, I can cover any bruising with makeup. As for Evie … well, as a teenager, I had some issues, mainly as a result of my parents dying, but also self-esteem issues. Evie knows I was anorexic for a time. If she needs to think that again, it's easier to deal with that than cancer. And I'm going to shave my head soon, hopefully before it starts coming out in clumps. I've already contacted someone who will make me a wig, maybe using some of my own hair. She's really good. I don't think Evie will ever know."

"If you die, she will know."

Lila turned a few feet inside her bedroom. Her gaze slid to the plush white carpet between us. "I know. *If* that happens, she will grieve. She will get over it. She will go on being a wife and mother. If she finds out now, she will suffer. Evie doesn't deserve to suffer anymore. Your kids deserve a happy mom. You deserve a happy wife."

I wasn't sure I had a happy wife at the moment, but I didn't say that to Lila because I feared my issues (that stemmed from Lila) were the reason. Lila didn't need to suffer anymore either.

"You're not going to die." I didn't know that. I just hoped if I thought it and said it aloud enough that maybe she would believe it too. My knowledge of life, death, other lives, other universes ... well, it wasn't extensive. I knew nothing more than the belief that anything was possible. If Lila believed she would live, she would live.

When our gazes locked, her mouth curled into a familiar smile. "We're all going to die, Ronin." With a shrug, she released a tiny chuckle. "But ... hopefully not today."

"Not today." I matched her smile.

"I was going through these boxes the other day." Lila disappeared into the closet, which was bigger than our master bedroom, and returned with two floral hat boxes stacked on top of each other. "Photos from homecoming and prom. And my best friend winning the science fair two years in a row."

I chuckled. "Sounds about right."

Lila set the hat boxes on the gray tufted bench at the end of the king bed adorned in thick white, silver, and baby blue bedding. I sat on the other side of the hat boxes as she opened the first box and thumbed through the messy stacks of photos.

"This is Maverick." She handed me a photo of Evie and her date for one of the dances.

He looked like a sweaty mess. The dude's disheveled brown hair stuck to his sweaty brow covered with pimples, only slightly deterring from his crooked black tie. Evie wore a simple pink strapless dress that fell just below her knees and shoes dyed to match it. Her hair was a bit longer and not quite as blond, and she had bangs curled and heavily cemented in place with hairspray.

"Maverick looks a bit nervous. How long did they date?"

"Oh …" she giggled.

She. Giggled.

It felt good. Lila felt good. I felt good.

"Maverick is the poodle photobombing right there." She pointed to the caramel poodle poking its head into the shot. "I don't remember the boy's name. Evie was super pissed off at her ex-boyfriend, Brandon, so she said yes to the first guy who asked her to homecoming that year. I think his name was Todd? Tye? Travis? I don't know. Something like that."

She continued to go through the photos, handing some to me while discarding others back into the hat box. Lila not only made me feel good, she made me feel closer to Evie.

"Oh, you *have* to see all of these." She hugged a stack of photos to her chest, blue eyes wide and filled with excitement like those of a child. "They're from my eleventh birthday. My parents took me and Evie skiing."

She crawled onto the bed and plopped onto her back with her head on one pillow.

I followed her, resting my head on the other pillow.

"I'm not sure we have any photos of her standing upright." She giggled more, handing me photo after photo of Evelyn on her butt, her face, her side. One ski on and one ski off. Ski patrol helping her on and off the lifts.

Those photos made me miss my wife. They made me fall in love with her all over again.

"This … this was her favorite thing to do." Lila handed me a photo of Evie with a hot chocolate mustache. "She endured the awfulness because she's always been the very best friend a girl could ever have, and she loved hot chocolate and warm cookies in the lodge."

Lila sighed. "My accident … it happened because Evie wanted to let us—you, me, and Graham do what we loved to do. Had she been selfish, not thinking of other people before herself, I never would have been on skis that day. Isn't that crazy?"

I never thought of it that way.

"She should be more selfish." I handed the photos back to Lila.

"She really should." Rolling to her side, she set the photos on the nightstand. When she rolled back toward me, her smile faded.

We stared at each other in silence for a minute or so before she lifted her hand and rested it on my face. "You came here for this," she whispered.

That one touch. When Lila touched me—when I touched her—it felt like the first time I touched Evie and she touched me. My eyes drifted shut, and I let her touch be Evelyn's touch. I let the pain vanish. I embraced the silence. Each thought brought an image of my wife and all the perfect moments we'd shared in our nearly six years together.

Lila's thumb traced my cheekbone the way Evie's had done so many times before. I covered her hand with mine, keeping it pressed to my cheek. Every second we stayed connected gave me more time. More time to get home to Evelyn and feel *good*. More time to take my wife in my arms and feel only us, even if it didn't last. I just …

Emotions burned my eyes, and without opening them or blinking, I felt a few tears slide down my face.

Lila said nothing, but her thumb chased each one, erasing it with her beautiful, magical touch.

I just … I just wanted her to be Evelyn. I wanted Evelyn's touch to feel that way.

That warm.

That necessary.

That perfect.

There was no dignity in addiction. I stumbled and fell flat on my face when Evie called me out on my opioid addiction. I swallowed my pride (what little I had left) and got the help I needed.

Lila's touch became my new addiction. More addictive than any pill I had ever popped. I *needed* her touch to survive, to keep from losing everything. Yet … it was *so so so* incredibly wrong.

"I love Evie," I whispered.

Lila started to pull her hand away. I opened my eyes to her face wrinkled in regret. Easing my head side to side against the pillow, I swallowed my own regret. I needed to *need* my wife's touch again, and only Lila could give me that chance.

"I miss Graham," she said softly.

I wasn't Graham. She wasn't Evelyn. But we were … something. And sometimes something for a breath in time could be absolutely everything.

Ignoring what was left of my instinct to do what was right, to turn away from what was wrong, I slid my arm between Lila's waist and the mattress, pulling her into my body. She rested her cheek on my chest and her arms encircled my neck.

Her thinner body, the familiar scent of Evie's shop in her hair, the way she molded into my body like Evie always did so naturally, it *felt* like my wife in my arms, so I closed my eyes and let it be Evie. And I hoped that Lila closed her eyes and let it be Graham.

We fell asleep in each other's arms. Three hours later, my phone vibrated in my pocket, waking us up. I reluctantly let go of Lila and the best sleep I'd had in many months. We sat up, Lila rubbing her eyes while I slid my phone from my pocket.

> **Evelyn:** Tami just texted me. She wants to go out tonight. We're meeting a few of her friends for dinner and drinks. Please make sure you're home in time to relieve Sue and get dinner for our kiddos. Thanks xo

I had one hour to make it home in time, but I couldn't get to Aspen from Denver in one hour. Evelyn didn't know about my trip to Denver. I'd shut off my location on my phone. Half of the time we couldn't locate each other because of poor signal in the mountains, so not locating me never raised suspicion.

"Everything okay?" Lila stood, straightening her blouse and running her fingers through her long blond hair.

Scratching the back of my own messy hair, I nodded, glancing back at the screen. "I need to be home in an hour." I grunted a laugh.

"That's not possible."

"Yeah …" I brought up my contacts screen. "I know."

Ronin: I need a huge favor. Can you be at my house in an hour and watch Franz and Anya for a couple of hours?

I pressed send and typed out a quick second message.

Ronin: And can you not tell Tami, Evelyn, or any-one for that matter? And can you bring them dinner? They love pizza.

Noah: Hey, buddy. Sure. Is everything okay?

Ronin: Yes.

I didn't elaborate. What was I supposed to say? Noah owed me a few favors after he ran into an old girlfriend who was in town for a week skiing last year. She wanted to have dinner with him one night and drinks the next night, and more than that. He didn't cheat on Tami, but he also didn't tell her about the old girlfriend. When Tami called looking for him twice, I covered for him. I *lied* for him.

Next, I texted Sue to let her know that Noah would be there to relieve her and watch the kids while I grabbed some groceries. She wouldn't know how long Noah was there, so the chances of her mentioning it to Evie were pretty slim.

I slipped my phone into my pocket and climbed off the bed. "I don't know what to say." I twisted my mouth, giving Lila a slight cringe.

She latched her hands behind her back and shrugged. "There's nothing you have to say."

I felt so fucking good—so normal—the guilt didn't stand a chance. It wasn't like I did anything truly inappropriate with Lila. Over and over I reminded myself, convinced my conscience, that her touch wasn't anything more intimate than getting a massage from a therapist.

It felt good.

I didn't want it to end.

And I'd leave feeling like a whole new person … even though it wouldn't last.

"How do you feel?" she asked.

"Frustrated that Evie won't be home when I get there, but hopeful that this good feeling will hold on until she does get home."

Three hours. I had three hours in Lila's embrace. In the world of energy and unexplainable phenomena, that had to mean something. Right? Like charging a battery. I hoped I was leaving with a full charge of whatever the hell Lila gave me just by touching me.

"I hope so too." Lila smiled and averted her gaze, like all of a sudden she felt shy around me.

"How do you feel? I don't want you to feel bad or guilty or … anything negative about this … about us."

She shook her head, keeping her gaze averted. "I don't. I feel … strong."

"What do you mean?"

Her eyes shifted to my face. "Graham makes me feel weak. Sick, broken, and weak."

I frowned. "Have you told him that?"

She grunted. "No. I think he needs it to feel strong. You know? I think he likes to feel like I depend on him. He is the giver. I am the taker. But I feel like you *need* something from me, and it feels ..." Lila drew in a shaky breath, the essence of tears glistening in her eyes for a few blinks. "It feels incredible to feel needed."

I took the opportunity to hug her again because I thought she needed it, and she was right—I definitely needed her.

"Thank you," I murmured. "You *are* needed."

"Go." She stepped back and took a deep breath, releasing it with a smile. "Go home to your family. Go love my best friend. I think she's felt neglected."

My eyes narrowed. "Did she tell you that?"

"Not in those exact words." Lila's nose wrinkled. "Just ... *show* her how much you love her and need *her*. Okay."

I nodded slowly. "Yeah. I can do that."

Thanks to Lila ... I could do that.

CHAPTER SEVENTEEN

Evelyn

I TOOK A Lyft home, grateful that the next day was Saturday, Sophie was handling the store, and Ronin had the day off to take care of the kids if I had a hangover to nurse. It wasn't that I was plastered, but it had been a long time since I'd had anything to drink. Being a responsible shop owner, a mom, and a wife to a man who no longer wanted to touch me didn't leave time to enjoy a glass of wine or six.

Then there was Graham—my owner. The warden of my life. The Grim Reaper.

His confession.

His threat.

Him.

I had better judgment than that. There was no way he was the same guy I met in college. Something happened to him, turning him into a villain, a rabid animal that needed to be put down. Only ... he had me cornered at every turn, holding my best friend hostage. And Ronin? Well, I didn't know what Graham might do to him.

A little before midnight, I turned the key to the door and slipped inside, closing it behind me and wobbling a bit to get my shoes off without falling into anything. I ambled to the sink and filled a glass with water, gulping down copious amounts along with a packet of natural remedy stuff Tami gave me—some sort of electrolyte and liver cleansing concoction. She swore it would prevent a hangover. I hoped so.

With my clumsy, inebriated version of tiptoeing, I made my way to the closet to grab some clean panties and a nightshirt. Feeling a *need* that hadn't been met in a long time, I eased the closet door shut and opened a shoe box of a pair of ankle boots and retrieved my old pink friend, Madonna. She had batteries in her.

Her.

Yes, my vibrator was a her, and her name was Madonna. A true, trustworthy friend like Lila, not an actual dick like Graham. And sadly, Madonna was the only one there to meet my needs since my husband was unable to get and sustain an erection for me.

Leaving my fitted gray and oil-stained tee on, I slid out of my skinny jeans and panties. From my other old ankle boot, I retrieved a bottle of lube, the warming kind that made me tingle. I concocted it myself in my lab, but I didn't sell it at the shop.

Dropping to the floor in the most uncoordinated fashion, I leaned against a stack of drawers, legs bent and spread wide. My heart raced, making a whooshing white nose in my ears, proof of how long it had been. The thought of tingling lube and Madonna had me very turned on. The wine might have helped too. I wasn't really a Zinfandel person, but after the second glass, it tasted pretty damn good.

With one hand, I applied some warming lube, rubbing tiny circles over my clit and my opening. I closed my eyes and imagined Ronin's mouth down there. He was *so* good at that—definitely an expert in that department. After a minute or so, I flipped on my Madonna, only … she didn't move.

I opened my eyes and frowned at her under the dimly lit closet light where two of the three bulbs had burned out. Wiping my lubed hand on my already stained shirt, I removed Madonna's batteries and put them back in, but she still didn't work.

"Just my luck," I whispered.

Fuck my life.

Really, if sitting in a closet close to midnight and getting stood up by a vibrator wasn't the lowest of lows, then I don't know what could have beat it. Maybe my next move …

"Fine, Madonna, we'll go old school tonight," I murmured, lubing her good and inching her into me while my eyes closed again. Not going to lie … I was tired. I really needed her to do some of the work, but I also needed to get off. So I worked my clit with one hand and Madonna with my other hand.

Stupid, terrible thoughts warred in my mind, like Graham gloating about giving me orgasms with his mouth. I pinched my eyes shut tighter and willed those away. I had no intention of getting off on the Devil that night. Instead, I thought of my first night with Ronin, the nights by the fire, the times (pre-kids) in the kitchen.

Yes … yes …

Those were the images that moved my hands faster, made my knees spread wider. I wasn't ashamed of my needs as a woman. Humans were sexual creatures, even the ones dressed in robes, carrying crosses around their necks. If Ronin couldn't give me what I needed, I'd capture it myself. It wasn't the same. Madonna wasn't Ronin no matter how hard I tried to make her mimic his rhythm, but six glasses of wine made her good enough.

Good enough felt really damn great at that moment.

"Need help?"

I jumped and my eyes flew open.

In one horrifying second, I sobered up.

I yanked Madonna out of me and clawed for absolutely any item of clothing to cover myself and hide my pink friend—the nearest thing being Ronin's dirty shirt. The bottle of lube tipped over onto the carpet beneath my legs as I hugged them to my chest beneath his shirt.

All the blood in my body went to my head, filling my cheeks with fire and pushing beads of sweat out along my brow.

So.

Unbelievably.

Embarrassing.

Six years. In our six years together, Ronin had never seen me masturbate alone. He didn't know I owned a vibrator. And I knew my selfish, drunken, late-night behavior had to make him feel like a failure.

He squatted in front of me, wearing a pair of silk boxers, resting his forearms on his legs. The corner of his mouth twitched as I panted like I'd just finished running a race.

What was I supposed to say?

Sorry.

Please forgive me.

Can we agree to raise the kids without ever making eye contact again?

"Can I get you new batteries? Three of my fingers? My mouth? My *dick*?"

I coughed a bit, parched from so much heavy breathing, or maybe his words choked me as I attempted to digest each one.

Did my eyes look as huge and dilated as they felt? Probably.

"I'm so sorry …" I whispered, scrunching my face and biting my bottom lip really hard.

His head cocked to the side as he squinted. "Sorry for what?"

Why did he have to completely humiliate me?

Making my point, he pulled his T-shirt from my legs, exposing Madonna and the lube. "You're sorry about this?" He held up my dead vibrator. Poor Madonna.

I nodded, keeping a full cringe glued to my face.

"I have spare batteries in the garage." He held it in front of his face, giving it a close inspection as if he hadn't ever seen a vibrator before. And it's possible Madonna *was* his first close encounter. That was something that hadn't ever come up in conversation.

I snatched it from his hand and grabbed the bottle of lube while trying with clumsy effort to stand. "Please just forget you saw this. I need a shower."

Ronin grabbed my naked hips as he dropped to his knees. Still, I couldn't look him in the eye.

"Evie ..." he whispered. "I don't want to forget what I just saw."

My face flushed all over again as I resigned myself to the fact that he wasn't going to let me get away with a simple "forget about it." I tried to keep my breath steady, tried to hide how his hands on my hips did things to me.

The rough pads of his lumberjack fingers slid up the sides of my torso, taking my T-shirt with them.

I dropped the vibrator and lube. "Roe ..."

"Shh ..." He pulled my shirt over my head. "Look at me, Evie."

Embarrassment turned into pain. Weeks of loneliness and heartbreak over my husband ... my friend ... Lila ... it all rushed to the surface, bleeding out with a single look at the *one* person I needed more than anyone else to feel me.

"*I'm* the one who's sorry, baby." His mouth claimed mine, his tongue sliding against mine in slow, deep strokes as he removed my bra.

My hands dove into his hair, hoping with the deepest desperation that he would be able to take it all the way. I didn't touch him *there*. I couldn't bear the rejection, so I took the kiss. I took his hands on my body, caressing my skin, cupping my breasts, giving me pleasure. I took everything he offered without asking for anything in return.

We kissed forever. The more we kissed, the more I feared it was as far as he could go. I willed myself to keep from crying, silently mourning that deepest intimacy.

"Touch me, Evie." He held my head as his lips moved from my mouth to my jaw, my ear, and down my neck.

I kept my eyes closed, feeling intoxicated all over again, but it wasn't the wine; it was all him. My fingertips traced the lines of his abs so slowly. Each muscle contracted beneath my touch. The instant I reached his waistband, I felt him almost breaking through the thin fabric.

Relief washed along my body with a renewed urgency between us when my hand slid along his erection.

He moaned, and his kiss became more demanding as he sucked and bit his way along my skin to my breasts. I let go ... I let go of everything. We turned into the lovers we were that first night in his condo.

Two frantic bodies incapable of getting close enough, moving together fast enough, penetrating deep enough ... hard enough.

His touch was rough, but so was mine. He marked me with his mouth sucking my neck and breasts and his bruising grip on my ass. I marked him with my teeth planted into his shoulder as I used him to muffle my cries when I orgasmed—also marking him with my nails along his back.

I love you. And I will never belong to anyone but you.

My body fell limp beneath the suffocating pressure of his naked torso collapsed onto mine. We were nothing but sweaty, breathless deadweight on the floor of the closet. And I didn't want to ever move. I wanted that moment to last forever. I wanted to stay that connected to Ronin for the rest of my life.

My fingers tickled the nape of his neck as the warm air from his mouth brushed along my shoulder.

"Again," I whispered.

"Again," he echoed, climbing off me and carrying me to the shower where we did it all over again.

After we ran out of hot water, he wrapped me in a towel. I lifted onto my toes and kissed him slowly. The towel slipped from my body. "Again," I whispered over his lips.

"Again." He grinned against my mouth before hoisting me up to his waist and carrying me to bed.

We slowed it down.

We whispered all the words except those three words that still hadn't made an audible debut between us.

We softened our hold on each other, leaving behind all the desperation, letting every kiss linger, letting every touch spread along our naked bodies and seep into our intertwined souls. And while we eventually reached the point of release, it wasn't about that. It was about making amends, healing wounds, and tightening those invisible bonds that had always held us together.

Ronin held me the rest of the night, and I said a silent prayer to God, imaginary or not, asking her to help us navigate the road ahead. It scared me. It scared me so very much.

CHAPTER EIGHTEEN

Ronín

I WOKE UP at four in the morning. The ringing in my ears had returned, but I didn't feel bad ... yet. In fact, I felt pretty damn good with naked Evie's naked backside spooned into me. Under normal circumstances, I would have been a kind husband and a patient lover, letting my wife sleep—after all, we'd only had two hours of sleep— but I didn't know how long the feeling would last. And at that moment, a certain *part* of me wanted Evie very much.

I wanted to fill my hands with her.

I wanted to fill my mouth with her.

I wanted to fill every void in my entire body with Evelyn.

And then *I* wanted to fill her *everywhere.*

Slipping out of bed, I locked the bedroom door—just in case. Then I grabbed my phone and wireless headphones, two scarves, a bandana, and that bottle of lube she had in the closet. I maneuvered her slowly and carefully, keeping her asleep until I was ready to wake her up.

Standing naked at the end of the bed, I smiled, feeling a thrilling jolt through my veins, giving me a rush of life that I knew would disappear all too soon. The scarves restrained her hands. The bandana rested loosely around her neck, ready to be slipped into her mouth to keep her from screaming and waking up the kids. The headphones rested on her ears. My wife looked so fucking beautiful spread out on the bed, naked, and sleeping like an angel with her blond hair fanned out along the pillow. But it was time to wake my angel. Whether she would understand it or not, I *needed* her.

I didn't want to waste an ounce of *life* that Lila gave me.

Pressing play on my phone, Evie's blue eyes popped open and her arms jerked at the restraints as "One Track Mind" by Thirty Seconds to Mars flowed through the headphones. I pressed a finger to my mouth to keep her quiet as my other hand slid the bandana over her chin and into her mouth.

She bit down on it. Eyes wide. Chest heaving with each exhilarating breath.

I worked my way down her naked body, sucking her taut nipples and dipping my tongue into her navel as she writhed beneath my touch. A twisted, aching part of me needed to erase the memory of another woman in my arms. Although Evie knew nothing about that, I still needed to make it right in my own head.

The seductive song played for her as I took my *one-track mind* between her legs. Her back shot off the bed into the most beautiful arch of flesh as I took her to the edge.

Over … and … over … again.

As soon as I released her restraints and the bandana from her mouth, she tore off the headphones and grabbed my face, kissing me harder than I had kissed her … possibly ever. Every time her tongue thrashed against mine, she moaned.

A hungry.

Needy.

Starving moan.

She shoved me onto my back and navigated down my body. I closed my eyes for a few seconds and let her take me to another world … one of her parallel universes where all I felt was pleasure.

Her mouth wrapped around me.

Her eyes peering up at me, making me feel like a king—not the man who needed to touch another woman before he could fuck his own wife.

Before she took me to the finish line, I tugged her hair and sat up. She perched on her knees between my spread legs. I had never seen anything more beautiful than my Evie with mussed hair, on her knees naked for me, and her tongue making a slow swipe along her full lips. I reached for her bottle of lube and stared at it for a few seconds before shifting my gaze to her.

She did the same thing, trapping the corner of her lower lip between her teeth for a breath before relinquishing a single nod.

I died *again*. Who knew it could happen so many

times in one life? I wasn't sure if it was the Devil giving me permission to take *any* kind of pleasure in my wife's body or if some higher power was giving me one last hurrah before taking my last breath.

Either way, I didn't question it. Instead, I smiled at Evie as she eased onto her hands and knees, looking over her shoulder at me.

Screw the ringing in my ears.
To hell with my cursed life.
I embraced the "madness."
One. Track. Mind …

Evelyn

"MOMMY!" ANYA CLIMBED into the bed.

I peeled open my tired eyes, feeling a little disoriented, a lot sore *everywhere,* and utterly panicked about my current situation. As she hugged my neck, I took a quick inventory of everything.

The bedding was neat like Ronin had made the bed with me still in it. I couldn't remember putting my nightshirt back on, but it was there along with a pair of (thankfully dry) panties. No lube, scarves, or bandana in sight.

"Good morning, sweetie." I sighed, hugging her squirmy body.

As quickly as she ran into the room and woke me up, she jumped off the bed and ran back out to the living room.

Apparently, mission accomplished.

Filling the doorway was my sexy as hell husband with his hands tucked into the pockets of faded ripped jeans, a white wrinkled tee stretched across his broad torso, and a cocky grin hiding his secrets.

"Good morning." He stayed in the doorway, shoulder pressed to one side.

I pushed myself up to a sitting position, cringing a bit.

"Sore?"

My gaze shot to his. I wish I could have seen a flicker of regret on his face … but I didn't. If anything, he looked pretty proud of himself.

I rubbed my wrists. They weren't bruised or marked in any way, but they were a bit tender to touch. "Nope. I'm good."

I lied.

Seriously … *every part* of my body had been thoroughly *enjoyed* by him before he left me for dead. Okay, maybe not dead, but I'm pretty sure at some point I just passed out from exhaustion.

"You?" I tipped my chin up, feigning confidence and strength.

He pulled the neck of his shirt to the side, exposing some impressive bite marks, but not nearly as impressive as the carved lines he showed me when he turned and lifted his shirt, revealing the marred skin on his back.

"Not bad. Does it hurt?"

He released his shirt and turned back toward me,

grunting a tiny breath through his nose while maintaining his shit-eating grin. "No."

I nodded slowly, giving him a tightlipped smile.

"I made waffles. You coming?"

Standing sounded like a great idea, my backside was sore, but I sure wasn't going to let Ronin know that. I eased out of bed, trying hard to keep a straight face. It was all fun and games until real life demanded things like … functioning body parts.

When your husband goes weeks without getting an erection for you, holding you, kissing you … you don't say no when things start working properly again. And that was why I couldn't move. I didn't say no. Not once.

Not to anything.

Part of it was my own desire, my own need to feel as close as possible to Ronin. The other part, that made me completely submissive, was the look on his face every time I gave him a nod, a yes, and did exactly what he wanted me to do.

"You dressed me." I eyed him while slipping on my robe, hoping my statement might distract him from seeing my tiny grimaces.

"I did. I cleaned you up. Forced you to take two ibuprofen and sang you a lullaby."

I tied my robe sash and walked into his waiting arms, glancing up at him while wearing a grin. "A lullaby, huh?"

He nodded, grabbing my ass, forcing me to grimace. He eased his grip, grinning as if confirmation of my discomfort pleased him.

"Sadist." I narrowed my eyes at him.

There it was … the look. It shone in his eyes like a beacon of hope, silently begging for me to say yes. For me to let him say it—those three words.

"Don't." I shook my head.

"You have to let me say it."

"I will." I lifted onto my toes and kissed the corner of his mouth while whispering, "Just not today. Now, feed me. I'm starving."

Ronin led me to the kitchen by taking my hand the way he took my hand the day we met, just like he took my heart. Six years later, I continued to give him both.

"You should be hungry, after all that alcohol and … *stuff* last night." He shot me a grin.

Stuff. It was definitely the stuff that made me feel famished.

I loved the *stuff* and the man serving me breakfast.

I loved the two kids on the floor, rolling themselves up in blankets like burritos. I loved the house, my job, Aspen, the start of fall, and my life.

On the days I wasn't forced to think about Graham or acknowledge our past and our mutual connection to the present, I loved my life.

Every. Single. Second.

CHAPTER NINETEEN

T WO DOZEN ROSES arrived Monday at Clean Art.

"Who are they from?" Sophie clasped her hands at her chest and jumped up and down like they were for her. "I bet they're from Ronin."

No. They wouldn't have been from him. Mr. Worst Gift Giver Ever.

Unless it was our anniversary or Valentine's Day, which it wasn't.

I pulled the note out of the envelope.

I opened myself up to you. I let you see the love—the good love and the ugly love. We will always be friends, and I will always wish it could be more. This is on me, not you. I should have said all that needed to be said before you found Ronin, before Lila came home from Europe. I'll take you in my life any way I can have you. Please forgive me for ruining our lunch.

XO, Your Graham Cracker

"Well, who sent them?" Sophie prodded, trying to peer over my shoulder at the card.

I pulled it to my chest, every word a knife into my heart. He never referred to himself using my pet name for him. "Ronin," I answered in a weak voice and nervous smile.

"Gah! You married the sweetest, sexiest man alive. It's not fair." A groan escaped with her long sigh as she went back to dusting the displays.

"I did," I murmured, ripping the card into tiny pieces. "I'm going to do some inventory in the back if you need me."

"Uh-huh …" Sophie hummed in her pouty tone.

Tapping Graham's name in my contacts, I brought the phone to my ear while closing the door to the back room.

"Hey, Evelyn, give me a second …" he answered. His voice muffled in the background, but I made out the "everyone please leave the room" part.

Graham loved me.

Graham sent flowers.

Graham cleared rooms to make me his priority.

Graham could save the world, defy gravity, and walk on water … but he would never be Ronin.

"I'm back. I take it you got my apology?"

"I feel like you threatened the people I love. In the bathroom you said, 'For everyone's *safety*, this needs to stay between us.' That felt like a threat. When you said I would eventually have to give you something in return and that something was me … that felt like a threat. That's not love, Graham. Friends don't threaten friends like that. True friends give unconditionally or not at all. I can't accept your apology unless you take back all those things you said to me. And even then, it's going to take time for you to earn back my trust. My trust can't be bought."

"Can I steal it?" He chuckled. "If I can't buy something or steal it, how do I get it?"

"Good deeds."

"I write checks for good deeds. That's how it's done right? How else do you do a good deed?"

I couldn't play his joking game. The things he said to me in the bathroom, the *way* he said them to me, wasn't a joke. He meant them. The truth could right the wrong of a lie, but nothing fixed the truth. His love was ugly and so was his truth.

"I've been replaying every word in my head, formulating a plan. Figuring out what's the worst that could happen if I told Lila she should leave you, if I confessed everything to Ronin, if I walked away from the shop and gave you back your building, if I told my sister she took a gift from the Devil. Then what? What would you do to me? To my family? To Lila?"

After a good thirty seconds of silence, I wondered if we were still connected. Just as I started to say something, Graham said four simple words that I never expected him to say. "I would be devastated."

No begging.

No new threats.

No attempting to call my bluff.

His reaction left me feeling my own kind of devastation.

There were a lot of what-if's that I imagined before confronting him, but I never expected to feel sorry for him. Not even a little. Yet, that was exactly how I felt. I imagined what it would be like to love Ronin and know that he didn't love me the same way. Just a few weeks of not feeling like he physically wanted intimacy with me nearly brought me to my knees.

Graham spent *years* pining for me from near and afar. He dug himself into such a deep hole he must have felt the improbability of ever seeing light again. But he took my best friend with him, and that still felt unforgivable.

"I love Lila as much as I love my own sister. How am I supposed to live with myself when I know she's in a loveless marriage? She could have a chance at true love, a family, the life her parents always wanted for her. Not some rich politician who married her to make some other woman jealous, not a second-place trophy."

"She's not a second-place trophy and you know it. You know me better than that."

I didn't.

Since Graham became governor, most days, I didn't think I knew him at all.

"She's miserable. I can tell."

"When my term is up, I'm out. She can do whatever she wants. Go back to work. Travel. I don't care."

"But I want you to care!" I closed my eyes, pinching the bridge of my nose. "If you love her, then you care. You don't ask her to wait for happiness. Give it to her now."

"So you want me to resign?"

"I want you to give her a family or give her the chance to return to her career now. She deserves to pursue her dreams before they're too unreachable."

"What if she doesn't want what you think she wants?"

He had a point. I didn't understand Lila all the time. It wasn't just Graham who I didn't always recognize. Lila had changed too.

"Love her," I whispered. "Love her with your whole heart or let her go."

"Okay."

Why, Graham? Why do this?

He played head games better than anyone else. Okay what?

"I have to go," I sighed, drained of all desire to play the game any longer.

"Are we good?" he asked.

No. We would never be good. I would never look at him again and not think of the words he said that could never be forgotten. Him referencing how I still *smelled* familiar after I married another man and had two kids.

"Just make things right." I pressed *End*.

Graham

THE ONLY THING I disliked about my wife was her name—Lila. Not Evelyn. She resembled Evelyn, but not enough. And she tried too hard to be a perfect wife, not like Evelyn's fuck-you-Graham attitude.

Fine. Technically, there were three things I disliked about my wife, but they all could be summed up in three words—she wasn't Evelyn.

I liked the chase.

Lila was fun until she said yes. Damn ... I loved that chase. My attraction to Lila nearly exceeded my attraction to Evelyn because Lila wanted nothing to do with me.

The truth? I loved Lila. It wasn't even intentional at first. But she made me fall in love with her. It just never equaled my love for Evelyn. I loved how she loved me, maybe I even loved her out of a sense of duty. The tears I cried after her accident were real. But I also hated that love. I blamed her for it.

My wife's blue eyes shifted to me as I stood in the doorway to her office. Her condition kept her from fulfilling some of her public duties which was fine. Out of sight, out of mind. We made excuses ... like she was writing a book. She let her personal assistant go, claiming she was too strong and independent to need help.

The spin. It was always how you spun the lies to fit a desired truth.

Lila eased her laptop shut and slid her hands from the vintage desk to her lap. Even at home, she wore designer dresses and short skirts or the occasional pant suits.

I took slow steps toward her desk, not missing the fear in her eyes. "No visible marks today."

She answered with silence.

Easing into the gunmetal gray leather armchair opposite her, I steepled my fingers and tapped them against my chin. "I'm sorry you're going through this. No one plans for their life to go in this direction. Yet, here we are. We can't change what has happened, but we can go forward with the best intentions and hope for better days."

Lila flinched. I wasn't a monster. Part of me regretted that flinch. Part of me took responsibility for that flinch.

"I don't want to be owned," she whispered.

"You own me."

She shook her head one tiny inch at a time. "Evie owns you."

"I didn't marry Evelyn."

"Why?"

I narrowed my eyes. The world. I gave that woman the world.

More money than she could ever spend.

A closet the size of a small apartment.

Houses.

Yachts.

Maids.

Assistants.

Cooks.

Really … if her definition of "owned" meant a life of luxury, then sure … I owned her.

"Evelyn and I are friends."

Lila nibbled the corner of her lip. The problem with her? She questioned shit that didn't need to be questioned.

"A friend you've been intimate with."

I shrugged. "So have you."

"That's not the same." Her gaze fell to her lap.

"Come here." I held out my hand.

Lila stared at it, silently defying me.

"Come. Here."

After a slow sigh, she stood and made her way around the desk.

"Closer." I spread my legs, nodding to the open space between them.

She held her ground.

"How can I *make things right* with you?" I used Evelyn's exact words.

Her empty gaze shifted to meet mine. "You can let me go."

"I don't think I can." I wrapped my hand around her wrist being careful to not bruise her. Sometimes it was hard … sometimes she fought me. Sometimes she tried to deny me. Sometimes I liked it when she tried to deny me.

In silent acquiescence, my wife let me pull her between my legs.

"I think your cancer treatment is working." I loosened my grip, rubbing soft circles with my thumbs along her wrists and up her forearms, common areas to see bruising on my wife. Of course a part of me felt bad for her and her situation. She didn't ask for such unfortunate things to happen to her. And if I wanted to get closer to Evelyn, I needed to find a way to get the four of us together more often. My days of lunch and watching football with my best friend were most likely over.

Just thinking about Evelyn made my dick painfully hard. I couldn't stick it in her, *yet*, but I could find the next best thing, which happened to be standing right in front of me.

My hands released her wrists, finding the hem of her short skirt much more tempting.

"No." Lila grimaced with her weak protest, and I slid her skirt up her legs. "Please … not now."

"Long blond hair, short skirt, tight blouse … I think you're asking for someone to take notice. And who better to do that than your husband?" With her skirt gathered at her waist, I slid down her delicate black panties.

"Graham … please …" She reached for her panties.

I shot her a look. That was all it took for her to relax her hand and let me remove her panties. Fuck … nothing compared to a woman in high heels stepping out of black lace panties. "Sit."

Swallowing hard while wearing that stupid cringe like she wasn't going to enjoy it, when we both knew that wasn't the case, she eased her backside onto the edge of the desk. I unfastened my pants. Just because I couldn't fuck her without leaving marks didn't mean I wasn't going to get off.

I knelt on the floor, guiding her feet to rest on my shoulders. Why? Why did she give me that look? For the love of god, I was on my fucking knees in front of her, seconds away from pleasuring her. It almost ruined the moment. But then I imagined making a surprise visit to Evelyn's shop. I imagined her stainless-steel benches instead of a wooden desk, her legs spread wide for me as I knelt on the soapy, gunky floor. Evelyn would give me that same look, pretend she didn't want my tongue teasing her, until my fingers entered her.

Lila stiffened when I kissed her there. She wriggled on

the edge of the desk, but she had nowhere to go. I fought the urge to grip her hips to hold her still and force her legs farther apart as her knees attempted to collapse inward.

No marks.

I had to leave her without a single bruise.

She left me with no choice, just an uncontrollable need to channel my energy and frustration into something. My eyes closed and returned to Evelyn's lab. I wrapped my hand around my dick and let my thoughts go where they needed to go.

CHAPTER TWENTY

Lila

H E SAID MY name.
Graham pleasured me when I didn't want it, but he said my name. I hated myself for clinging to that. After *everything* he had done, he didn't deserve a pat on the back for saying the right woman's name during sex.

Still, I had nowhere to go. He trapped my best friend, my only family, and his control reached further than I could even imagine. I wanted to tell Evie everything. But I didn't trust Graham—not as a husband, not as a friend. It wasn't just me and Evelyn. She had a husband and two kids. I would die before letting Graham destroy her family.

The irony of my own part in destroying Evelyn's life didn't escape my conscience. Her husband needed to touch me to feel good, to be a better husband to his wife.

How did our friendship—the four of us—turn into such a toxic mess?

I had fallen the furthest down the rabbit hole of lies. I kept all the secrets—Graham's, Ronin's, my own.

After I washed Graham's semen from my cleavage, I stood in front of my full-length mirror and contemplated my next move.

"Long blond hair, short skirt, tight blouse ... I think you're asking for someone to take notice."

I no longer cared if anyone ever took notice again. Gripping a pair of scissors in my right hand, I grabbed a chunk of hair pulling it taut with my left hand while cutting it as close to my scalp as possible. Tears filled my eyes. The point of no return embraced me, swallowing the pain of each handful of hair I cut from my head.

I had cancer.

I could wait for it to fall out or I could cut it on my own.

On my own ...

Graham could fuck me at will, mark me, degrade me, and wish I were someone else, but he would never own me. He would never have the final say in my destiny.

When the bulk of my hair rested at my feet, I padded to the opposite end of the hallway, where Graham slept and showered. In a cabinet next to his sink, I retrieved his beard trimmer and retraced my steps to the pile of hair beneath my sink.

The trimmer hummed when I turned it on. It vibrated next to my scalp as I made slow strokes from my forehead to my neck.

Numb.

I felt nothing.

The feeling of nothingness comforted me. It prevented me from blinking and kept my hand from shaking as I sudsed my entire scalp and took a new razor to it. I knew why some cancer patients shaved their heads before all of their hair fell out on its own. Dignity—they wanted something to be on their terms. They needed to control some tiny part of themselves in the midst of something so out of control.

Everything in my life felt out of control.

"What have you done?"

My gaze lifted from the mess on the floor and in the sink to Graham's reflection of complete bewilderment in the mirror. Did he sound regretful? Was that remorse on his face? The numbness blocked my ability to feel him the way I used to … before he became a different man.

"People going through cancer treatment lose their hair. You said it yourself."

"What have you done?" Graham repeated, threading his fingers though his hair, clenching and tugging at it. A very unusual reaction from him.

Lucky him. He still had hair to pull.

He warned me that my life would change. I would not get to do the things I used to do. And he said it too … I would lose my hair from the cancer treatment. Why did he look so shocked?

Interesting note: Sounds stayed with me, like the sound of Evelyn's mom's voice when she told me my parents had died.

"What have you done!"

Sounds … oh the sounds …

I never forgot the click of Graham's dress shoes against the tile floor or the high-pitched slap of the back of his hand across my face. But sounds faded faster than the slow destruction of a heart grieving death or the sting from flesh and bone colliding.

It knocked me back several feet. It always did.

"I don't even recognize you," he sneered.

That made two of us.

I would—eventually—recognize my husband. He turned and clicked his shoes across the tile to leave me alone with the resonating sounds, with the mess on the floor, with my thoughts …

Later, he would return, wearing his favorite mask of regret. He would hold me, kiss my wounds, and on a long sigh, he would say, "How did we get here?"

We.

He was the hero.

I was the villain.

And *we* were innocent victims of … something.

What?

I really didn't know. How *did* we get there?

When did our passion turn into rage?

When did our connection become so destructive?

When did our love turn into resentment?

My phone on the vanity rang. I contemplated not answering it. Ronin … he must have felt that. Felt me.

My fingers feathered along the sensitive skin. I would tell him something, but I couldn't make it believable yet. Instead, I knelt on the floor and gathered as much of my hair as I could—my long blond hair. My mom used to braid my hair, and my dad used to give my pigtail braids a few tugs when he called me his lovely Lila.

I hugged my hair to my chest, rocking back and forth, remembering a much simpler time in my life when love came in the form of gentle touches, adoring smiles, and unbroken promises. A time when candy trumped everything and my biggest worry was forgetting to wear my retainer. Sometimes a good cry made everything tolerable again.

After five or so minutes, I finished cleaning up the mess and slid my journal out from under my mattress. Graham would be gone ... maybe an hour. When he lost control, he took off in his car. Maybe time alone and creating distance between us brought back a tiny bit of clarity. At the very least, it usually bestowed a sadness upon him that I took as his temporary version of regret.

Opening to the back of my journal, I read through my exhaustive list of *reasons* ...

Reasons for bruises on certain parts of my body. I never imagined I'd need a list of excuses for the riddling of bruises on my arms and back, a black eye, half a swollen face, and his fingers imprinted in red, blue, and purple on my neck.

The hardest part?

Some weird, desperate, self-loathing part of me thought I still loved him, but I knew how things would end, eventually, because the scale had tipped. Flipping back to that date in my journal, I let my gaze reacquaint my broken heart with the words that marked the end of us.

JOURNAL

I feel so stupid. So blind. So trapped.

He manipulated me. It's not rough sex. It's not a physical need. At least ... not anymore. I blindly fell for his excuses because he hurt me during sex. He justified it. He made me feel like my orgasm righted any sort of wrongs. It's always left me confused because I love Graham. I love our intimacy, and sometimes I love the intensity, even when a little pain is the price to pay for pleasure. My desire to please him blinded me.

Today, everything changed. It's not a fetish or a preference. It's a sickness. Only a sick man breaks his wife's nose because she playfully grabbed his phone when he wouldn't give her his attention. I wanted him to notice me, my new white dress. Now, that white dress is in the trash, covered in blood.

He apologized immediately. And I honestly think he felt remorse. He cried. It's the first time I have ever seen Graham cry. Today was the "tennis ball incident." At least, that's what we told the doctor at the hospital owned by the Porters. No one questioned it. Not even my best friend, but she's pregnant with her first child, so I can't tell her that her other best friend broke my nose. It would destroy her. And I would feel responsible if anything happened to her unborn child.

Graham did more than break my nose today. He broke a piece of us. I don't know if we will ever be the same. I don't know why he's so angry.

I flipped to the back page again and chose the bookend excuse. The two-story Porter library had bookends, some very expensive and *heavy* ones scattered on different shelves. If I reached for a book on a shelf above my head and accidentally pulled the bookend off the shelf with the book, it would hurt. A lot. And it would leave a significant bruise and swelling.

Opening my nightstand drawer, I retrieved a pen and put a line through the bookend excuse so it didn't get reused in a moment of mental confusion. It was the eighth excuse in six years. Not all marks required an excuse, just the ones I couldn't hide with things like a pretty scarf, long sleeves, or layers of makeup.

"What happened?" Ronin answered his phone with grave concern weighing his words.

I drew in a shaky breath to steady my own words. His concern, his touch ... it reaffirmed how lucky Evelyn was to have found him. It also reminded me of everything Graham was not.

"Ugh. I'm so sorry." I faked a tiny chuckle. "You should see my face. Be thankful you only felt it. I'm going to look like a boxer who lost a fight for the next week or two."

"What happened?" he repeated. No other question mattered at that point.

"I was getting a book from a high shelf in the library. It caught the edge of a bookend—an expensive one I fear—and it landed on my face before tumbling to the floor and cracking into three pieces. I was clumsy and weak from the chemo. I should have asked for help.

Again, I'm so sorry. I'm icing it now."

I closed my eyes, tears stinging behind my eyelids. It sounded believable, even to me. Never … never did I imagine I would—could—be an abused wife making excuses. *Listing* them. I had a list. That was … soul crushing in a way I couldn't articulate, even to myself.

"Did you see a doctor?"

"Yes."

No.

"So you did start chemo?"

"Yes. And I shaved my head. The shedding started clogging the drain."

"Lila …" Ronin sounded broken in his own way. "I'm sorry. But how are you going to explain this to Evelyn?"

"Well, I have access to the very best wigs. I'm not sure she'll know. And if she does. I have a plan B."

Yes. I had a plan B. Just like I had a list of *reasons* and a husband who abused me. Oh, and I was an orphan who kept secrets from the one person who loved me and treated me like family. I hated lying to Evelyn, but she would forgive me … eventually.

"What is plan B?"

"Hannah Ellis. A young girl in foster care with cancer. She thought I was beautiful … that I looked like a princess. I told her she was the princess, but she said she didn't have the hair of a princess. I said hair didn't make a princess. And to prove it, I shaved my head and swore to not let it grow long again until Hannah could grow long hair again too."

"You said that?"

I smiled, in spite of the ache on the right side of my face that needed some ice. "No. But if you believe me, Evelyn might too. Right?"

He groaned. "Lila ... we need to tell her. She's stronger than you think she is. A phrase she has said to me many times during our marriage."

"Tell her what? That I have cancer? That I could die? Or we tell her that the only thing that stops you from feeling my pain is when we're *together?*" I couldn't say "holding each other" or "touching." It felt too intimate.

Ronin's arms made me feel safe. I needed that. I made him feel whole and normal. He needed that. We needed each other in a way that nobody else could understand. Not even Evelyn. In a small way, I already felt the devastation of a husband needing something from another woman that his wife couldn't give him. Except Graham didn't simply need something from Evelyn; he thought he needed all of her. I could be *like* her, but that wasn't enough.

"It will destroy her, Ronin. She will never look at us the same way again. Even if she manages to put on her favorite brave face, I'll see through it. And it will eat away at my relationship with her. It will eat away at your marriage. This won't last forever."

"What does that mean?" he whispered. "What won't last forever?"

"This pain. Either I'll get better—you'll get better. Or I'll ..." I couldn't say it. I thought it. I thought about it a lot. Saying it, though ... that was different. Words had many powers. They shaped perception. Sometimes they cut. Sometimes they healed. But every once in a while, words brought actions to life. The law of attraction.

Even if my fate felt unchangeable, I couldn't put it out there and give it life before its time—before my time.

"You're not dying."

With my heart in my throat and my lips trapped between my teeth, I nodded. A few tears spilled over, tiny drops of fear I let go. "Of course not."

"Can I …"

I didn't make him finish. He could feel me. And as crazy as it seemed, I wondered if a part of me could feel him too.

"Yes," I whispered.

He needed to see me, to touch me. I needed it too. That need carried its own pain because we loved Evelyn. That was why she didn't ever need to know. That was how I knew it wouldn't last forever. It couldn't. I wouldn't let it.

"When?"

I wiped my tears and swallowed a bitter dose of my new reality. "Graham will be out of town this weekend."

"I'll figure out something to tell Evie."

A lie.

Ronin had to lie to Evie because of my pain. I may not have had cancer, but in many ways, I'd become a cancer in their lives. And I hated it.

"I will protect you."

"Protect me?" he questioned.

"You and Evelyn … Franz and Anya. I won't let anything happen to you."

"Lila, you don't need to protect anyone. You need to take care of yourself. Get better. Let's never have to tell Evie."

"Okay," I sighed.

"Ice your face more. I'll see you this weekend."

"What about your face?" Yet another thing to add to my guilt list: my predicament caused him an untreatable pain.

"Nothing some hugs from my kids and a kiss from my wife can't heal."

"I hope so." I frowned.

"Goodnight, Lila."

"Night."

I wrote several more raw, painful pages in my journal before tucking it back into its place and digging a scarf out of my closet. With a renewed sadness, I brushed my hand over my shaved scalp as if I had to touch it to truly believe the lie and the great lengths I went through to sell it. After a few seconds of acquainting myself with the stranger in the mirror, I tied the black and yellow floral scarf around my head and headed to the stairs to get some ice and something for the pain.

"Where do you think you're going?" Graham's voice startled me just as I made it to the top of the stairs where he climbed the last two steps to tower over me. Loose tie. Wrinkles around his concerned eyes. And a frown aimed at my scarf-covered head and red face.

"Ice. I wanted to get some ice for my face," I murmured, unable to keep from shrinking as he glowered at me.

"Elaine is in the kitchen. Your face raises too many questions. And don't even get me started on your head."

"A bookend fell onto my cheek. I shaved my head in support of a young child I met who's battling cancer."

Graham blew out his signature breath of frustration. "Christ … I can't believe how well you've planned this out. Go. I'll get you ice."

You should. You did this. You. Did. This!

"Thank you," I whispered, nearly choking on the words. Planned? I couldn't believe he had the nerve to act like my excuses for the things he did made *me* the unbelievable one.

We pivoted in opposite directions. I waited in the bedroom for him to bring me ice and something for the pain … like divorce papers. No such luck. A few minutes later, Graham returned with a bottle of ibuprofen and a gel cold pack.

"Come here." He sat in the chair by the fireplace, gesturing to his lap.

Once upon a time … I used to love his lap, his embrace, his affection. He used to scoot back in his desk chair at the office and pat his leg for me to climb onto his lap where I'd nuzzle my face into his neck and inhale him. One thing often led to another, and we'd turn into a frenzy of torn off clothes, desperate hands, and passionate kisses. Afterward, he'd hold me once more in his arms, like a small child.

I felt loved.

I felt cherished.

I felt like the most important person in his life.

Feelings changed. I no longer wanted to crawl onto his lap or get anywhere near him. Too bad I didn't have a long list of other options, so I gave in, submitted, confirmed to him that I was weak in that moment. But I wouldn't always be that weak. One day, I knew my confusion—the guilt—would lift. And he wouldn't be able to hurt me anymore.

I would be free.

"That's my girl." He pressed his lips to the top of my head, against my scarf, and held the ice pack to my swollen cheek while my opposite cheek rested against his chest, giving me a brief reminder that he still had a heart—or at least a beat.

"I have a lot of stress in my life ..." He began his usual spiel. It fit as an excuse for many things—headaches, sleep issues, the occasional grumpiness, maybe even snapping out a few regretful words with a raised voice in a heated moment. I gave him a pass for storming out of a room. Driving off and not returning for hours. Hanging up on the phone with me.

But he didn't get a pass for hitting me. Even if my temporary submissiveness led him to believe otherwise.

"It won't always be this way. When my term is up, we'll reset. Take a long trip. And things will be better. Maybe we'll take Evelyn and Ronin with us if they're still together."

What the hell?

I pulled my head away from his chest to look at his face. "What's that supposed to mean?" He could beat me and break me, but he would never destroy my instinct to protect Evelyn.

He shrugged. "I'm sure it's nothing."

It wasn't nothing. It was something.

"What's nothing?" I tried to climb off his lap, but he grabbed my arms. Having met my quota of injuries for the day, I surrendered so he'd ease his grip.

"A friend of mine thought he saw Ronin at a bar with Adrianne Craig."

I squinted at him, angry like it was his fault. Evie shared her concern over Adrianne, but I knew … just knew Ronin would never take the bait.

Graham rolled his lips together and nodded. "It's true."

"Evie must have been there too."

"My friend never saw him with anyone else except Adrianne. He said they were huddled together in a small booth at the back of the bar. Supposedly, they looked quite infatuated with each other."

"Did you say anything to Evie?" The muscles in my jaw tightened. I knew Graham talked to Evie more than his own wife some days.

Graham frowned. "No. I'm not one for breaking up marriages."

Except his own.

I couldn't believe it. Not Ronin. No way.

"Good. There's no way there's any truth to it, so there's no need to stir up trouble."

"Why would I stir up trouble?"

Emotion burned my eyes. *Why …*

I asked myself that multiple times a day.

Why marry *me*?

Why keep me?

Why hit me?

"I don't know," I whispered.

Graham pressed the cold pack to my cheek again. "I think I'm going to have to tell Evelyn about your cancer."

My head eased side to side.

"You shaved your head. She's going to know. I think it's best if I tell her. You're not in the right frame of mind to break the news to her."

"I *don't* have cancer."

I swore at times he had this look on his face like he'd come to believe the lie as much as Ronin, like he *wanted* it to be true.

"So you're just going to what? Not see her until your face heals and your hair grows back?"

"If you tell her the lie, I will tell her the truth."

His expression turned to stone again. "You won't."

"Yes. I will."

"She won't believe you."

I grunted a tiny laugh. "She's my best friend. She will believe me."

His lips twisted as he cocked his head a fraction and narrowed his eyes. "You? A crazy person who lied about having cancer after Evelyn's mom died of cancer? She'll think you're fucking mocking the tragedy that happened to her mom. She'll see a crazy person who cut off her hair to make it more believable. She'll see the bruises you inflicted upon yourself to sell the lie … to hurt her."

I shook my head over and over. What was he talking about? I wasn't crazy. It was all him. "I would never hurt her."

"No?" He cocked his head to the other side, studying me like the crazy person he tried to make me out to be. "I think if she thought you were jealous of my feelings for her, it would make this all very believable. You're human. Humans can be vengeful … even the good ones. It's an instinct we can't deny. We are created in the likeness of perfection but thrust into a world of sin. No one is immune from its affects. Not me. Not you. Not Ronin and Adrianne Craig."

"You can't do this," I hated my voice for shaking.

Keeping one hand pressed to the cold pack on my cheek, he slid the scarf from my head with his other hand. "Lila … I didn't do this. You did."

Swallowing the fear that he could hurt me even more, I whispered, "You hit me."

The tiniest flinch wrinkled the skin on his forehead. "I'm sorry. I chose the wrong reaction. I just …" He frowned while his gaze spread along my shaved head. "I never imagined you would hurt *me* like this."

My stomach twisted as my heart shriveled in my chest.

"I don't expect an apology tonight." He kissed my forehead. "It's been a wash. Wrongdoing on both sides." He set the cold pack in my hand.

I couldn't speak. Disbelief and shock paralyzed my words.

"Hop up." He nudged me from his lap like a dog no

longer needed for any sort of comfort. "I have to shower. Tomorrow will be a fresh start." He stood, a disappointing grimace spread across his face. "I thought today was the fresh start. It felt that way in your office." He brushed his knuckles over my cheek. "I knelt at your feet." The corner of his mouth curled upward a fraction. "I worshipped you. And you enjoyed it. I could *taste* it."

The physical abuse hurt less than the emotional degradation.

CHAPTER TWENTY-ONE

Evelyn

"**I**'M PREGNANT!" KATIE squealed over the phone as I finished my early morning jog, slowing to a walk as I reached the end of our long drive.

I needed to find an exercise routine again. My mom's cancer and dealing with her death made it hard to feel motivated. Ronin's onset of depression, which he refused to acknowledge, made it necessary for me to find time alone to exercise, breathe in the mountain air, and clear my mind. A mind filled with self-doubt and uncertainty. Since the night Ronin caught me masturbating in our closet, he'd been back to his no-sex-drive self. Of course he never said those actual words; he masked the truth with excuses like migraines and fear of a cold setting in that he didn't want to give to me.

"Oh, Katie. I'm really happy for you."

She laughed. "Wow. Could you have said that with any less enthusiasm? What's up with you?"

I used to do a better job of selling my act, my fake enthusiasm. Married life. Mom life. Friendships-falling-apart life. They'd worn me down. The act felt like too much work.

That ... and Graham's money made Katie's pregnancy possible.

"Whatever. I won't let you rain on my parade today, Evie. Oh, if it's a boy, we're naming him Porter. If it's a girl, Porter will be the middle name. I promised Graham I'd use his family's name. And honestly, I think Porter is a really cool name. I love surnames as first names. What do you think?"

I stopped, resting my hands on my knees, feeling nauseous and ready to pull my ear pods out of my head so I didn't have to hear any more about Graham. "I think if you didn't put it in writing that you'd name your child Porter, then you name the child whatever you want to name him or her. Maybe something special to our family or Tanner's family."

"Tanner loves the name Porter too. Besides, Graham and his family have done *everything* for our family. Sometimes I feel like we both owe him more than a name, we owe him ... our firstborn." She laughed.

I wretched but nothing came up.

"Kidding. I'm not suggesting you give Franz to Graham." More laughing from my blissfully ignorant sister who had no idea the Devil impregnated her.

Standing straight, I tipped my chin up, pointing my face at the sky and the shards of light breaking through the trees.

Mom.

I needed our mom.

"I just finished a jog, and I'm out of shape. So I'm sorry if my enthusiasm didn't carry through the phone. Of course I'm thrilled for both of you. I can't wait to have a little niece or nephew."

"Thank you, Evie."

"Give Dad a hug for me." I made my way toward the house again, dragging my tired feet along the gravel.

"Will do. Bye."

Before I made it to the front door, the garage door opened. I backtracked to the side of the house. Ronin slipped on his jacket as he stood at the door to his Subaru.

"How was your jog?"

"Fine. Where are you going? I thought you had the weekend off."

"I did. But Andy called. He's sick. I said I'd teach his first aid and CPR class today—in Denver." Ronin frowned. "The kids are still asleep. I put our sheets in the washer, and oatmeal is warm on the stove."

"You're a good man." I stuck out my lower lip. "But I'm not going to pretend that I'm not a little bummed. There's a nip in the air. I thought today might be a good day for a fire. Hot chocolate. Books. Puzzles. Snuggles." My hands curled into his jacket as I lifted onto my toes to give him a soft kiss. "If I'm even more honest, I was hoping the kids would still be asleep and you'd shower with me this morning." I grinned against his mouth.

"Later. I'll definitely want it later." He turned toward the car door without so much as a returned kiss or a hug goodbye. I hid my disappointment underneath my captive breath, the creeping of self-doubt into my fragile conscience.

As he opened the door, I couldn't keep my feelings completely to myself. "It's okay for you to *want* it now, even if you can't have it now."

I knew ... I really did know he didn't mean to make me feel unwanted. Just like I hoped he knew I wasn't trying to make him feel bad. Sometimes censoring every emotion took too much effort. We exchanged vows. We brought two lives into the world. Surely that meant we could let a little vulnerability leak into the space between us without it ruining everything we'd worked so hard to build together.

Ronin paused before sliding into the car. With his back to me, he dropped his chin to his chest for a few seconds before he turned back to me.

"Right?" I shrugged, offering a half smile so that he'd know I wasn't mad, just ... I didn't know. I wasn't sure what word described how I felt in that moment. Maybe a little disconnected from my husband.

"Probably." When he smiled, I caught a glimpse of the Ronin I married. The unrelenting flirt. My partner in crime and all shenanigans. Before I could cry from relief or even take my next breath, he kissed me.

Ronin kissed me like he needed me. He kissed me like we were the center of the universe. He kissed me like everything was fine and would always be fine. It wasn't sexual like the night he caught me with Madonna.

This kiss said I love you.

"I needed that," I whispered, more breathless than I had been on my jog.

White teeth peeked out from his soft lips. "Me too."

"Drive safely."

He slid into his car and winked at me. "Always. Um … I'll have my phone on vibrate during class, so if you try to reach me and can't, don't worry. I'll get back with you during a break."

I returned a nod after he shut the door.

"Oh!" I knocked on the window.

Ronin rolled it down.

"Katie called. She's pregnant."

"That's great. I'll call her later and congratulate them."

Ronin loved me. He loved my family. I married the perfect man. Why the hell did I struggle to have the perfect life with him?

After a quick shower, I called Lila since the kids were taking full advantage of sleeping late.

"Hello?"

"Hey! Haven't talked with you in a while. I miss you."

"I … well, I miss you too."

"You should come to Aspen for the day. Ronin was supposed to have the day off, but he's driving to Denver now to fill in for a friend who got sick and can't teach his CPR and first aid class. We could do hot chocolate. I'll make cookies. The kids would love to see you."

"Oh, I can't. I'm sorry. But that sounds like fun."

"Why not? Come on!" I begged, laughing at my maturity level which reached maybe that of a ten-year old.

"Soon. I just can't today. I have other obligations.

Graham is out of town, but I'm not off duty."

"Fine."

"Everything else okay?" she asked. "You and Ronin doing better than the last time I talked with you?"

"I'm not sure. I think so. He still seems so depressed. And I also think he's experiencing pain some days even though he denies it. Are you feeling okay? I know not everything he feels is directly related to you, but my mind still goes right to that connection when I know he's not well."

"I'm good. So I'm not sure why he's been off. Are you two…" she cleared her throat "…intimate?"

"Well, about that … the last time we had sex, it was …"

"It was what?"

"Intense."

She hummed. "Intense is good, right?"

"Intense is 'I could barely walk or sit properly the next day.' It was this weird angry kind of passion. Possessive. It lasted most of the night, and we did … everything." Biting my lower lip, I wrinkled my nose. "And we haven't done *everything* in a long time. Not since we were first married."

"O—kay."

Squeezing my eyes shut, I shook my head. "Sorry. That was clearly too much information. I guess my point is that we had the most intense sex of our entire married life, but he hasn't showed any interest in having it since then—not even plain old forty-something sex."

"What about Adrianne Craig. Any more from her?"

"No. I haven't seen her since the day she drove him home. And Ronin hasn't mentioned her. I'm hoping she got the hint and moved on."

"Yeah … me too."

"Oh, and Katie's pregnant."

"Evie! That's great! Tell her congratulations from me."

I rubbed small circles on my forehead to release the tension. "Yeah. I will. A slight catch or caveat to that good news."

"What's that?"

"Graham paid for Katie's IVF."

"He … he did?"

Clearly he didn't tell Lila.

"Yes."

"Well, that's okay. Good. Right? I mean … if she couldn't afford it. That's a good thing that he helped her out."

"Sure."

After a few silent seconds, Lila cleared her throat. "You don't think so."

It wasn't a question. She knew me. She knew my complicated and emotional relationship with Graham—most of it.

I blew out a long breath. "It's not that I'm ungrateful. It's just …"

"It's just that he's done so much for your family."

"Yes," I whispered.

"And you feel indebted."

"Yes."

"If he didn't ask for anything in return, then he can't expect anything. He can't hold this over her head. He wouldn't ..." Lila's words faded before she finished her thought.

He wouldn't what? Hold it against Katie? No. He would hold it against me or Lila. The need to say more clawed at my conscience. I wanted to say so much to her.

Are you really happy?

It's okay to leave him.

I will be fine.

I choose you.

Please forgive me for pushing you into his life.

"He had one request." I let her unfinished thought die because I didn't like the reality of what she started to say any more than she did.

"What was that?"

"He asked her to use Porter for the first name if it's a boy or the middle name if it's a girl."

"Jesus ... figures. Please tell me she's not seriously thinking of doing it."

"I ... I don't know. It's your last name too. You give the Porter name dignity."

"Dignity ..."

"Listen, I don't want to keep you. But we miss you. Let's make sure we get together soon. Just the two of us. I miss *us*."

"Me too." So much sadness bled through her words.

"Lila?"

"Yeah?"

Nibbling the inside of my cheek, I weighed my

words, choosing them carefully, finding the right tone to deliver them with a welcoming sincerity. "If something … *anything* was wrong, would you tell me?"

Silence.

Her delayed response answered my question.

"Li … tell me. There isn't anything you can't tell me."

"I love you, Evie."

Closing my eyes, I let her words wash along my entire being. She meant them. But she also used them to hide what she wouldn't tell me—maybe couldn't tell me.

"If he's not your forever, that's okay. Do you hear me? It's. Okay."

Tell her.

The truth swirled in my head like an unpredictable storm. Tell her that Graham loved me?

Love … that wasn't the word. Infatuated? Obsessed? God … that made me sound so conceited.

"I know. I said until death do us part."

"They're just words, Lila."

"And this is all just an experience. Right? You told me that years ago when we were talking about parallel universes."

"Yes. But you have a say."

"Well, I say I have to go. Love you. Talk soon?"

"Sure. Bye." I pressed *End*.

CHAPTER TWENTY-TWO

Lila

I WAITED FOR Ronin in my bedroom.

Earlier that morning, I showered and shaved my legs and arm pits to match the rest of my bare-naked body. I wasn't sure why. It wasn't a date. We weren't having an affair—at least not one of a sexual nature. After covering my head with a scarf and dressing in a pair of soft leggings and a fitted tee, I called Ronin.

"Hi," he answered on the first ring.

"Are you close?"

"Ten minutes."

"The code to get in is 483562. Can you remember that?"

"483562. Yeah."

"I'll be upstairs."

It took a few seconds for him to respond. "Okay."

"Ronin?"

"Yeah?"

"This isn't wrong … like cheating. Right?"

"I … I don't know."

Tears stung my eyes. "I'm sorry."

Another few seconds passed in silence. "I'll be there soon." He ended the call.

I pushed a button that closed my room-darkening blinds. Then I sat on the bed, taking a deep breath. My heart, body, and conscience battled for a sense of reason. Maybe I needed an escape, a place where I didn't crave the attention and affection of my best friend's husband. A place where I felt a sense of hope that bloomed inside of me instead of the growing dread that everything around me was about to blow up in my face.

Before I exploded with anticipation, the bedroom door opened slowly.

"Lila?"

"On the bed. I … I don't want the lights on. If … that's okay."

I felt his approach even though I could barely make out his footsteps on the carpet. The hair along my skin stood on end.

Did his?

My heart raced.

Did his?

The bed dipped, and I could see a faint outline of his body as he sat with his back to me.

"You're nervous," he murmured.

He felt me.

"Yes." I hugged my arms to my chest, refusing to touch him first. This was all on me—his pain, the guilt, a shared life.

My life.

Ronin shared my life in a way I never imagined possible. Yet, he put my feelings into words. I couldn't hide the darkest parts of myself from him.

"You feel hopeless."

I swallowed my nerves. "Sometimes."

"But not now."

"No," I whispered.

"Because you want this."

When I didn't answer, he turned toward me. I hoped the darkness hid my tears. "I don't know what I want."

Ronin laid his tall, warm body beside me. I jumped when his fingertips ghosted along my right cheekbone. His touch didn't hurt, at least … not on my face.

My reaction didn't deter him from keeping his fingers connected to my skin, gently wiping away the tears. Ronin didn't speak about those tears. And he didn't ask permission to remove my scarf.

I swallowed a lifetime of heartache when his lips pressed to my head where I used to have hair. No man had ever made me feel so safe … so cherished … so *needed*.

The feathering of his touch, the way it regarded me as something special, something that could break, it did things to me it should not have done. It was my job to make him feel better, not the other way around.

Warmth radiated along my skin, settling into places it didn't belong, not with Evie's husband in my bed.

Ronín

NO WORDS EXISTED to fully describe how I felt touching Lila.

Calm?

Whole?

And desired.

I felt her desire for me. Not in the way I felt Evelyn's desire for me, and not in a way I'd ever felt my own desire. It flowed through me just like her pain, her depression, all the guilt, and every aching drop of fear. I *needed* her touch, but that wasn't a singular gift. I could have all or nothing.

"Turn the other way," I whispered.

Lila rolled to the other side so I could hug her back to my chest. Her breath caught in her chest, paralyzing her whole body as I froze in place too. I had an erection. And I couldn't explain it.

I loved Evie.

I desired Evie.

I needed Lila to take away the pain, the depression, the thoughts of hopelessness.

My reaction to her surprised me as much as it surprised her.

It was *her*. But how could I say that? How could I accuse her of making me hard? Lila had cancer and an injured face. Lila risked her own marriage to refill the bottomless void I felt from saving her life. A lifelong friendship with Evie hung in the balance, vulnerable to complete destruction if anyone ever found out about us.

As we held our breaths, I felt the desire—*her desire*—growing. My breathing turned ragged like her breaths. My flesh heated beneath my clothes, like her flesh. I felt it in my chest and along my thighs. I felt engorged. Her need to be filled collided with my need to fill someone. There was no way *I* was turned on by her. I didn't think of her that way. And yet ... there we were. And I fucking couldn't pull myself away because Lila was my new drug. My new Oxy.

She took away my pain. I felt weightless with her in my arms. Lila did something to me that took me to a place I never even approached with the Oxy. I tried to stop myself from moving my hips forward—desperately feeling the need to rub my goddamn erection against something ... literally anything.

I couldn't explain it. It *wasn't* Lila I wanted, yet it was so much Lila. Her desire flowed through me triggering my desire, and I felt both. I felt how she felt. I knew where I wanted to be touched and where *she* wanted to be touched. The two felt inseparable, too much, too strong to pull apart. I needed her to ... god ... I didn't know what. Not be turned on by me?

"Ronin ..." she whispered, her chest expanding and collapsing so hard I could feel it.

"Don't talk. Don't move. Don't feel *that*, Lila," I *begged* her to not want the things I knew she desired, to not feel an attraction to me.

I should have just died all those years ago. If I would have run out of her house right then, it would not have mattered. The damage was done. The irreparable damage.

Her body shook with silent sobs.

Guilt.

Pain.

Heartbreak.

I felt *all* of it. And I hated it.

I turned her toward me and held her as close as possible. My fucking erection didn't even matter at that point. She knew it was there. I knew it was there.

"I'm sorry ..." she cried.

"Shh ..." I kissed her forehead. And when I kissed her forehead, I felt as though someone I loved was kissing my forehead. I felt Evie's love.

It felt incredible.

Lila fisted my shirt and nuzzled into my neck, radiating comfort like the way I buried my face into Evie's neck, her soft skin, her flowery scent.

It felt incredible.

I kissed along Lila's face, being gentle with her cheek. When my lips reached her lips, I stopped. Again, we remained still, our lips a breath away.

"What do you feel?" Lila whispered with her voice weak from crying.

"I feel Evie." I also felt Lila's desire to kiss me, a physical ecstasy and an emotional torture. I knew if I kissed her mouth, it wouldn't stop there. Like the Oxy, feeling her desire *and* mine would be too much for any human to resist. We were breathing, yet it felt like a slow death.

"I feel her too," Lila rested her good cheek on my shoulder.

Over the next few minutes, my erection disappeared,

along with all the pain and the guilt. I knew it might return later, but I felt too complete with Lila in my arms and Evie in my thoughts to think about anything beyond that moment.

After sleeping with Lila for nearly four hours … I eased my arm out from underneath her and sat up on the edge of the bed. It wasn't normal to sleep that long during the day unless you were exhausted.

"The chemo is draining you."

She didn't respond, but it was the only logical explanation.

"You felt me … you felt what I felt, didn't you," she whispered.

The desire …

I nodded without looking back at her.

"I'm sorry."

"Don't be. Nothing happened."

Something happened. However, my Lila-high prevented me from making more of it. Worrying about it. And our time together did something to her as well. I felt her sense of peace too. Maybe we should have felt more regret. There were a lot of maybes.

Maybe I should have died.

Maybe Lila should have died.

Maybe life was far more complicated than anyone could fully comprehend.

I stood. "Thank you."

Just as I reached the bedroom door, Lila whispered, "You're welcome."

I messaged Evie before pulling out of the Porter estate, letting her know I'd be home in time for dinner. While I had no right to feel good, not after what happened with Lila, I couldn't help it. I had a high and I wanted to ride it until I crashed to the earth again.

Just as I pulled into the city limits of Aspen, Evie messaged me. I veered off the road to read it.

> **Evie:** Broken shipment arrived today. Sophie's at our house watching the kids while I figure out what to salvage. I'll be home in about an hour. Tell Sophie thanks and that I'll see her Monday.

Fate winked at me, and some greater power—a need—steered my car in the direction of Clean Art. I dug out my key since it was after closing time and let myself inside, locking the door behind me.

Music played from the back room. Twenty-one Pilots "My Blood."

Evie glanced up at me, wiping the outside of an amber glass bottle. Something—maybe lemon or grapefruit—hung heavily in the air.

"Hey! What are you doing—"

I grabbed her head and kissed her hard, making her stumble back into the opposing stainless-steel bench. Until I tasted the recesses of her mouth, I didn't fully understand how badly I needed my wife. *All* of her.

Evie could right wrongs, even if she didn't fully understand it. And from the way she gasped for breath when my mouth gave her a short second of reprieve, she didn't understand anything happening at that moment.

"Roe ... what the... Roe ..." I had her sweatpants

and panties at her ankles in under two seconds and my mouth between her legs.

"Jesus … Roe …"

Evie clenched my hair in her hands to steady herself as we shared drunken gazes. Maybe she didn't know why I drove to her shop, why it couldn't wait, but no words questioned my intentions in that moment. She didn't question my need to fill her, fucking her from behind, on the table, and one more time just for good measure against the bathroom sink after she cleaned herself up.

"Ronin …" She finally relinquished a concerned expression as I wordlessly put back on my clothes and fished my keys out of my pocket.

"See you at home." I winked, leaving her with a half-sorted shipment of broken products and a million questions. I also left her with three pretty spectacular orgasms.

Evie wouldn't find a bottle of Lila in my pocket, but she knew something wasn't normal. Normal felt like an unreachable goal by that point in our marriage.

CHAPTER TWENTY-THREE

Evelyn

AFTER THE SEX ambush at my shop, I arrived home to dinner on the table and the kids ready for bed. That meant one thing ... I wasn't going to get much sleep that night. Ronin sang his karaoke heart out in the shower while I put the kids in bed.

"I think you have some explaining to do." I crossed my arms and leaned against the side of the bathroom doorframe as Ronin toweled off.

"About what?" He smirked, sauntering in my direction.

"You know about what."

"Oh, that? Well, we can talk about that later." He hung his towel on the hook before bending down to whisper in my ear, "Because I'm not done yet."

I followed his naked body into the closet, knowing the only thing keeping him from ripping off my clothes was the fact that Franz had only been in bed for ten minutes.

"At the risk of sounding forty, is there a reason why

we can't have normal sex three or four times a week, instead of Tarzan and Jane sex every couple of weeks for like … seven hours straight?"

Ronin slid on a pair of boxer briefs. "Is there something wrong with Tarzan and Jane sex? I like it … a lot."

I liked it too. Although, by the time he lifted me onto the bathroom vanity at my shop and rammed into me for round two, like a robot with an endless battery supply, I longed for the days of quiet, slow, missionary sex with a child in our bed sleeping and oblivious to our actions.

"I didn't say there was anything particularly wrong with it, I just asked if there was a certain *reason* for it."

He shrugged, shouldering past me (but not without swatting my ass) to brush his teeth. "I've been plagued with so many headaches and whatnot that a moment of reprieve feels like a chance to seize the moment—show my wife how much I desire her. Is there anything wrong with that?"

Wrong? No.

Right? Also no.

It was just … odd behavior.

"Have you thought about seeing a doctor? Why are you getting so many headaches? Do you think Lila is having headaches?"

He brushed his teeth and shrugged again. "Maybe," he mumbled over his toothbrush. After he spit, he dried his mouth. "How do you feel about sixty-nine tonight?"

Who is this man?

Ronin grinned, delighted with the embarrassment seeping into my cheeks.

"How do you feel about a back rub and spooning?"

"Sixty-nine. You on top." He kissed me long and hard again.

It didn't persuade my tired ass to do that. "Back rub. Just you. And spooning with me behind you."

"Sixty-nine and we watch your favorite horror movie." Ronin tossed the decor pillows from our bed and pulled down the sheets.

"Missionary and no horror movie," I changed into my nightshirt in the closet.

"Blowjob and we can be done negotiating." He poked his head in the closet and gave me a single raised eyebrow with his head cocked to the side.

I curled my hair behind my ears, parking my hands on my hips. "How about you sleep on the sofa and I sleep in peace?"

Ronin rolled his eyes. "Fine. Missionary sans horror movie. Brush your teeth and get in bed."

I brushed my teeth, took a shower, applied facial cream, and prayed Ronin was asleep. No such luck. He grinned and lifted the covers as I padded toward the bed, rubbing lotion on my hands.

"Don't," he said as I reached for the hem of my nightshirt to remove it. "Just get in bed."

After eyeing him for signs of sincerity or ulterior motives, I turned off the light and slid into bed. He turned on the TV, illuminating the room again. *IT* started playing.

"We agreed on missionary and no horror movie."

He rubbed my back as I watched the screen. "Horror

movie. I rub your back. No sex."

I love you, Ronin.

I smiled over my shoulder at him. "Thank you."

Kindness bred more kindness.

Ronin gave me a long back rub. Then he fell asleep before the movie ended. After I turned off the TV, I slid out of my nightshirt and panties and kissed him all over. The Ronin I married awoke with gentle hands and patient lips. We made love—missionary—and it was perfect.

THREE DAYS LATER, things returned to their new normal. Ronin lost his sex drive, and he spiraled into a depression.

"Have you thought about antidepressants?" I cringed while saying the words as he filled his canteen with coffee for work.

Ronin sighed. "I'm not going down the medication road again. I've taken some herbs, they haven't helped. I'm sure it's temporary. Sorry you have to deal with me." He rubbed his left shoulder, face contorted into a grimace.

"What's wrong?"

He shook his head. "I don't know. I woke last night with serious shoulder pain. It hurts to move my arm. Not sure what I did."

I screwed the lid on his canteen for him and kissed his cheek. "Hope it feels better soon. Have a good day. Okay?"

"Yeah," he replied with another long sigh.

When he wasn't on a one-to-two-day sexual rampage, he spent most of his time sighing, frowning, and complaining about aches and pains. His interactions with the kids were forced, at best, and his interactions with me were nonexistent, unless I made him speak and acknowledge me. It was like he ran out of effort to engage after giving what little he had to work and the kids.

I waited for a fake smile, a tiny wave, even a simple glance before he walked out the door.

Nothing.

After the door closed behind him, I released my one exasperated sigh. "Enjoy your day to yourself," I mimicked the words the old Ronin would have said. "Hope you get a lot done."

Sue agreed to watch Anya at her house while Franz was in school so I could have a day alone to thoroughly clean the house and go through the kids' closets to evaluate what clothes they needed before winter.

Loud music.

Caffeine.

And chocolate.

I didn't let Ronin ruin my time. As soon as I had the house to myself, I found a great playlist and dug into the mess.

Before I could get one toilet cleaned, my phone rang. I turned down the music and answered it on speaker so I could keep scrubbing. "Yes?"

Graham laughed. "Why the attitude?"

"I took the day off to get some stuff done at home while everyone else is gone. What do you need?"

"I'm concerned about Ronin. Something showed up on my desk this morning. I'm not sure who it's from or why they sent it to me. Maybe because people know about my relationship with you and Ronin."

"What is it?"

"I don't want to say over the phone."

"Then why did you call me?"

"To find you."

"Well, you found me. So either tell me what it is or let me get my shit done."

"Down girl. Really, what has you so pissed off? Is there trouble in paradise? I fear there might be."

I tossed the toilet brush into the bucket and sat back on my ankles, glaring at my phone on the bathroom vanity and the voice inside it. "I don't need this today."

"Evelyn, there's never a good time for shitty things to happen in your life, but they happen anyway. I'll see you soon."

"What? No!"

Too late. He disconnected the call.

I turned up the volume and let my frustration feed me as I tore through my house, cleaning every little corner and crack. Just as I started to go through Franz's closet, the doorbell rang.

"Please don't be Graham. Please don't be Graham." I opened the door.

"Graham." I gritted my teeth, shooting his security guys a tight smile.

He stepped past me and shut the door, leaving his team outside.

"Evelyn." He glanced around. "Looks good. Smells clean. I've always loved your domesticated side." His creepy gaze gave my body, clad in ripped jeans and a tight tee, a slow inspection. "But if I'm being honest, I've loved all your sides."

"Whatever you came to say or show me, just do it. Franz will be out of school in three hours. If you fuck up my day, I'll kill you."

He opened a large envelope. "I have a meeting at three, so I can't fuck you or your day, given my time restraints. Maybe I can pencil you in next week."

Smack!

I hugged my hand to my chest. It stung after connecting so hard to Graham's face. He rubbed his cheek and had the audacity to grin.

"I am married and so are you. What the hell is wrong with you?"

"Nothing is wrong with me." Graham pulled a handful of photos from the envelope. "But something definitely doesn't feel right about this." He shoved the photos into my chest.

I squinted as some of them were fuzzy, but others were quite clear. Adrianne getting into Ronin's car. Ronin going into her apartment. Them coming out of her apartment. The photos were timestamped. He spent an hour in her apartment.

"He's not a cheater." I let the photos fall from my shaky hands to the floor.

Graham bent down and picked them up, maneuvering them back into the envelope. "I think he loves you.

But just because a man loves his wife doesn't mean he's immune to temptation."

I crossed my arms over my chest, trying to ignore the twisting of my stomach, sending waves of nausea along my skin and burning the back of my throat. "Have you cheated on Lila?"

He smirked. "You know the answer to that."

"How would I know the answer to that?"

"Because you'd be the first to know."

"You should go."

"You're right." He tossed the envelope on the counter. "Maybe find a place for those where the kids won't find them."

"They're in the same support group. That's how they met. I've met her. She was actually at the house not that long ago. She's changed. And Ronin is a nice guy who does nice things for other people. She probably needed a picture hung or something like that."

Graham blinked several times, returning a blank expression. "I like Ronin. You know this. But if he hurts you, I'll end him."

I nearly choked on the irony of the most hurtful person I knew pointing fingers and making threats against the most loving person I knew. But I couldn't find the right words to say because I didn't understand why Ronin was at Adrianne's place, and I didn't recognize the protective side of Graham. My world flipped and everything felt upside down.

Graham rested his hand on the back of my neck and kissed the top of my head. I felt too numb to react to his touch.

He brushed his lips down my cheek, and I barely felt that either. "I love you," he whispered in my ear. "I would never cheat on you."

But Lila … he would cheat on Lila with me.

Fuck my life.

Ronín

LILA ANSWERED HER phone by the third ring. What I wouldn't have done for a few pills to numb the pain.

"Hi."

"What happened, Lila?"

"Wh-what do you mean?"

"My shoulder aches. My head hurts. I feel like I broke my wrist. I'm depressed as fuck. And Evelyn is taking the brunt of my misery. What. Happened?"

"I'm sorry. I felt weak and nauseous after my treatment. On the way to the bathroom, I fell and dislocated my shoulder and broke my wrist. I'm … really sorry."

I stared out my window, debating whether or not I should go to the meeting or go home. "I'm sorry." I sighed. "I didn't mean to sound so harsh. Are you okay?"

"Yeah. I'm fine. My wrist is wrapped and my shoulder is in a sling. I have a few stitches in my head from it catching the corner of the bathroom cabinet, but … I'll be fine. Do you *need* anything?"

Yes. I needed to see her. I needed to touch her. I

needed the pain to subside.

"Lila …" I grunted a partial laugh. "I'm not going to let you do anything for me while you're healing."

"It's not just for you."

I touched Lila. Lila felt good. When Lila felt good. I felt good.

"Lights on. Daytime. Sofa instead of a bed. Maybe you read me a book. Or we work on a crossword together. Do you like crossword puzzles?"

"Yeah," I whispered.

"If it doesn't rain Saturday, Graham's planning on golfing with his dad since snow is predicted next week. Can you come to Denver?"

Another Saturday away from Evie and the kids. She wouldn't like it. But she didn't like me at the moment, and a few hours with Lila would change that. I'd be my old self again, even if it didn't last.

"Maybe. I'll call you."

I sent off a message to Evie to let her know I was going to a meeting. She replied with a simple OK.

"Hey." Adrianne caught sight of me the second I walked through the door. "You look unusually distraught."

I shook my head. "It wasn't a usual day."

"Wanna talk about it?"

I shook my head again. "The meeting will suffice."

"Thanks again for helping me put together my new bed."

I shouldn't have helped her do that, but she asked me in front of three other people from the group. And she asked me after I'd already confessed to having no plans that night beyond playing with the kids. While I fumbled for excuses, she jumped to the assumption that the answer was yes and gave me an unwelcome hug. To make matters worse, *her* car had slashed tires that night, so I gave her a ride to her apartment, but not before calling the police to let them know they should patrol that area a little more.

After the meeting, I tried to be the first one out of the building, but Mark stopped me to chat. Adrianne exited without as much as a look or wave. I breathed a sigh of relief, very willing to chat with Mark at that point if it meant Adrianne would be gone by the time I walked out to my car.

Ten minutes later, I wormed my way out of the conversation and the building.

"Fuck," I whispered to myself.

"Mark sure knows how to talk your ear off, huh?" Adrianne smirked, sitting on the hood of my car.

"He's fine. If I were you, I'd hop off before I drive off." I unlocked my door.

"I have a surprise for you." Adrianne slid off the hood and crooked a finger at me.

I tried to hide my annoyance and pain, but I couldn't. Not with her, not with my coworkers, not with my wife.

"Don't look like such a grump. You're going to thank me." Adrianne unlocked her car and opened the back door. "Meet your new family member." She pulled a puppy out of a crate and hugged it as it licked her face. "You've been incredibly kind and helpful to me when so many people see me like the plague. I know it's just a dog, but I hope your wife and kids love her and that she'll bring as much joy to all of you as what you've brought to me."

A dog.

She got me a dog.

You didn't gift people things like dogs that required care, training, vet bills, food, toys, time …

"I haven't named her yet, but if I'm honest, I think she looks like a Bella." Adrianne handed her to me.

"I'll set the kennel in your backseat, and I have a sack of toys and food to get you started. I really wish I could see the look on your kids' faces when you take her home." She rolled her lips between her teeth and wrinkled her nose. "But I suppose that might be crossing a line, huh?"

Crossing a line? I felt certain she'd crossed a line by gifting me a dog, asking me to put her bed together, and knowing my address.

"We're not ready for a dog." I tried to give back the wiggling puppy, but Adrianne held up her hands like no take-backs.

"Nonsense. Your darling little ones are the perfect age for a dog. And you have the perfect location, big yard, lots of sticks and trees …"

"I can't."

She shook her head. "Just take her home. If it doesn't work out, I'll take her back to my breeder friend."

Take her back? Sure. There would be no taking her back after I showed her to the kids. And I would never have sex with my wife again if she found out Adrianne Craig gifted us the dog.

"Adrianne—"

"Enjoy!" She hopped into her car and pulled out of the parking lot before my brain could make sense of anything that just happened.

I contemplated taking the dog to a shelter or seeing if Noah wanted it. Then I thought maybe the dog would be the perfect distraction for my family from me.

Me and my fucked-up emotions and physical ailments.

The kids were outside in the yard, playing with toys while Evie split firewood—the job I should have been doing—as the sun crouched behind the mountains.

"Daddy!" Franz and Anya ran to greet me.

The puppy barked.

"Is that a dog?" Franz's eyes bulged from his head as he gasped in excitement.

"Um … yeah." I opened the back door and let the puppy out of its kennel, handing her to Franz.

He giggled as she licked his face, squatting to release her to the ground. She took off toward the yard, sniffing everything along the way.

"Doggie!" Anya squealed chasing her brother and the puppy.

Evie made her way toward the dog, wiping her brow with the sleeve of her plaid shirt as she glanced up at me.

I smiled.

"Wow … a puppy. Did we um … discuss this?"

I slipped my hands into my pockets and shrugged. "Yes. We've discussed getting a dog."

She couldn't be mad. The kids went crazy over her. I

was mad ... mad as hell at Adrianne for ambushing me like that.

"What kind of dog is she? We discussed a small dog, *if* we ever got a dog. Right?"

"Yeah. But I did a little research, a lot of the smaller dog breeds can be a little snippety with kids. So I went with a Bernese Mountain Dog. She'll be great with them."

Evie's eyes widened as her lips parted. "Uh ... yeah. She'll also be big. That's a large breed. Did you know that?"

"So what do you want to name her, Franz?" I ignored Evie's line of questions.

"Mrs. Humphrey."

Evie rolled her eyes and laughed as Franz chased the puppy and Anya tried to throw a pink ball at her. "Franz, that's your teacher's name, not a dog name."

"I want to name her Mrs. Humphrey!" he insisted.

"Franz—"

"That's her name!" he yelled.

Evie turned toward me for help.

"It's not an awful name." I gave her a tight smile before retrieving the dog's things from my car. I needed to rest my arm and shoulder. Franz could name the dog Big Bird for all I cared at that moment.

After depositing everything just inside the door, I dragged ass to the bathroom and turned on the shower, adjusting the temperate to hot.

"Thanks for the dog. She's peed on my rug already. Did you happen to notice I cleaned the whole house today? How did you know I was *really* secretly hoping you'd surprise us with a dog tonight?"

I closed my eyes and let the water wash the suds from my hair.

"I'll return it."

"Ha! Okay. Great idea. It's like taking back the kids' Christmas presents the day after Christmas."

Shutting off the water, I reached for my towel, grimacing at my fucking shoulder.

Mrs. Humphrey cried from the other room. Evie must have kenneled her.

"Your shoulder hurts because Lila fell last night. Tripped on the tiny threshold between the bedroom and bathroom. She dislocated her shoulder and fractured her wrist."

I rubbed the towel over my face. "She told you that?"

Evie, narrowed her eyes. "Yeah. Why are you saying it like that? I'm her best friend, of course she told me."

Nodding slowly, I finished toweling off.

"So now we know why you're sore. I'm still not sure why you're depressed. It's not like I surprised you with a dog. Or spent an hour at a whore's apartment."

I tied the towel around my waist and brushed past her to get my clothes from the closet. "She needed help putting together her new bed. I tried to get out of it, but she put me on the spot with a bunch of other people from the group, and I caved. How did you find out?"

"Oh … how did I find out? That's the direction you want to go?"

"It was nothing." I pulled a white tee over my head

and combed my fingers though my hair.

"It was something ... because someone took photos of you coming and going from her apartment and anonymously gave them to Graham. *That's* how I found out."

Again, I brushed past her and sat on the end of the bed, letting my body deflate after a long day. "I'm not having an affair. I have no idea who took the photos or why they would take them."

"She was getting out of your car."

"Someone slashed the tires on her car."

"Oh ... another tire slashing. Seems odd."

"I thought so too, so I notified the police and they're going to keep a closer eye on that area. Now ... can I just rest for a while without getting the third degree?"

"Sure. You rest. I'll go take care of dinner, bath time, and the *dog* you brought home."

"Evie ..."

She marched out of the bedroom. I deserved that. I just didn't have the energy to plead my case.

CHAPTER TWENTY-FOUR

Graham

"W HAT DID YOU say?" Lila asked me as we ate dinner in the formal dining room. Just the two of us at a table for twenty.

"Say to whom?"

"The doctors and nurses who treated me at the hospital. Do you really think it's not going to end up in the tabloids in the next few days?" She picked at her food with her good hand.

My wife looked like hell—bruised, broken, emaciated. She for sure pulled off the cancer look. Too bad it did nothing to make my dick hard.

"I told them you were mugged, and I didn't want it made public."

"And my hair?"

"I told them it was none of their business."

Her shoulders curled inward as she dropped her head. "I told Evie I fell."

"And your hair?" I parroted her words back to her.

"I have wigs. If she notices, I have it covered."

"Well, maybe you should enlighten me so we're on the same page." I took a bite of salmon.

"I shaved my head in support of a little girl with cancer."

I nodded. "Think she'll believe it?"

Lila glanced up. "You better hope she does."

"What's that supposed to mean?" I dropped my fork onto my plate and blotted my mouth with the cloth napkin.

I had to give my wife credit; she didn't back down.

"Either she believes me, or she suspects I'm being abused."

"It was an accident."

"You pinned me to the wall and twisted my arm to the point of breaking my wrist and dislocating my arm!"

I pounded my fist on the table and made her jump out of her disrespectful rage. "Enough!" Taking several slow breaths, I let my anger settle into control. "Did you not enjoy it?"

"I didn't enjoy it," she gritted between her teeth.

"You orgasmed."

"If I give you a blowjob before slitting your throat, is it still murder?"

I really wasn't trying to break anything. I just needed a release. It was, in fact, an accident. We'd had plenty of rough sex over the years. How was I supposed to know her screams were pain instead of pleasure when I *did* go out of my way to make sure she enjoyed it too?

Nothing.

Nothing was ever fucking good enough for her.

"If I left tomorrow … what would you do?" she asked, just above a whisper.

The legs of my chair whined against the hard floor as I scooted it back and stood. Leaning forward, I rested my fingertips on the table and cocked my head to the side.

"What would I do to you? Or what would I do to Evelyn and Ronin? Or maybe you're concerned about the rest of her family. I believe sister dearest is pregnant. Although our mutual friend has failed to disclose that information to me yet. I'll have a word with her. And the last I checked, her dad has a kidney I paid for, and those borrowed organs don't last forever. So please … clarify whom exactly you're referring to so I can give you the grim details of my plans for *if* my wife thinks she's going to leave me."

I wasn't a total bastard. When she blinked, releasing a stream of tears, I plucked the napkin from her lap and dried them from her face before leaving her in the mess she made all by herself. As I reached the stairway, I called Jeremy.

"Bleach blond. Long hair. Five-six. Thin. Not too much makeup. And she needs to be wearing some sort of natural perfume that smells like flowers. Pick me up in an hour."

I had a few drinks before Jeremy picked me up. It took impaired vision to overlook the fact that the woman waiting in the hotel room wasn't actually Evelyn, just a knock-off. Although not a cheap one. The kind of woman who would let you do absolutely anything to her without ever leaking a single detail cost a fuck ton of money.

Good thing I just so happened to have had a fuck ton of money always at my disposal.

My Evelyn knock-off stood at the end of the bed in the dimly lit hotel suite. I poured myself another drink and paused the glass an inch from my mouth. "Your name is Evelyn. Do you know how to make soap, Evelyn?"

She inched her head slowly side to side.

I took down the entire glass of whiskey. "You do. You know how to make soap." I tugged at my tie as I crossed the room. "You know how to marry the wrong fucking guy. You know how to come in my mouth then act like it meant nothing. So why don't you get on your knees and show me some goddamn respect for once?"

Evelyn got on her knees without me having to ask twice.

About damn time.

I unfastened my pants, grabbed her hair, and shoved my dick into her mouth. Closing my eyes, I leaned my heavy head back and let Evelyn treat me like I deserved to be treated after all I had done for her.

THE NEXT DAY I felt better. More controlled.

I signed two new bills into law and had a budget meeting.

"See this?" My chief of staff showed me an online publication with a photo of Lila and me leaving the hospital after her accident. There really wasn't such a thing as a secure entrance. "Your secretary told me they called several times looking for a statement. Why am I just now seeing this? What happened?"

I continued walking toward my office, giving my tie a slight adjustment. "Do you want the official statement or the unofficial statement?"

"The truth."

"She was attacked while jogging."

"Shit ... how did that happen? Where was her security detail?"

I sighed. "You know Lila. She's a strong woman. I can't tell you how many times she escapes without anyone knowing. Sneaks out a back entrance. What am I supposed to do? We're just lucky it wasn't worse. She'll be fine."

"Was she ..."

I glanced back at him, internally rolling my eyes at his unfinished question. "Raped? No."

"Do you want me to have an official statement released?"

"Do we really need one?" I nodded at my secretary before I opened the door to my office.

"Uh ... yes. We need one. Otherwise you leave yourself open to speculation. And as charismatic as the world thinks you are, someone will start a rumor that you abused your wife."

"Lila is spoiled."

"Won't matter."

I plopped down into my chair and sighed. "Fine. Release a statement. Then get something else in the news cycle pretty fucking quick. Lila won't like this attention."

"Pictures will help too. Maybe the two of you at a restaurant looking happy. Take her to dinner tonight."

I didn't respond, but I was sure he took my frown as a reluctant yes. After he shut the door behind him, I called Lila.

She answered her phone with silence. Not a single hey or hello.

"Hey, sweetheart. Do something nice with your hair—er … wig—and makeup. We're going to dinner tonight." A term of endearment and a dinner invitation. If she sulked about it, that would be her problem. I did my part, giving her what she longingly referred to as "the old Graham." I missed that guy too. The old Graham spent his free time with his best friend, Evelyn. They watched sports, drank beer, and fucked.

Just once. And that was the tragedy that led to new Graham. New Graham had more responsibilities, which left so little time to undo all the shit Evelyn had done— like marrying the wrong fucking guy and pushing me into marrying her best friend.

Such a mess to clean up.

"I'm not in the mood to go out for dinner. This cancer treatment has left me feeling weak and unsocial."

My dear Lila liked to fight me at every turn, and fighters knew if they threw a punch, they'd get one or two in return. She made it hard for me to feel remorse for longer than a day. Most of the time, I liked the fight. But sometimes I just needed her to be obedient. Lila failed at obedience.

"I'm not asking for an RSVP. I'll be out front at six."
I disconnected the call.

Checking the time, I decided to call Evelyn, hoping she'd be at her shop and able to talk without the ankle biters disrupting her. Don't get me wrong; I loved those kids. Their biggest flaw? They weren't mine. One day soon, I'd make her pay for that—most likely naked and tied to my bed.

"No time for you," she answered.

I'd make her pay for that too. I'd make it my life's purpose to assure I was the only person she had time for in her life.

"You failed to mention Katie's good news. And you're welcome, by the way. I'm sure you'll adore your new little niece or nephew."

"What do you need? I'm running late because Mrs. Humphrey shit all over the carpet. I need to get a shower while Anya's asleep and get Franz picked up from school."

I could hear her turn on her shower.

"Mrs. Humphrey?" I laughed, making my way to my office door and locking it. I wasn't to be disturbed when the door was shut, but occasionally an intern with mush for brains would sneak past my secretary.

"Our dog." Her voice muffled.

I sensed she had me on speakerphone, just as I sensed she was undressing. Taking a seat on my sofa, I unfastened my pants and scooted back, already stone hard from just the sound of her voice. Catching her getting ready to take a shower may have been the highlight of my whole damn week.

"When did you get a dog?"

"Did you call about my dog?"

Imagining Evelyn naked made it difficult (hard) to remember my reason for calling. "Did you confront Ronin about the photos?"

"Yes." Her voice muffled more.

"And?"

"He helped her put something together. She kind of manipulated him, and he felt like he had no choice."

"Sounds like a lame excuse. Are you comfortable with the ease at which your husband can be manipulated by another woman?"

"I don't know, Graham. Should Ronin be comfortable with the ease at which you manipulate me?"

Really, the shower and imagining her naked in real time was just a bonus. Evelyn admitting that I had a certain amount of control over her could have gotten me off all on its own merit.

"Friends don't manipulate. They ... encourage and plead their case. Maybe on occasion there's a little begging involved. Call it influence. It's a much better word than manipulate. Believe me, you manipulate or have more influence over me than any woman has ever had over a man."

"Bullshit."

"It's true."

"Okay. Great! Then I need you to come train Mrs. Humphrey. Let Lila go back to the job she loves. And stop saying and doing inappropriate things around me. Do I have *that* sort of influence over you, Graham?"

It took me a few seconds—a few strokes—to answer because I liked Evelyn and her signature benevolent smile. Everyone adored the nerdy soap lady. But I *loved* the bold and lively side to Evelyn. A lightweight with a real punch.

"Anything for you—"

"That's the crap I'm talking about." The water stopped. Which meant … naked Evelyn drying her wet, naked body. "I don't want you to do anything for *me*."

Women … really … why did I like them so damn much? As a whole, they were a gigantic thorn in my cock. "I meant … anything for Mrs. Humphrey. Does she like bones or tennis balls?"

"I have to get dressed. I'm going to be late."

I reached for a wad of tissues on the table because confirmation of her nakedness took me straight to the finish line.

"Graham? Did you hear me?"

"Yeah …" I panted.

"Why are you out of breath?"

"Treadmill."

"I'm driving to Denver to visit Lila tomorrow. She'd better be the happiest wife in the world." Evelyn ended the call.

I chuckled, wiping off my dick and hands before tucking everything back into my pants. I had a meeting on sexual harassment in an hour—funny timing. "Good talk, Evelyn," I said to the air.

To my surprise, my wife greeted me in a long-sleeved dress that hugged what few curves remained on her underweight body, a wig that looked one hundred percent believable, and makeup covering all residual bruises on her face. The cast and sling were unfortunate, but perfection at that point felt unachievable. After all, she wasn't Evelyn.

"You said to meet you out front." Lila glared up from the ottoman where she used her good hand to put on her high heels, but she struggled to keep her dress from catching her other foot.

I sauntered toward her, kneeling at her feet. "I saw someone today," I said in my most somber tone as I slid her shoes onto her feet, feathering my fingers along her calves as I gave her my most sincere expression of regret.

She stiffened under my touch, and her eyes narrowed. "What do you mean?"

"I don't like what has happened between us." I dropped my chin to my chest, closed my eyes, and slowly shook my head. "I need to fix us. I hate what's happened. You deserve better. And I know I can't erase the past, but I can make sure we don't repeat it. So I'm going to do the work to be a better husband and get help. I just ..." I sighed, glancing up at her. "I just need you to give me a chance to be a better husband. I miss spending time with friends and traveling together. I don't know how things got so out of control, how I let this job consume me ... change me. But it stops now."

Tears filled her eyes. "You can't make things right. It's too late."

"No!" I grabbed her arms then immediately loosened my grip. "It's not too late. You have to let me prove it to you. I'll do anything ... *anything*."

"Tell Evelyn what you did to me."

Fuck ...

"Baby ... if I tell her, she'll never forgive me. So even if I fix us, there will always be a wedge between the four of us. Is that what you want? A strained relationship between your husband and your best friend?"

I wiped her tears as soon as they broke free.

"You ruined us," she whispered.

"No, baby ... we're stronger than that. *You* are stronger than that. If I keep getting help, if ... if I let you go back to your old job, we can fix this. I believe it with my whole heart. Just give me time. If I don't change, you can pack your bags and leave. But you have to promise to not tell anyone. I want *us* back. Not rumors and scandal. Not broken friendships. We can have everything again if you just trust me."

"You lost my trust."

"I'll earn it back." My urge to force an answer warred with my need to channel my anger. "Baby steps. Let's start with dinner. Okay?" I stood and held out my hand.

Lila stared at it, void of any sort of emotion. She needed to happy that shit up before visiting with Evelyn.

"Evelyn and Ronin got a dog. Did you know that?"

Her brows lifted a fraction, not quite hitting the happy mark, but curiosity opened the door to the possibility of a real smile. Baby steps.

She rested her good hand in mine, and I helped her to her feet. Lifting her hand to my mouth, I gave it a soft kiss. "I love you. And I'm going to make you love me again too."

CHAPTER TWENTY-FIVE

Evelyn

"You're too thin." I hugged Lila, trying to keep from bumping her shoulder. "But your hair looks fabulous. Lowlights?"

"Uh, yeah. And you have no room to talk about being too thin." She nodded toward the formal living room just off the foyer. A tiered tray and tea for two adorned the coffee table.

"Well, this is fancy." I lifted an eyebrow at her.

Lila, dressed in her sophisticated yet adorable burnt orange and gray jumper, took a seat in one high-back navy velvet chair while I sat across from her. "I miss afternoon tea. I had it when I traveled—many moons ago." She pointed to the goodies on the tray. "Pink rhubarb shortcakes, cheddar pecan scones, blood orange sticky buns, Earl Grey teacakes, and avocado toast with smoked salmon. Tea?"

I nodded as she poured us both a cup of tea. "Is this tea set a Porter relic?"

Lila shrugged with her good shoulder. "Probably."

"Are you eating?" I questioned her. "I'm genetically curve-less. Boy-shaped. Brilliant artists sculpt figures like yours ... the one you used to have. And ... don't get mad at me, but you made me promise to kick your ass if I noticed you falling victim to anorexia again."

Lila grabbed a shortcake and shoved half of it in her mouth. "No anorexia," she mumbled over a mouthful to prove her point.

"Are you going to stick your finger down your throat when I leave?"

"No." She laughed. "I've just been busy and injured. And Graham had me taking a self-defense class. So my curves disappeared. I'll get them back over the holidays."

"Well ..." I leaned back, sipping my tea and assessing her with my most scrutinizing gaze. "You look good. And it's not your figure or even that amazing jumpsuit or your new hairstyle. It's your smile. I haven't seen the real one for quite a while. It's nice."

"I'm meeting with a few people about starting my own engineering firm again. I was going to find someone looking to add a partner, but Graham insisted I be my own boss. Have financial control."

"You signed a prenup. So technically Graham is funding it and controlling it."

"True. But he agreed to a contract giving me full control if we'd ever divorce."

"That's ... surprising." I plucked a cheddar pecan scone from the tray and took a bite.

Lila twisted her lips. "Yes. Definitely surprising. I'm not sure what to make of his recent change of heart. I didn't think he'd entertain the idea of me going back to my job until his term ended. And honestly, I anticipated him making some excuse to run again or run for the senate … president. Who knows?"

Me.

Graham made things right with Lila because I told him to do it. I wanted him to do it for her, for them. But the smile on Lila's face was enough to let me overlook the other details, at least temporarily.

"How are you and Ronin?"

"Good question." I frowned. "I'm not sure if he's bipolar or feeling pain from someone else. He hasn't told me about saving anyone's life since he saved you. But he's not right. One day he's insatiable, and then he goes weeks without touching me beyond a quick goodnight hug and kiss. Then on a whim he brings home a dog without saying anything to me."

"A dog … yeah. Graham mentioned that." Lila smirked.

"Yep. We talked about getting one, but I assumed we'd decide together the actual *when* part. Nope … he just showed up one night with a dog. Basically dropped it in my lap like a third child then escaped to the bedroom because he wasn't feeling well. He takes Mrs. Humphrey on walks in the morning and when he gets home. He feeds her and occasionally picks up poop. But for the most part, it's been my job to housebreak her and train her to play with her toys instead of eating Anya's stuffed animals and Franz's Legos."

Lila giggled. "Graham said you named her Mrs.

Humphrey. How did that name come about?"

I couldn't hide my shock that he told her. That made me happy. It meant he found it interesting or funny. It meant he wanted to share it with his wife. "It's Franz's teacher's name. I discouraged it. He had a fit. Ronin said it wasn't a terrible name. It's growing on me, but Franz keeps asking to take her to show and tell. I can't. The kids will laugh at her name, and I'll look like the disrespectful mom that allowed her kid to name the family dog after his teacher."

Lila didn't laugh as much as I expected her to. "I'm sad for you and Ronin. I feel responsible."

"No." I shook my head a half dozen times. "You didn't know you were going to fall off the side of a mountain. It's a miracle you lived. We don't regret miracles. And Ronin is a paramedic. He's wanted to save lives since he was a little boy. Even after his accident and his *experience* … he chose to save lives. Some firefighters never make it out of a burning building. Some soldiers come home with permanent wounds. People who do extraordinary, brave things do it knowing it could kill them or change them forever. They don't want our sympathy; they want to know that the people they protect and save don't waste their second chance at life. If you want to thank Ronin, be happy. Okay?"

Lila dabbed the corners of her eyes and bit her lips together as she nodded. I kept my own emotions in check, just barely. Even with all the anger I felt sometimes toward Ronin, those words flowed effortlessly from my mouth. I loved him for a million reasons, saving my best friend was just one. However, loving him wasn't the problem.

"I'm trying. This past year has been unimaginable. But Graham took me to dinner last night. Then we walked down the street to that ice cream place that has the mango-lime gelato. He held my hand like we were just a couple in love strolling under the evening lights. I didn't think of the security tailing us or the occasional photo snapping. He didn't look at his phone. Not once. Then he ordered rocky road and told me how his grandma introduced him to rocky road. He told me about the first pet he owned—a rabbit. It's crazy how long we've known each other and I never knew he had a pet rabbit. Did you?"

I smiled. "No." Graham told her something he never told me. That didn't erase his indiscretions, but it was a step in the right direction to redeem the man I'd come to think of as unredeemable.

"He also had a stuffed dog named Moolah because his dad complained about all the things a real dog would destroy and how much money it would cost to replace them." Lila grinned. "Why did he wait so long to tell me these things? To open up to me? Why did he wait so long to be the man I thought I was marrying?"

"Better late than never?" I wrinkled my nose.

Her gaze rested on the tiered trays. "I'm not sure. Do you ever …" She trailed off a million miles away.

"Do I ever what?" I leaned forward, refilling my cup of tea.

"Do you ever wonder if Graham is truly …" When

her gaze lifted to mine, it filled with a dark emotion.

Pain?

Regret?

Fear?

"Truly what?"

"Trustworthy."

No. He was not to be trusted. The voice in my head screamed, "RUN!" Then another voice started listing the things he'd done for me and my family.

That Porter-Taylor scoreboard flashed in neon.

His whispered threats.

My pregnant sister.

My father with a kidney that would not last forever.

The Clean Art building.

"What don't you trust about him?"

"He's just different. I mean, we're all different. Older. Married. Kids. Different jobs. Responsibilities get in the way. We don't shut down the bars anymore. I don't get to Aspen as often to make soap with you. You don't watch games with Graham anymore. But you're still you. And on good days…" Lila gave me a half smile "…I'm still me."

"You don't think Graham's still Graham?"

He wasn't. I questioned not only his loyalty to his wife and friend, I questioned his sanity. But while my best friend remained married to him, those words sat nervously idle in my gut. Approaching the "your husband may be a psychopath" subject required absolute proof. Loving me, desiring me, didn't necessarily make him a psychopath, just a terrible husband. Sniffing me … that rode the line, but it also fit into the pervert category. Not all perverts were psychopaths. The worst part? I would have told Lila about his inappropriate behavior had it not been with me. As ridiculous as it sounded, I felt like I could rehabilitate him, steer him back on course. Avert an affair that would have happened had it been anyone else but me whom he pursued.

"Sometimes he's Graham. Sometimes he's unrecognizable. One moment he's kind and his amazing self, but other times I feel like he wishes he hadn't marry me. And please, *please* don't tell him I said that. I know you've always felt responsible for our happiness together, but you're not. And after last night, I don't want to do anything to jeopardize his generous mood. I'm just expressing my thoughts ... my fear that it won't last."

I nodded slowly. "W-what has he done to make you question if he really wanted to marry you?"

Lila shook her head. "It's nothing. Silly actually."

"It's not silly. Just tell me."

Her nose wrinkled as her gaze met mine and several pregnant seconds passed. "Occasionally, I think he wishes he would have married you instead of me."

Those words evoked strong nausea. Had she seen something? In the Hamptons, did she see one of the multiple occasions that Graham crossed that line by the length of an ocean? "Me?" I laughed a little, as much as I could with my scone churning in my stomach, pushing bile up my throat. "He's made it his life's goal to remind me how imperfect I am compared to you. He encouraged me to pursue Ronin. He knows our drunken mistake in college proved we would never work well as anything more than friends—"

"But what if ..." Her nose remained wrinkled.

I couldn't blame her. Graham's feelings toward me fell into the cringe-worthy category. My grimace tried to claw its way to the surface as well. I held it back.

"What if *you* thought it was a mistake, but he didn't? I know ... I know it sounds crazy, but what if he's secretly been pining for you all these years? And what if his insults were high school antics, reverse psychology to get you to like him ... to encourage you to prove him wrong by getting him to like the very things he said he didn't like about you?"

My jaw dropped, feigning shock. How could I expect anything less from my best friend? She noticed guys eyeing me before I spotted them in a room. Her intuition was right nine out of ten times. Lila graduated with honors, navigated the world by herself for years, started her own company that she later sold to be the governor's wife. Beyond her endearing traits of kindness and loyalty, my friend possessed a wicked intelligence and razor-sharp intuition. When Lila seemed blind to something, it wasn't because she didn't see it; it was simply because she purposely turned a blind eye to it.

"I don't know what to say, except, *if* there's any truth to your theory, *if* Graham had feelings for me beyond friendship, he knows I'm happily married. In the pining scenario, he has no chance of being with me in that way. So it makes no sense to ruin his marriage for ... misplaced feelings from the past."

No lie.

It *didn't* make sense to risk his marriage for a fantasy. Graham had no chance of ever being with me.

"I know. Trust me, I know it's ridiculous. But sometimes the ridiculous is real. Have you ever sensed it? Even a little bit?"

Yes. When he rubbed his erection against me, sniffed my crotch, and announced that I was his endgame or challenge in life, I sensed a bit of *pining*.

"You know I'm oblivious to little signs, subtle gestures. So, if there's any truth to it, then I don't know what to say. If it were the case, I'd feel terrible. Devastated even."

I did. I felt terrible. And the times he crossed that line, I felt complete devastation.

"And if you knew it for sure or could prove it, what would you do? I mean … what *do* you do if your husband longs for something he can never have? Clearly, he won't ever cheat on you with me. But you also have to know that I support you and your happiness without preexisting conditions. I told you to love *you* first. And that hasn't changed. *We* are forever, even if you and Graham are not."

She scraped her teeth along her lower lip several times, pointing her gaze to her teacup. "I'm not leaving him. And if you ever told him about this conversation, he would never forgive me."

"Lila, I will never say a word to him."

"I just need …" When she glanced up, tears filled her eyes.

"Your friend," I whispered.

She nodded.

I set my tea on the table and moved to her side, giving her a gentle hug and a kiss on the cheek. "It killed me to keep the truth about Ronin from you for so long. I needed to tell my friend, but it's hard to tell your friend if that friend is then put in the position to feel responsible. I get it, Lila. I understand completely. But *we* have to always remember that this is more than friendship. We are family." I released her hand and knelt on the floor beside her chair, resting a comforting hand on her leg.

Lila relinquished a sad smile. "I know. But sometimes family hides the truth to protect the ones they love for as long as they can."

I wanted to say, "Not us." I wanted us to swear we would never keep anything from each other, but I couldn't. And Lila didn't suggest a complete honesty pact either, which meant I wasn't the only one holding back a piece of the truth.

Sometimes we loved with lies and protected with sins.

"Yes." I returned a single slow nod. "Sometimes we start wars and throw ourselves into the line of fire to protect the ones we love. But let's try to avoid starting a war and stay out of the line of fire."

Lila rested her good hand on mine and squeezed it. "Agreed."

ON MY WAY back to Aspen, I called my mom.

You've reached Corey and Madeline. We're too lazy to answer your call. Please leave a message.

I redialed three times and ended the call before it gave me the chance to leave a message. Her voice. It was all I had left of her. When I heard it, the reality of her death didn't seem possible. I mean ... she was *right there* on the other end of the line.

Happy.

Healthy.

Alive.

After the fourth time calling her, I left a message. "Hi, Mom. Are you tired of my crazy messages? I hope not. Maybe you should be glad that you're not here to deal with my life right now. It's so weird ... having everything yet feeling like every day is a struggle. I don't know how to put the pieces of my life together. So I try to focus on the kids. I know that's what you would have done. It's what you did. Even when you were sick, you focused on me and Katie. Franz and Anya. Sometimes the only *truth* I can still feel is that you raised me to be a good mom. I wish I could be to Ronin what I am to the kids. He's in so much pain. I see it even when he tries to hide it. Maybe it's Lila, but I don't see the same pain on her face. Maybe it's something more ... something beyond our control. But I feel like ..."

I wiped a few tears. "I feel like I'm losing him a little every day. So I hug my babies, and I tell myself over and over that they are enough. It pains me to imagine a life without Ronin, but I feel so helpless. And if I'm honest, I'm just tired. I'm tired of not knowing what version of my husband will walk through the door. Not knowing where he is or who he's with. I'm tired of feeling responsible for Graham and Lila. I just … some days I just want to pack up the kids and leave. Maybe go stay with Dad or find a beach where I can cast away my pain into the vast ocean. I don't know …" I sighed. "Franz is out of school. I'll figure this out. But I appreciate you being here for me. I feel you. Your smile. Your arms around me. Your voice reminding me to take it one day at a time. I love you, Mom. And I miss you beyond words."

CHAPTER TWENTY-SIX

Ronin

L ILA HAD CANCER.
I had lies. The healthy man's cancer.

Something had to give. I just feared it would be Evelyn … giving up on me. She gave me my space. Too much space. We worked. Played with the kids. Cooked and cleaned. And at night we crawled into the same bed, but it felt empty. I hoped in a parallel universe we were making love and living our intended life of bliss. Maybe in that other universe I didn't feel Lila. God … I hoped so.

In spite of her telling me that Lila seemed better when she last saw her, I knew the truth. I *felt* the truth. Nearly a month had passed since I'd been with Lila, and it showed in my level of enthusiasm for life. I called her twice, but she wasn't available to see me. Starting her own engineering firm consumed her time. That and trips for treatment. I didn't know how she did it or why Graham encouraged her when she clearly had no business doing anything but focusing on beating cancer.

"I think I'm taking the kids to California for Thanksgiving. I want to see Katie and my dad." Evelyn packed Franz's lunch as I packed my own lunch while Anya slept and Franz brushed his teeth.

"How long are you thinking? I'm not sure how much time I can get off."

She shrugged without looking up from the two slices of bread on the counter. "I'm not sure. I might let Franz miss a little school so we can stay out there for maybe … two weeks. I'm interviewing someone today to help Sophie at the store, so I should have plenty of coverage."

"There's no way I can take two weeks off around Thanksgiving, especially if we get the amount of snow they're predicting."

"That's fine."

I slid my sandwich and salad into my thermal bag and leaned my hip against the counter. Evie calmly spread peanut butter onto the bread.

"It's fine that I can't get time off or fine if I don't go at all? Come to think of it, you did use the word *I* instead of *we*. Do you not want me to go?"

"It's up to you."

"You didn't answer my question."

She wrapped his sandwich and packed it in his lunch box before giving me a direct look. "I don't want you to go," she whispered as Franz barreled down the hall toward the kitchen.

It hurt. Maybe more than Lila's pain—at least my heart felt a direct hit.

"Let's go, Daddy!"

"Shh …" I held my finger to my mouth. "I'm coming. Put on your shoes." I grabbed his lunch box and stuffed it into his backpack.

Evie crossed her arms over her robe-clad chest and stared at her feet. We needed something. I was tired of just existing. But suggesting I spend Thanksgiving away from my family was not the answer. I couldn't believe she suggested it.

"Will Sophie be at the shop with you today?"

She nodded, giving me a two-second glance.

"Meet me at Grinds at noon."

Another nod.

The rejection hurt and the suppressed anger I saw in Evie that morning poisoned my blood. I swore my heart stopped beating correctly. My body moved from one task to another, but I couldn't focus on anything but those words she whispered to me. By the time I made it to Grinds, Evie was already there sitting in our favorite booth, sipping her coffee and picking at a piece of coffee cake. I ordered a drink and wormed my way to the back of the cafe.

"Hey." I pulled out the chair across from her.

She returned a sad smile, more like a cringe. "Hey."

"Two kids and close to six years of marriage and I'm already being disinvited from Thanksgiving with your family. Not going to lie, Evie, I didn't see that coming."

"I need some space," she murmured, gaze stuck to her cup of coffee. That made it exponentially worse—she couldn't look at me for more than a blink, maybe two.

"Space? We're away from each other for a good eight

to ten hours—five, sometimes six, days a week. We take care of the kids and the dog without saying more than a dozen words to each other in the evening. And even on the weekends you find some excuse to run to the shop or take a two-hour hike by yourself. We have space, Evelyn. Maybe too much space. And I'm trying to work my way out of this depression or whatever's been dragging me down. But I'm not walking away. And I'm sure as hell not doing it on Thanksgiving."

"I can't breathe, Ronin. When I'm at work, I hold my breath, wondering if you'll be better or worse. When I'm at home, I tiptoe around you, putting on this "we're-okay" act for the kids, all while holding my breath. And I lie in bed at night for hours, just listening to you breathe, wondering if we'll ever be the same. Still … holding my breath. So maybe it's not space that I need, maybe it's distance. And maybe you need some distance too. Maybe part of your depression is the feeling, consciously or subconsciously, that you're being rushed to feel better, suffocated to act like everything is fine when it's not."

I started to speak, but I had nothing to say. Her painful assessment of our current situation wasn't wrong.

"Fuck …" I rested my elbows on the table and ran my fingers through my hair. "I'm sorry … I'm just so incredibly sorry. Sometimes I think I should have chosen to accept the short life this time around. The pain. As much as I try to contain it, shield you from it, I can't. I'm cursed and it's ruining my whole life."

She reached for my arm. "No one has been ruined. I'm not leaving you. I'm not giving up on us. I just need a little break to find myself again, to recharge my battery. This mom gig is exhausting, and you added to my responsibilities by bringing home a dog."

"Evie—"

"No. I'm not mad about that … anymore. Mrs. Humphrey is a great dog, and the kids love her. I'm only making my case for needing a break. I might even see if Katie and my dad will watch the kids so I can drive down the coast and truly have some me time to do a lot of things I've needed to do."

Grieve her mom. That was what she meant. I wanted her to have that too, but it still stung. My failures as a husband lingered in my conscience. I never thought this could happen to us. We had the perfect life.

"I'm going to see a doctor again. See if they can give me something."

Evie nodded, rubbing her lips together. Her skepticism showed, even if she held back her words. I wasn't hopeful either. It was like trying to cure Lila's cancer by me going through chemotherapy and radiation. Antidepressants weren't going to numb me everywhere like opioids. They were going to simply fuck with things that weren't out of balance. I knew they weren't a happy pill. I also knew I needed to prove to my wife that I was doing everything I could to fix our situation.

Lila … I needed Lila.

"Oh, hey!"

I closed my eyes. Someone was out to get me. Really … I should have died as a child. That slow death crap and torturing of my family had to stop. Opening my eyes,

I turned to the cheery voice. "Adrianne, hey. We're kinda in the middle of a private conversation." Rude? Yes. Desperate? Hell yes.

Evelyn's icy demeanor intensified. She eyed Adrianne but said nothing. The look on her face said it all—she hated her.

"I won't keep you. I have to get going too. I just wanted to see how Bella's doing. I know it's presumptuous of me to assume you named her Bella. Either way, do Franz and Anya love her?"

Kill me. Just fucking kill me now!

"Yes. They do. See ya around." I tried so hard to keep the tower of lies from crashing to the ground.

Evelyn narrowed her eyes at Adrianne and then at me. She didn't *know,* but realization raced to the finish line while I choked on my words.

Adrianne, however, had no problem articulating her words, which sounded like she wanted to ruin my marriage.

"Bernese Mountain Dogs are just the best. Ronin told me you two were thinking of getting a dog. I couldn't help myself. Ronin has done so much for me."

Those three sentences translated to: I just stopped by your table to completely fuck up your marriage. Have a nice day.

Evelyn pushed her chair back and stood, slinging her purse over her shoulder.

Not one look in my direction.

Not one word.

"Oops ... did I do something wrong?"

I ignored Adrianne as I chased after Evelyn. She took a sharp right after exiting the cafe, cutting through an alley toward Clean Art.

"Stop!" I grabbed her arm and she jerked it out of my grip, jaw set, hands clenched, and eyes brimming with tears.

"She gave you that dog? You brought home a dog from a whore. What the fuck is wrong with you?" With one blink, tears covered her face. "What exactly have you done for her—*with* her—that's made her feel so indebted?"

"You know the answer to that." My words came out a little harsher than I intended. We were cracked in many places from the heavy strain of life always bearing down on us, but we weren't broken. Suggesting I was having an affair meant she thought we were broken.

Evelyn shook her head. "I don't know anything anymore."

"I didn't ask her to get the dog. She just showed up and shoved it in my face. It's a dog."

"No. It's a lie. And since when are you so weak that you can't resist when someone shoves something in your face? What else has she shoved in your face that you can't resist?"

"This!" I grabbed her shoulders and made her look at me. "This is how she ruined so many marriages. You said it yourself. She didn't even have to fuck the men she pursued; she just had to make it look bad, cast doubt, drive wedges. We're better than this and you know it."

"But she did …" Evelyn whispered. "She slept with a

lot of those men. Good men. Family men. Men who no one thought would ever cheat on their wives. They just couldn't say no." She wriggled out of my grip and took long strides down the ally.

I followed her, grasping for what emotional energy I could muster. "I am not having an affair. And if you believe that, then the last six years have meant nothing. Would you just stop and look at me?"

"No!" She jerked away again when I reached for her hand. "You don't get to force this. You don't get to shove yourself in my face. I *can* say no. And right now the answer is no. I don't want to hear what you have to say. You had a chance to say it the day you brought Mrs. Humphrey home. You've had weeks to say it since then. Honesty after you get caught means nothing."

I let her go. Temporarily … I let her go. But instead of calling my doctor to beg for some drug I didn't need, I called Lila.

"Hey, Ronin."

"I need to see you."

"Oh. I have a lot—"

"Jesus, Lila …" I ran a hand over my head. "I wouldn't ask if I weren't really fucking desperate."

"Are you and Evelyn okay?"

"No." I leaned against the side of the building.

"Do you think it's a good idea to do this if you and Evelyn are having issues?"

I didn't answer.

"Ronin?"

"Lila …" Her name broke from my aching chest.

"Tomorrow. But you'll have to be here early. I have an appointment in the afternoon."

Lila

"I HAVE TO cancel my trip. Please take me back home," I asked my driver after talking with Ronin. My three-day trip to meet with a potential client from Chicago could wait. Ronin couldn't. And I owed him my life. If he needed me for a few hours, it was a price I could pay.

My depression lingered, in spite of Graham's extraordinary efforts to fix our marriage. He hadn't laid a hand on me in weeks, but I sensed his growing anger. Anger at what? I had no idea. But it leaked through in clipped words and clenched fists when I asked one too many questions about simple things like his whereabouts.

We agreed my cancer treatment would be successful. I would go into remission and it would never return. Problem solved.

Evie never needed to know, and Ronin could let go of his guilt over keeping the secret.

As for our sex life … I wasn't ready to revisit it. I wanted to trust Graham and forgive him, but I couldn't. He'd made several attempts to come into my bedroom, acting sweet and seductive. It always ended with me clamming up, feeling repulsed by his touch. I didn't say those words. Instead, I kept asking for a little more time.

He never forced himself on me, but I swear I saw it in

his eyes … the monster teetering on the edge of control.

"Oh, hello Mrs. Porter." Wendy, our maid glanced up from the floor where she worked to scrub black scuff marks. "I was told you were out of town."

I smiled. "Change of plans."

"Ah, well, it's a rare day that I get to see you and Mr. Porter."

"When did you see him?"

Graham left early every morning. Aside from our cook and his driver, the rest of the staff rarely saw him.

"He arrived about an hour ago. Went straight to his office. Said he wasn't to be disturbed."

"Oh. Okay." I contemplated going upstairs. My basic instinct continued to be avoiding Graham. However, sometimes playing the offensive worked best. Tell him my meeting was rescheduled at the last minute. Avoid an unexpected visit to my room later with twenty questions. If he didn't want to be disturbed, he'd most likely give me a quick, "Okay. Whatever."

I grabbed for the gold lever knob to his office.

"Fuck yes … wider … take it all." Graham's husky voice bled through the door.

I froze before opening the door.

I knew that voice. I knew those words.

My stomach twisted. On the other side of the door my husband was cheating on me. I wasn't sure what hurt the most—the betrayal or my lack of surprise. Confirmation of what I'd always suspected.

The tiny, barely audible voice in my head that represented what little bit of self-preservation I still possessed told me to go pack my bags and be a million miles down the road before he emerged from his office. Before *they* emerged from his office. The louder voice in my head convinced me to open the door, to be courageous enough to face reality so he couldn't twist it, deny it.

I inched open the door, one, maybe two inches, my world ending as I held my breath. It wasn't what I thought. In fact, I couldn't make sense of the scene before me.

Graham leaned back in his desk chair, stroking himself—lips parted, gaze glued to the TV screen on the wall adjacent to his desk, above the fireplace.

He grunted the way he did as he approached an orgasm. Only, it wasn't him in the chair. The sound came from the TV. My gaze shifted to the screen as he jerked off, oblivious to the cracked open door and my prying eyes.

The screen was fairly dark, except for the two people by the bed, dimly lit by a single nightstand light.

Her on her knees with her back to the camera. Graham with his dick in her mouth and his hand fisting her nearly white hair as he pumped into her. All I could think in that moment was, had I not known better, I could have thought it was Evelyn on her knees. The hair matched. The lithe figure. The way he looked at her.

"God ... Evelyn ... it's always been you. Right, baby?"

No. NO!

She. Her. My friend nodded even as she gagged a little. Silent tears spilled down my cheeks, blurring the couple on the screen, blurring the live version of Graham, twisting his face as he ejaculated onto himself.

I didn't try to close the cracked door. I just ... ran. I ran past Wendy, up the stairs, and straight to my room where I locked my door and fell to my knees before I could make it to the chair or the bed.

The tears. I waited for more tears, but they didn't form. I fell on my side and hugged my knees to my chest, staring unblinkingly at the wall. I wished Evie wouldn't have found me in my car that day. I should have died. My life had meant nothing. *I* meant nothing to the people I allowed myself to believe loved me.

Ronin shouldn't have saved me on that mountain.

Reaching toward my head, I clenched the wig in my hand and pulled it from my head. I wanted to have cancer.

I wanted ... to die.

CHAPTER TWENTY-SEVEN

Evelyn

H E DIDN'T CHEAT on me.

I knew it in my heart. It still hurt.

Everything hurt.

"Hello, dear. How was your day?" Sue looked up from the sofa where Anya sat on her lap holding a book.

Franz zoomed past me dropping his coat and backpack on the floor. We encountered an accident after school pick-up, and he nearly wet his pants holding it for the extra twenty-minute detour.

My day was terrible. "Good. How was your day?" I frowned at Mrs. Humphrey, begging for my attention. It wasn't her fault that Adrianne forced her into our family. Still, I wondered if I would forever look at that dog and think about the woman who tried to break up my marriage. I gave Mrs. Humphrey a few strokes on her head before turning my attention to Anya hopping off the sofa and barreling toward me.

"Lazy." Sue laughed. "We had the best intentions, but she quickly fell asleep after lunch. I wonder if she's running a low fever."

I kissed Anya's forehead. "You do feel a little warm, baby."

"Bye, Franz," Sue yelled as she slipped on her jacket and opened the front door.

"Bye!" Franz returned from the bathroom.

"Thanks, Sue."

"Of course." She closed the door behind her as I carried Anya to my room to take her temperature. Just as I set her on the bed, my phone rang. I jogged back out to the kitchen to retrieve it from my purse. "Hey, Noah."

"Hi, Evelyn. Don't panic, but I'm on my way to the hospital with Ronin."

I stumbled backward a few steps as a familiar fear gripped my lungs. "What happened? Did he save someone? Did he get injured?"

"No. Actually, we were having a meeting and he started clawing at his throat like he was choking, but we weren't eating or drinking anything. His coloring was fine. No obstructed airway, but he kept gasping and whispering that he couldn't breathe. Before the ambulance arrived, he gasped a full breath and fell to the floor, seeming better but really weak. We don't know what caused it, but they'll run all the tests and hopefully figure it out. He doesn't have any allergies listed on his medical form. Do you know of any?"

"Um, no." I grabbed my purse, but Franz was still in the bathroom, and Anya was still on the bed, only she'd lain on my pillow, a sure sign she wasn't feeling well.

"I already messaged Tami. She's on her way to your house to watch the kids. I'll see you in a bit. But he's better. He'll be fine."

"O-okay," I mumbled while fishing through things in my bathroom to find the thermometer. "Thanks. Tell him ..." What? I didn't even know, so I dropped my phone before officially ending the call.

"I want a snack," Franz declared, emerging from the bathroom as I took Anya's temperature. "Franz, Tami's coming over to watch you and Anya for a while. She'll be here soon and get you a snack. You can have your hour of screen time now if you want it."

"Okay." Man, that kid knew when to go easy on me, even if he could be so stubborn at other times.

"One hundred and one, baby. Do you feel okay?" I kissed her forehead again.

Anya nodded, but it didn't match her lethargy.

Within minutes, Tami arrived, reassuring me that Ronin would be fine and my kids were in good hands. I hated leaving my sick child, but something wasn't right with Ronin, and that seemed more serious than a fever. As I pulled onto the main road, I called Lila. The last time Ronin had this happen to him, he thought it was Lila. It wasn't. But I still had to know for sure that this wasn't him feeling something awful happen to her.

"Why aren't you picking up?" I murmured to myself as it went to voicemail. After redialing two more times and two more times it going to voicemail, I started to really worry. Once I parked the car at the hospital, I brought up Graham's number, but before I could press the call button, Lila texted me.

Lila: Sorry, I can't talk. Graham took me to the ballet and it's past intermission. He's the best!

What's up?

In the midst of my chaos, the last thing I wanted to do was give Graham Porter credit for anything good. But the relief of knowing Lila was not only okay, but at the ballet—something she loved—lifted a tiny bit of weight from my suffocating chest.

Evelyn: Nothing important. Have fun.

Until I knew more about Ronin's situation, I didn't need to alarm anyone else.

"Hey." Noah pulled me into his arms when I reached the waiting room at the ER. "They're running some tests. He said his neck is really tender and his voice is hoarse. But their initial exam didn't show anything. It's ... weird."

"Has he done any rescue stuff recently? Like CPR on anyone?"

Noah shook his head. "Why do you ask that?"

"It's ... nothing."

"He hasn't even taught a class for nearly a year. But still, I'm not sure where you're going with that anyway."

"Really, it's nothing. And actually he did teach a class not that long ago. Couple months ago he filled in for ... I think he said Andy? A CPR and first aid class in Denver."

"I filled in for Andy with that class, and it was over six months ago."

My eyes narrowed.

"I mean ..." Noah fumbled his words. "A couple months ago? Yeah, that might have been right too. Andy says yes to everything, but then he backs out at the last minute and begs us to help him out." He couldn't keep his gaze on me for more than a few seconds before averting it to anywhere else in the room.

Noah lied. He lied for Ronin.

If Ronin didn't teach a CPR class that day, then where was he? Or *who* was he with?

Adrianne.

It wasn't possible, but it felt like the only logical explanation, the only explanation that didn't make me look incredibly naive.

Noah said very little while we waited for nearly an hour to see Ronin in the ER. When the nurse took me back, sliding open the glass door, Ronin's tired gaze shifted right to me.

"You need to call Lila."

Lila … his scapegoat.

"I did. She's fine."

"She's not—"

"Ronin!" I sighed, hoping no one heard my outburst. "It's not Lila. I checked. It's something else. If they say it's nothing, then I think we need to take you to Denver and have you checked out by better doctors. Something is wrong with you. If you feel like you can't breathe, that's a serious problem. Don't you get that?" I didn't mean to let so much of my aggravation seep through, but I had nothing left.

Too many unanswered questions.

Too many lies.

Too much disconnect from the man I loved.

Doubt ran amuck in my head, and Ronin did nothing to stop the chaos.

"They already discharged me. We can go home." He sat up.

I reached to help, but he shook his head. "I'm fine. I've got it."

"So that's it. You can't breathe. They run tests. And send you home with nothing. What the hell, Ronin?"

"Not nothing. They wrote me a prescription for an inhaler," he mumbled his words as he stepped into his jeans, dragging them slowly up his legs. He failed at hiding his weakness.

I pulled them up the rest of the way, giving him a single look when he tried to bat away my hands. On a long sigh of surrender, he let me dress him. I finished tying his boots as he sat on the edge of the bed, legs dangling. When I stood between his spread legs, he pulled me in for a hug, resting one hand on the small of my back and the other hand on the back of my head.

There. Right there ... I felt his love. It just felt shackled to something. Like he couldn't give me all of it.

So much anger brewed inside of me. His touch couldn't tame that, but it did something. It *always* did something. And that something brought forth raw emotions that made me say the three words that I'd been feeling since the first time I called 9-1-1 in Ronin's condo before we were married.

"Please don't die," I whispered on a tight sob that clutched my chest and burned my eyes.

We weren't unbreakable.

I just needed to believe we weren't unrepairable.

CHAPTER TWENTY-EIGHT

Graham

Three hours earlier …

I KNEW I shut my door. Maybe I didn't lock it, but my staff didn't disobey me. Yet clearly someone had ignored my order. As I made my way to fire someone, I noticed Lila's suitcase parked inside the front door. Before I could pull my phone out of my pocket to check her location, the wavy brunette who cleaned the house—Mindy, Amy, something like that—came down the stairs carrying a bucket of cleaning supplies.

"Sorry, Mr. Porter, I should have carried Mrs. Porter's suitcase to her room. I got—"

"Is she home?"

"Yes. Her trip was rescheduled."

"Leave. Now. Ask everyone else to leave as well." I started up the opposite stairwell.

"Sir, what do you mean—"

"I mean get the fuck out. Tell everyone to get the fuck out and don't come back until you're called."

Well, all my hard work for nothing. I gave Lila permission to go back to work. We ate at her favorite restaurants. I let her wear those stupid short dresses, teasing my cock relentlessly, only to give me a meek whisper of, "I'm not ready," every time I started to undress in her room. Yet I forced nothing. As her husband, I deserved more respect, but in the spirit of making Evelyn proud of me, I left without a fight and spent a long shower jerking off like pussy husbands who fell for the headache line on a regular basis.

The biggest question ... how much did she see when she poked her snoopy head into my office? After watching the video I took at the hotel, I made several business calls and returned a few emails. It was possible she caught me on the phone and decided to not disturb me.

I tried to open her door. It was locked. "Lila?"

No answer. I retrieved a key to her door from under a vase on a recessed shelf in the wall a foot to the left of her door.

Just fucking fantastic ...

I found her in a fetal position on the floor, a blank stare focused on the wall and her wig resting a few feet away from her head. She saw the video. In all fairness to myself, that happened before we agreed to make things right between us. Since our truce, I hadn't fucked anything but my hand. Okay ... that was ninety-nine percent true. Kimberly, an intern who looked like a younger version of Evelyn, celebrated her thirtieth birthday after work the previous week. She had a little too much to drink, so I offered to give her a ride home like any gentleman would have done. It was her first time in a car with a divider between the front seat and backseat, supposedly not counting the one time she was arrested for protesting some female rights shit in college.

After giving my driver her address, I closed the dark glass divider and waited for her to make her move. After all, I was technically her boss, and women seemed sensitive to sexual advances in the workplace. My dad said he missed the good ol' days. I agreed with him.

It took drunk Kimberly less than ten seconds to bite her lower lip while unfastening my pants. For the record … I never touched her. If her idea of a good birthday present from her boss was letting her suck me off, who was I to rain on her birthday parade? The girl gave head like a champ. When we arrived at her dinky apartment building, I assured her she would have a bright future in politics if she kept up the good work.

"Can I ask why you're on the floor?"

No response.

I nudged Lila's ass with the toe of my shoe.

No response.

Why did she insist on always putting me in such a predicament? Thinking back to Kimberly had me hard as fuck. Seeing my bald wife on the floor with her wig doing its own thing did nothing for me. But Lila still had a killer body with tits for days. Evelyn had a mouthful at best. See? I always managed to see the good in Lila, even when directly comparing her to Evelyn.

"I sent the staff home." I scooped her limp body up off the floor. "I thought we could discuss what you saw earlier." I laid her on the bed, and her cold eyes affixed to me as I loosened my tie. "So … what did you see?" My fingers made quick work with the buttons of my shirt. After I shrugged it off my shoulders, I reached for the button of her light gray pants, half anticipating her batting me away.

She didn't move more than relinquishing a single slow blink. I removed her pants and underwear. Still, she didn't move.

"This looks nice." I traced my finger around her freshly waxed cunt. "I hope you did this for me and not someone else?"

While she held strong to her refusal to speak or move, I unbuttoned her top and shoved her bra up over her tits.

Yep, they were still quite spectacular.

"I normally like you a little more feisty … you know … I like to work for it." I removed my pants and briefs. "But it's been a long day, so I'm good with easy tonight."

"Y-you had s-sex with m-my b-best friend," Lila said just above a whisper as her lower lip quivered and a single tear trailed down the side of her face.

I didn't think about the video hard enough to anticipate such an unexpected change of events. The whore … she looked like Evelyn from the back, and I called her Evelyn. I wondered if Lila had called her BFF, but the genuine hurt and tears led me to believe that she never made it further than the floor of her bedroom. Did I want her to think it was Evelyn in that hotel suite? Good question. I had a little time to think on that.

"It was before you and I decided to kiss and make

up." I forced her legs apart, but it didn't require much force because she didn't fight me. She could have fought me. I didn't have her hands tied.

I camped out down low for what felt like hours ... or at least a good fifteen minutes.

Nothing.

It was the first time I failed at making her orgasm with oral. "You broken down there?" I sat up and fingered her, but it was the Sahara Desert down there.

Her dead gaze did nothing more than stare at me and leak tears.

"I guess we'll do it another way." I spit on my hand a few times and smeared it between her legs and along my dick. It still felt like sandpaper when I pushed into her. By that point I wasn't doing it for the release as much as I just didn't want to let her win. So she played the errant, limp child, refusing to cooperate while I did all the work.

It took *forever* to feel my orgasm approach, even using Kimberly and Evelyn as my visuals. The bedroom lights were on. The blinds were cracked open. And Lila's grotesque bald head occupied my line of sight.

On the verge of pulling out before finishing, admitting a rare defeat, Lila surprised me. She lifted her knees toward her chest, allowing me deeper penetration. Then she grabbed my head and pulled it to hers, kissing me slowly, teasing her tongue along my lips, turning her head slowly to drag her lips across my cheek—

"Fuuuck!" I reared back, ripping my cheek from her clenched mouth. Pain seared through my face, and I swear she had part of my cheek still in her blood-stained mouth. I started to pull out of her, readying my right hand to break her face, but then she smiled.

Crimson covered teeth. That hideous bald head. And her nipples erect like doing that to me turned her on.

Instead of making her the victim with a fresh dose of bruises, I opted to simply get rid of that fucking smile. I grabbed the other pillow and covered her whole head.

Problem solved.

All that remained was her perfect body, bouncing tits, and hands clawing at the pillow as I finished ... blood dripping from my face to her torso while her body flailed. I took my time, no longer feeling the pain in my face, just the release. The glorious release.

As her fight began to weaken, I pulled out, released the pillow, and walked toward the door.

Lila's high-pitched gasp turned into a fit of ragged coughs. I plucked her phone from the pocket of her purse discarded by the door and closed it behind me.

Blood from my face dotted the floor from her bedroom to the nearest bathroom.

"Jesus ..." I cringed. My cheek looked like a dog attacked it.

I took a picture of it and sent it to a friend. A plastic surgeon friend.

Graham: Come to the house. Bring what you need.

I couldn't leave Lila. Things were too unstable between us at the moment. I also couldn't let my face be scarred for life.

I taped gauze to my face while I waited for Dr. Peters,

a buddy from high school who needed some help settling a lawsuit and keeping his medical license after operating under the influence on a patient. The thing was ... Blake was an excellent plastic surgeon who just so happened to have a drinking problem. He had to sober his ass up as part of our agreement for me to help him.

When I returned to Lila's room, her lifeless body remained just where I'd left her. Only, she wasn't without life.

Unfortunately.

With my face mangled and her body untouched, my attorney could have made a solid case for self-defense. My psychotic wife (the one who faked having cancer) going crazy and attacking me. However, that would have been a hard sell to Evelyn. And if I couldn't have my trophy when all the bullshit finally ended, what was the point?

"Listen, Hannibal, I have a friend coming for a visit." I grabbed her arms. She made a weak attempt to fight me. "So I need you to stay in your room and not make a sound until he's gone." After restraining her hands and feet, I wiped the blood from her mouth so the tape would stick. "I'll let you out of your cage later."

Blake arrived within the hour. I messaged security to let him through the gate.

"What the hell happened?" he asked the second I opened the door.

I removed the gauze. "Dog attacked me."

"I didn't know you had a dog." He followed me to my office where I sat on the leather sofa, leaning back because the adrenaline started to leave my body, and I wasn't feeling well.

"This isn't a dog bite." He frowned while inspecting my face.

"No shit. If it were a dog bite, I wouldn't have called you to my house."

"We need a sink or a bowl so I can clean this good to see it and to make sure it doesn't get infected."

"Go find a bowl in the kitchen. I can't get up. I'm not feeling so well at the moment."

"Okay, can you hold the gauze back in place? It's hemorrhaging more than I wish it were."

I pressed the gauze to my face. If I passed out or had to be rushed to the hospital, Lila restrained with tape over her mouth might not look the best. It would be very difficult to spin that.

Blake returned with a bowl and opened a saline bag.

"Could this not end well? What are the chances of you rushing me to the hospital? I have some things I need to take care of that are time sensitive."

He chuckled. "Hold the bowl right here. Do you want to leave me instructions in case this goes south? Do you have a hooker locked in a closet?" He snickered more.

No hooker. Just my wife bound and gagged. No big deal.

"Fuck …" I grimaced as he flushed out my wound.

"Sorry." After torturing me for a good thirty seconds, he narrowed his eyes, inspecting my cheek. "For this to heal with minimal scaring, I think you need a skin graft."

"Whatever, just do it."

"Graham … no. I can't do a skin graft here in your

office. You need to come to the hospital."

"Then no. Just make it stop bleeding."

"It won't look right."

"You're the best, Blake. So do your fucking best. I can't leave."

He returned another frown. I closed my eyes and worked out my next moves while he repaired my face.

"It's going to be sore. Here's some pain meds for you. I can't get you more without you making an official visit to my office. Don't get it wet for a few days and change the bandage daily using this antibiotic ointment for the next three days. I'll check it in a week. Call me if you spike a fever, have increased swelling or redness. Got it?"

I popped a pill into my mouth and swallowed it without water. "Got it. Thanks."

He zipped his bag and squinted at me. "Are you okay? You don't have to tell me who bit you, but if you're in trouble or danger …"

"No trouble. No danger. See yourself out."

I waited for the door to click shut before sitting up.

"God …" I lay back down. I didn't do well with injuries to myself. They always made me nauseous and dizzy. After another ten minutes on the sofa, I sat up slower and remained sitting for another few minutes before climbing to my feet.

Taking slow deep breaths, I made my way toward the stairs, swaying a bit but willing myself to man the fuck up and stop being so queasy.

"What are we going to do about this?" I collapsed onto the bed next to Lila. "I'm too fucking weak to deal with you." I rolled onto my side so we faced each other.

Her wide eyes darted from my eyes to my face.

"A friend stitched me up. Apparently you ate part of my face, so there could be a scar. Remember when we were named Most Beautiful Couple of the Year? I fear that honor will not be bestowed upon us again. You look like you're dying of cancer and I look like a rabid dog attacked me. We are in such a pickle, babe. I just don't know what to do with you."

She wrinkled her nose and thrashed her head side to side.

"Do you have an idea?" I ripped the tape from her mouth.

Lila flinched. "Just kill me."

"I don't want to kill you."

"Then let me go."

"Go where?"

"Anywhere but here."

I rubbed my neck. "Doesn't work that way. We're not some low-class suburban couple who no one gives a shit about."

"Maybe I die in a car accident."

I inspected her face. It showed no emotion, just like her words. "Fake your death?"

Inching her head side to side, she whispered in that eerily calm voice, "Not fake."

"You want to die?"

Lila blinked a few times before giving me a single nod. She thought her husband was screwing her best friend. She had no family, no other friends. She lied to

Ronin about having cancer. Of course she wanted to die.

Could it be that simple?

That simplistic idea swirled in my head. Was the answer to simply untie her, go back to my daily routine, and wait for her to end things? Evelyn would be devastated. I would be there to comfort her ... I would need comforting too. It was brilliant. Well, tragic, but brilliant.

"After Christmas. I don't want to ruin the holidays for Evelyn, Ronin, and the kids. This is their first holiday season without her mom. I don't want to add to that grief until Christmas is over."

How did she do it? How did Lila talk about planning her death with the confidence of planning a dinner party?

"And how am I supposed to believe you won't say anything before then?"

"You don't. But you also don't have a better option than to trust me."

"You bit my fucking cheek off. And I'm supposed to trust you?"

"Then kill me. Put that pillow over my head again and finish the job."

Her words stirred up my nausea again. I wasn't a killer. Wanting someone out of your life or possibly dead (if that was the only choice) was different than killing them. It was why I pulled the pillow away from her head before she stopped moving. I just ... I couldn't do it.

What can I say? I was a nice guy. Nice guys didn't kill people. Neither did governors or men who wanted to be with Evelyn Taylor. I mean, Evelyn was spontaneous and reckless with her love life. After all, she quickly spread her legs for Ronin, married him without telling me, and got knocked up—twice. But spending eternity with a killer felt like a hard limit for her, even on her most reckless day.

Christmas. That was six weeks away. Six weeks. I spent years waiting for another chance with Evelyn. I could wait six more weeks.

"If you don't go through with it, I'll have no choice but to have someone do it for me."

"What do I have to live for?" she whispered.

I rolled to sitting, feeling more queasiness.

"I'm going to Chicago tomorrow afternoon. The meeting was rescheduled."

"I don't think that's a good idea." I glanced over my shoulder at her.

"Everyone thinks I'm going back to engineering. Appearance matters. You've said that a million times." No emotion. Lila had zero emotion in her voice.

"I'll be tracking you." I grabbed her bound arms and untied them. Then I untied her feet.

"You always do."

Before closing her door, I turned back to her as she rubbed her wrists, especially the one that had a cast on it just a week earlier. Did I feel bad? Sure. But life was filled with tough decisions and unfortunate situations.

Lila's parents were waiting for her in the afterlife. Maybe it was meant to be more than it was tragic. Maybe one day I would tell Evelyn about Lila's leukemia and how the accident probably saved her from suffering a far worse death.

Yes. I would tell her that.

I smiled from my revelation, but when Lila glanced up, she didn't share my excitement, and I was too lightheaded to explain it. I needed to get to my bed before I passed out.

CHAPTER TWENTY-NINE

Lila

M Y HUSBAND RAPED me. That wasn't a first.
He almost killed me. That wasn't a first either.
That brick wall … the end of denial. The point beyond repair and *all* hope. That was a first.

Me injuring him? That was new too. And it felt incredible. His blood tasted like sweet revenge. Had he killed me, I would have died a happy woman.

I fought back but not with my words. I physically proved to him that if he hurt me, I would hurt him too. However, Evelyn's betrayal to me, to Ronin … to her kids. That gutted me. It hurt worse than any punch or fall I'd ever taken at the hands of my husband. I tried every way possible to make sense of it in another way. Maybe he blackmailed her. Maybe he forced her.

But it didn't look like he was forcing her. She hummed as he fucked her mouth. Not grunts … actual humming.

Maybe it wasn't her. After all, the camera view only showed her back. And the footage was dark. But he said her name. And he said things to her that he wouldn't say to some whore who shared her name.

It was her. I knew it in my gut. Even if I didn't fully understand her reasoning for doing it, I knew it was her.

We all had secrets. We all experienced desires.

I wanted Ronin and he felt it. I wanted him even as my brain and my heart tried to convince my body I shouldn't want him. But he touched me like Graham had never touched me before. It wasn't a conscious decision to feel that attraction—that desire. It happened like lighting a match too close to gasoline. I ignited and I thought my inability to control it might burn everything to the ground.

But together, we controlled it. We did it for Evelyn. Would I be able to do it for her again?

"Hey." Ronin greeted me with a sad smile when I opened the door.

The staff had the rest of the week off, thanks to Graham. And Governor Porter had a full day of meetings and lots of explaining to do about his run-in with a mean dog.

"Hi. You don't look well."

"Thanks for the compliment." He sighed.

I padded my bare feet toward the library, a place Graham rarely visited. We agreed no bedroom, and while my loyalty to Evelyn shattered the previous day, I owed Ronin more than going back on my word.

"I had a scan yesterday. What they thought was working is no longer working. After the news I had a panic attack. I couldn't breathe. Did you feel that?"

"Landed me in the hospital."

I grimaced, closing the door to the two-story library while Ronin sat on one of four custom fabric sofas. "I'm so sorry, Ronin."

"Don't be. Your news is much worse than my short visit to the ER. I'm ... god, I'm so sorry."

His apologies—his sympathy crushed me. "You're miserable." I sat next to him, tucking my bare feet beneath me and running my hands over the skirt of my navy wrap dress with white piping. "I can see it on your face and in your eyes."

He grunted a laugh, running his hands through his hair instead of touching me, the one thing I knew he needed. "I'm ..." He shook his head, fisting his hair. "Somedays I swear I don't feel this instinct ... this will to live. And I don't understand it because I have a wife who loves me and two beautiful children. It makes no sense unless it's ..." He opened his eyes.

"Me," I whispered. "I ... I'm sorry. It's the treatment. The bad news. It's the stress of going back to work to a job I love but feeling guilty, like I'm abandoning the things I took on as First Lady."

"Please ..." He sighed. "Stop apologizing. I don't blame you. And I hate that you feel responsible for any of this. I know you can't help what's happening to you or your feelings. I'm such an asshole for even asking for you to see me. To ..."

As he released his hair, letting his arms flop, I rested my hand on his leg. He dragged in a shaky breath. Just that quickly, he felt it. Our connection. And I felt needed. By that point, Ronin was the only person in the whole world who made me feel needed. But his need for me was toxic. Toxic like Graham's love for Evelyn.

The four of us lived a tortured existence, just in very different ways.

"When I die, you'll be free."

"Jesus, Lila … I don't want you to die, no matter what it might mean for me."

"Well, we can't control what's happening to my body."

"I can't talk about this. I don't want to think about your cancer or my depression. I don't want to talk about Graham or Evie. I just want …"

"Lie back." I climbed off the sofa and pulled a book from one of the shelves.

Ronin spread his legs, and I situated myself between them, reclining back onto his chest.

"*Desolation Angels?*"

"It's one of my favorites." He wrapped his arms around my waist, hugging me to him as I started reading Jack Kerouac's words.

With the turn of each page, his grip on me tightened, his hands moved softly along my abdomen, his legs closed in around mine, and his mouth hovered over my scarf-covered head.

I tried to stay focused on the words, not the warmth of his body. But my mind jumbled, drifting from the story to the video of Graham and Evie, and back to the warm body wrapped around me.

My heart started to beat faster and harder. My skin felt flush. My voice took on a husky tone, breathless and wanton.

"Focus on the book, *please*," Ronin begged. He felt my desire, and I felt him hard at my back.

I swallowed and then cleared my throat, trying to add some true character to the narration. Anything to distract my body from wanting something more. My legs squeezed together, like holding their breath, but it didn't work. Knowing Evelyn and Graham had an affair only multiplied my desire for Ronin. Knowing I had very little time left in my life multiplied it even more.

"Lila ... please." Ronin's breaths sounded ragged like mine as he adjusted slightly beneath me. It felt like him rocking his hips into my back was more than a simple adjustment.

My nipples were hard. The hairs on my skin stood at attention. And I felt a trickle of desire between my legs in spite of how tightly I clenched them together.

I knew it was wrong, but once you stopped caring about life, you stopped caring about all the stupid moral beliefs that dictated it. Once you saw your best friend sucking off your husband, you no longer gave a fuck if her husband touched you. I pulled the tie to my dress.

"Don't ..." Ronin rocked his hips against me in spite of his weak plea.

How did it feel to him? It had to be the best drug ever. Feeling his desire *and* mine. It had to be stronger than any drug. Impossible to resist.

I eased open my dress so he could see my dark blue lace panties and the matching bra.

"We have to stop ..."

I ignored him, certain that the truth would one day come out, and he would look back and realize I was giving him what his wife was giving another man. Only … they had no otherworldly excuse.

I took his hands and placed them back on my stomach, my bare stomach.

He let me.

I guided his right hand to my breast, slipping it under my bra until the rough palm of it pressed to my nipple.

He let me.

A gravelly groan rumbled his chest, and again he pressed his erection against my back as his hand squeezed my breast so hard I almost lost it from that one touch. Ronin's breaths pulsed against my ear, and sometimes his lips would brush it, and I felt it everywhere.

"L-Lila …" He panted like a wounded animal.

"Tell me … tell me what to do." My hand squeezed his hand that rested idle on my stomach. "Tell me how to make you feel better."

I could have died right then, and Ronin's touch would have lingered on my skin for a million eternities.

He couldn't speak. His heart wouldn't allow it. His deep love for Evelyn only intensified my desire for him. It made me want to give him my last breath.

When he didn't utter another word, I guided his other hand under my panties, a half inch at a time. The muscles in his arms tensed, and he paused his hand before reaching the place I needed him to touch so badly no death could be worse than waiting for him to decide where we'd take it.

I inched my legs apart as far as they would go with his legs on each side, and I waited. He squeezed my nipple at the same time his hand moved on its own between my legs. Taking it slow, he made tiny circles over my clit with the pads of his fingers as he pistoled his hips against my back in the same slow rhythm as his fingers.

My hips lifted from the sofa, silently urging him to move his fingers down and inside of me, filling a void only he could fill. Erasing the intrusive trespassing of the man who, in all honesty, raped me the previous night.

Feeling completely out of my skin with need, I pushed his hand lower and moaned as the pad of his middle finger pressed to my entrance.

I wanted him inside of me *so* badly.

Before I could silence my need, he had me flipped onto my back, his shirt shrugged off. His jean-clad lower body wedged between my legs, thrusting against me, as his lips attacked my mouth and his hand shoved my bra up so my breasts pressed to his warm chest. Both of his hands gripped the arm of the sofa as he dry-humped me, the denim giving me so much friction I saw stars behind my closed eyes when I orgasmed.

Ronin's moves were hard, almost violently so, and he yelled as he found his own release.

It brought instant tears to my eyes because he yelled *her* name.

Completely out of breath and sticky with sweat, Ronin collapsed onto me, tucking his face into my neck as his body started to shake.

He was crying. Ronin was crying.

"No. No. No …" His words destroyed me.

It reaffirmed what I knew in the deepest, darkest depths of my soul—I wanted to die. The pain would stop for me *and* Ronin. My time was near.

Something I mistook for reason whispered to my conscience, telling me to tell Ronin the truth about Evelyn and Graham. But I just couldn't. Their fate wasn't mine to decide. I let Ronin cheat on his wife of his own accord. I had to let fate take care of the truth in its own time.

I waited, emotionally preparing for him to climb off me and run out of the house without so much as a glance back. But he didn't. Once his sobs subsided, he moved us so we were on our sides, hugging, legs intertwined … and then we slept.

Two hours later, I woke from a deep sleep all alone with a blanket covering my half naked body and no sign of Ronin.

CHAPTER THIRTY

Evelyn

OH THE NEVERS …
I never imagined falling in love at a bubble tea cafe in Vancouver.

I never imagined marrying a man after knowing him for only a few months.

I never imagined that man would cheat on me.

But more than all of those nevers put together and multiplied times infinity … I never imagined my best friend screwing my perfect husband.

The truth?

I didn't know anything for sure. I just knew something in my gut caused me to leave my kids with Sue and have Sophie cover the shop while I followed my husband. Honestly, I imagined him driving to Adrianne's apartment. I *never* imagined the trail would lead me all the way to Denver, to the Porter estate. Yet that was where it led me.

I waited outside of the gate, just down the street. I waited for *three* hours. And while my mind tried to play tricks on me, forcing me to think the unthinkable, I never truly imagined I'd peek through the gate *three* hours later and see him practically stumbling out the front door, pulling on his shirt and jacket and carrying his shoes.

That day marked the beginning of the end, just not how I imagined it. Life never went in the imagined direction. It traipsed through the mud, climbed impossible mountains, and leapt the widest oceans. But usually not without getting muddy, slipping off a few cliffs, and drowning in the current.

Where to go?

What to do?

I didn't know that answer. Our actions affected two children. Packing a single bag and skipping town or tossing Ronin out of my house held consequences for Franz and Anya.

Instead of busting into Lila's house, demanding answers, I made the long drive home, being mindful to stay far behind Ronin's car. I needed the time to think, to let my knee-jerk reaction calm into something less hostile.

I made it to Franz's school twenty minutes early. Twenty more minutes to let my emotions make sense. When we arrived home, Franz hopped out excited to see Ronin's car.

"Daddy's home!"

"Daddy's home," I mumbled to myself.

Mrs. Humphrey greeted us as Ronin held a finger to his lips. "Shh … she's sleeping."

My baby girl wasn't well yet—another reason I needed to be meticulous with my words and actions.

Everything we did had aftershocks that could be felt for many miles.

"Go wash your hands, Franz." I shooed him toward the bathroom, and Mrs. Humphrey followed him.

Keeping my eyes on Anya, in spite of feeling Ronin's gaze heavy on me, I kissed her warm forehead. Before I could stand straight again, Ronin pressed his free hand to my cheek.

It hurt. That look in his eyes hurt more than his touch, more than the memory of him leaving Lila's house, more than anything. I had never seen so much torment and regret with one look.

"How was your day?" he whispered.

It felt like my mom died all over again.

I shrugged. "How was your day?"

He released my face and drew his bottom lip into his mouth, eyes slightly narrowed. "I've had better days."

"Want to talk about it?"

"Maybe later."

Later …

It felt like the longest evening of my life waiting for later.

Making dinner.

Walking Mrs. Humphrey.

Washing dishes.

Baths for the kids.

Bedtime stories.

Rocking Anya to sleep.

When later came, I didn't get a confession or a long description of Ronin's day.

I got a kiss. A hard kiss.

I got needy hands tugging at my clothes.

I got pushed against the bedroom wall as if the bed was just too far.

Ronin stole my breath, my words, my fight.

Tears begged to be set free. Words fought for their voice. All thoughts evaporated as he suffocated me with his need. That need broke my heart as tiny pieces of the puzzle started to align. This explosive need came from Lila.

The day he said he was going to Denver for CPR—he went to see Lila.

They shared something I couldn't completely understand. He felt her ... but on what level?

I couldn't believe he'd cheat on me. I *refused* to believe Lila would do this to me. There had to be some other explanation. But why the secrecy? If they weren't having an affair, why lie to me?

So many questions. Ronin didn't give me a chance to ask a single one before he had half of our clothes ripped off and his cock buried inside of me on a painful grunt. A bed ... we had a bed. But he chose the wall as if to prove the depth of his need, the urgency to be inside of me.

I kissed him because I loved him and needed him— needed us—so much that the idea of losing what we had made jagged cuts into my heart, tearing away pieces of my soul.

Over the next few hours—into the early morning hours—I tried to approach the subject of Lila, but Ronin silenced me with his mouth, his hands, his whole body manipulating mine, giving me pleasure but not without pain.

After he passed out a little before two in the morning, I set my tears free and muted my sobs with my pillow. Many years earlier, I'd helped Lila concoct a custom scent for all of her bath products—a very distinct scent made just for her. I knew that scent well.

That scent was all over Ronin.

The next morning, I woke to an empty bed. When I peeked in the garage, Ronin's Subaru was there, so he must have gone for a hike. As I shut the door, I heard a familiar *thunking* sound. I shoved my feet into my boots and put on my coat. The kids would likely sleep for another hour.

Pulling my fuzzy pink cap onto my head, I rounded the corner of the house. Mrs. Humphrey darted toward me as Ronin reared the ax back and heaved it forward, splintering a large log.

I wasn't sure why I felt the need to go outside with him. My mind and my heart still couldn't agree on the words I needed to say to him.

"Good morning." He wiped his brow with the sleeve to his coat.

"Morning," I tried to smile, but it hurt too much.

"Are you all set to leave next week?"

Thanksgiving.

"Anything I can do to help you pack?"

I shook my head, not because I didn't want help. I just couldn't *think*.

As much as I needed time away, even more after recent revelations, the worry over where Ronin would be, *who* he would be with, felt like a chain around my heart, holding me in place.

"What's wrong?" I asked.

He swung the ax again, slicing through the wood. "Nothing. Why?"

"Because we have enough wood chopped to last five years. So you must be out here working through something. And I know this because I've added plenty of wood to the pile while dealing with … *life*."

The sadness in his eyes intensified with each blink. On a long breath, he dropped the ax and sat on the tree stump, lacing his gloved hands behind his neck. "When we were in the Hamptons over the summer, I stumbled upon something. A discovery of sorts."

"What's that?"

"That first day when I took Lila's purse to her, she was having … a moment. In an attempt to comfort her, we hugged."

My stomach twisted. I didn't want it to be true, but Ronin was making it true. I hugged my arms to my chest.

"Something happened. The pain, the depression, the ringing in my ears, everything I'd been feeling from her just … vanished. I felt like myself. I felt good. And I don't know if she needed someone's arms, unconditional kindness and understanding, or what it was, but I only felt *her* feeling good too. At peace." Closing his eyes, he shook his head. "I could breathe. I felt normal."

My mouth opened to speak, but my heart strangled the words. I knew if I tried to say anything, I would fall apart.

"The normal feeling felt like a high. It lasted for a while, but eventually it faded. Starting with the ringing in my ears and then the pain ... the depression."

I didn't realize the depth of Lila's depression.

Ronin rested his forearms on his knees. "When things start to get really bad, when I feel it affecting you and the kids, I visit Lila."

Swallowing hard to keep my emotions in check, I whispered four words. It was all I could get out while remaining in one piece. "What does that mean?"

"We talk, but mostly we hold each other. Usually, we fall asleep."

Curling my cold lips between my teeth, I nodded slowly.

"Jesus, Evie ... I know this hurts. And I should have told you when it first happened. I loved the high. I loved the husband and father I was after seeing her."

"You saw her yesterday."

His eyes reddened as he returned a barely detectable nod. Why? Why did yesterday make him emotional but the rest of his confession did not?

I deserved to know the truth. The entire truth. Yet asking for it felt like confessing my lack of trust in him. And I couldn't forget how much it hurt him when I questioned his fidelity with Adrianne. If he didn't cross the line with a whore, how could I question him about Lila—my best friend?

Had I not suggested we go skiing to make up for how I'd treated Graham, Lila wouldn't have fallen off that mountain. Ronin wouldn't have saved her life. And they wouldn't have made a connection I couldn't understand. How could I be mad about something I created?

Still ... I needed to know. Not knowing for sure would destroy me. It would destroy us.

"You only—"

"Mom?" Franz called in a sleepy voice.

I turned, dragging my heavy heart toward the front door. "Morning, sweetie. You're up early." Mrs. Humphrey and I herded Franz back into the house. Ronin followed a few minutes later. The rest of our morning fell back into routine. Anya's fever broke. Franz fought with Ronin over what he was going to wear to school. And Mrs. Humphrey vomited some bile and one of Anya's socks.

There was never the perfect time to let our marriage fall apart, to stop swimming against the current, to forget about responsibilities in life that didn't care if your husband had an affair.

While I was changing Anya's diaper, the door shut. By the time I put on her clothes for the day, Ronin's car was gone. He and Franz left with no goodbye.

"Have a good day," I whispered to the empty spot in the garage.

When I arrived at my shop, I called Lila. She didn't answer. I sent her a message.

Evelyn: Can we talk soon?

She didn't reply.

"How's Anya?" Sophie asked the second she walked

309

through the door, wearing her signature youthful smile.

"Better. Her fever broke." I unlocked the register drawer.

"You excited for your trip? I think hiring Abby was a good idea."

"Yeah. The kids will love spending time with my dad and Katie."

"Maybe you and Ronin can have a date night with such willing babysitters."

"Ronin's not going."

"But it's Thanksgiving."

I nodded, turning the music on in the shop. "We'll be gone for almost two weeks. Snow is expected here. He couldn't take that much time off."

"That sucks."

Yes. A lot of things sucked at that point in my life. Sucked might have been a monumental understatement if my worst fears turned out to be true.

RONIN FELL BACK into his hole quickly over the following days. He found every excuse to arrive home late, fall asleep before I got Anya to sleep, and leave in the morning without a goodbye. His behavior made it easy to leave. If he was having an affair with Lila, not going to San Francisco wasn't going to stop it. But more than my fear of infidelity, I just wanted my husband and my best friend to not be in so much physical and emotional pain all the time. My distrust and accusations would ruin all of us, and I wasn't prepared to blow up my world.

At least, not until I had time to myself to figure some things out. And not until Lila returned my messages or called me back.

The Monday before Thanksgiving, Ronin drove us to the airport in Denver in spite of my insistence that I could leave my car there so he also didn't have to pick us up.

"Be good for Mommy, okay?" He hugged and kissed Franz while I unfastened Anya from her seat. After he unloaded our luggage, he kissed Anya on the cheek. "I'm going to miss you like crazy."

Tears stung my eyes. Why did our leaving for two weeks feel so final? Why did he have unshed tears pooling in his own eyes as he grabbed my face and kissed me? I tried to hold it, but I couldn't. I choked on a tiny sob as my emotions broke free.

"Shh … no, baby. Don't cry." Ronin hugged me as Anya tugged my hand and Franz sat on his suitcase.

I couldn't speak past the lump in my throat. Ronin wiped my cheeks and kissed me one last time. "Call me … every day. Okay?"

I nodded, holding my breath and the rest of the emotions threatening to break the dam.

"Mommy, don't cry." Franz wedged himself between us, hugging my waist.

I pulled my suitcase and guided Anya to the door with Franz pulling the other suitcase beside me. After we made it to the entrance, before the glass doors shut, I gave one glance back at Ronin, but he was already pulling away from the curb.

CHAPTER THIRTY-ONE

Lila

"THERE WILL BE thirty of us for Thanksgiving," Graham announced, opening the door to the library.

I was surprised he found me there. Equally disappointed. I liked having a safe haven. I also liked snuggling under a blanket with *Desolation Angels* on the sofa where Ronin touched me. *That* would be what I thought about before I took my last breath.

My attention shifted to him as he perused the shelves of books. "I called Evelyn yesterday. Did you know she's in San Francisco with the kids? Ronin stayed home. Something about not being able to get off work."

"No. I haven't talked to her in a while."

"Oh ... are you two having a tiff?" Graham's ridiculous game of ignorance usually angered me, but I had no more anger left inside of me. The recent infidelity between the four of us used up the rest of my give-a-fucks. Ronin stayed for me. There was no way he'd miss Thanksgiving with his family because of work.

"That would please you, wouldn't it?" I said.

"No. I like my girls to be happy." He pulled a book from the shelf, glanced at the back of it, and returned it to its spot before continuing his stroll around the room.

"I'm not your girl."

"You're my wife."

"I'm the person who will haunt you for the rest of your life."

He chuckled, brushing his fingers over the thin strips of tape along his scarred cheek. "Like a ghost?" Graham found our situation amusing. A perfectly healthy woman planning her suicide wasn't funny. It proved I married a psychopath. Maybe it also proved I wasn't "perfectly healthy." Emotionally damaged? Depressed beyond words most days? Yes. My biggest problem? I lacked the will to live most of the time. Except with Ronin. With him, I felt a spark of hope.

I didn't kid myself; that spark would die. *I* would die.

"More like Karma," I murmured.

"How ungodly of you to wish bad luck upon me."

I closed my book and rested it on my lap. None of it felt funny to me. Everything felt tragic. "I don't wish you bad luck. I pray for you. I pray for us."

"Is God not answering your prayers?"

I shrugged. "Time will tell."

"You know ..." Graham sat at the opposite end of the sofa.

I drew my knees toward my chest, letting the book fall aside as I tightened the blanket around me.

"In a perfect world, we could just swap."

"Swap?"

"Spouses."

What?

I inched my head side to side. That made no sense. "That's ridiculous."

"Is it?" Graham gave me a look.

I couldn't decipher it, but it brought bumps to the surface of my skin. It made my spine tingle with a cold chill.

"I think I failed to mention inside those two lovely statues anchoring the books on the middle shelf are security cameras." He clucked his tongue three times. "There's some expensive art in here that we must protect. The cameras are motion activated. And recently … there was a lot of motion happening on this sofa that we're sitting on."

My heart took a nosedive into the pit of my stomach, forcing a surge of acid up my throat. I couldn't breathe, let alone speak.

"Gotta say … I've never seen or imagined a guy could fuck a woman with so much vigor yet wear the most tortured expression on his face. You were sleeping, but you should have seen the look on his face when he left. In fact, I'd be happy to show it to you if you'd like to see it."

"He didn't fuck me," I whispered.

"No? Huh … definitely looked like it from both camera angles. Christmas came early. I honestly thought I'd have to work harder. I thought Adrianne Craig was my best bet. But even she proved to lack what it took to bring Ronin to his knees. Joining his junkie group. Befriending him. Gifting a dog. Hell, she even had his and her tires slashed to force more time together. Ronin is such a fucking Boy Scout, or so I thought.

"But who knew? Really … all this time the bait was right in fucking front of me. So much money wasted on a professional whore when I could've gotten one to do the dirty work for free. Family discount. Thanks, babe."

Adrianne …

He paid her to break up their marriage. Still … it didn't excuse everything.

"You have a video of you and Evelyn. I saw it. You have nothing. The two of you already ruined everything on your own."

"Evelyn …" He laughed again.

I married Satan in the flesh. How … how did that happen?

"I wanted her … I *requested* she look like Evelyn." He smirked.

What? No. No, no, no!

Tremors attacked my body while a cold sweat trickled down my back. The vein along my forehead throbbed. And my racing pulse suffocated each breath.

I thought my world ended when I saw that video. I was wrong. My world ended with his revelation.

It. Wasn't. Evelyn.

I let that happen. Revenge made me the temptress.

It. Wasn't. Evelyn.

"Aw, baby … are those tears on your cheeks?" Graham leaned forward, reaching for my face.

I swatted his hand away. "DON'T … touch me."

He paused, teeth clenched.

"You will *never* have her. Because deep down she knows what a fucked-up psychopath you really are." The never-ending tears blurred my vision. "She will *hate* you."

Whack!

Blood replaced the tears in my right eye as darkness and squiggly lines stole my vision. I think my eyeball exploded.

Thunk! Thunk! Thunk!

His knuckles connected with my jaw.

One. Two. Three.

The force of his anger knocked me onto the floor. A metallic taste spread along my tongue while a part of my tooth fell from my partially mangled mouth.

That's it … just kill me. I know you have it in your fucking evil soul. Just … finish it.

He didn't.

Graham didn't kill me.

He locked me in my room and boarded the windows. I waited to bleed to death, but that didn't happen. Completely blind in my right eye and unable to form words from my swollen mouth, I crawled from the floor to the bed—choking as my tongue worked to swallow the blood from my wounds mingling with stomach acid.

Silent sobs racked my chest.

Please let me die. Take me to my mom and dad. Take away this pain. And forgive me. Please forgive me for what I did.

I prayed over and over, shaking, chilled, and on the verge of losing consciousness. I prayed never to awaken. It was my time. I had *nothing* left.

Ronin

MRS. HUMPHREY'S WET tongue painted my face. I didn't blackout, but I felt like the one on the losing end of a street fight. Blurred vision, numbness in my tongue, a debilitating pain along my jaw that made it hard to speak. The only word I tried to say was Lila.

I moved my phone in front of my face, focusing with my good eye as I brought up Lila's number. It rang and rang.

My thumbs moved across the screen, texting her.

Ronin: Call me! What's happened?

"L-L-Li-la," I tried to say her name, but my mouth fucked up the word. I dropped my phone onto my chest, closed my eyes, and waited for the room to stop spinning, for the pain to subside, for my lunch to stop crawling up my throat.

A few minutes later, my phone vibrated. My hands fumbled it a few times before I got ahold of it bringing it to my good eye.

Graham.

Something very bad happened to Lila. That was what he was calling to say. I knew it.

I slid the bar across the screen and brought it to my ear, having no clue if my mouth would give actual coherent words. It didn't matter; he spoke first.

"Lila left her phone. Sorry, buddy." Graham's words held a different tone than I had ever heard from him before. Eerily calm. "I don't know when she'll be back. She was pretty torn up when I told her about the surveillance cameras in the library."

No. Fuck …. Please no …

"But some of those books are incredibly rare, first editions. Not to mention the priceless art scattered throughout the room." He sighed. "Anyway, she left. No phone. No suitcase. Her car is still here, so apparently she took an Uber or just ran off on foot. My people are looking for her. Do you want to leave a message? I'm sure she'll eventually turn up."

"Wh-what did you do?" I slurred the words, trying to say them without moving my jaw.

"You're breaking up, buddy. Listen, I have to go. And for what it's worth. I have no hard feelings toward you. We married the wrong people. Shit happens. I think what matters at this point is the world is on the precipice of righting those wrongs. For all I know, Lila's halfway to some other state by now. Preparing to start a new life. Maybe you should think about doing that too. Maybe you should return to Canada. Great skiing there. I'll handle things here. Best of luck." He ended the call, the way he ended my world.

I heaved my phone across the room. It knocked a family photo onto the floor, shattering the glass. So very symbolic.

Mrs. Humphrey barked and jumped up on the sofa

with me, whimpering a few times while situating herself between my legs and resting her head on my chest.

"I f-fucked up …"

When my family returned, I had planned on telling Evelyn everything. I never planned on Graham. I didn't know what my chances were of her forgiving me, of her not leaving me. But after that call I knew the number.

Zero. Zero chance of not losing everything.

CHAPTER THIRTY-TWO

Evelyn

FRANZ WANTED TO call Ronin the second he woke up on Thanksgiving. Ronin didn't answer his phone the previous day. They received almost a foot of snow, so I assumed he was too busy to respond until after the kids' bedtime. A text would have been nice.

I couldn't keep my mind from wondering if he was with Lila.

Touching her.

Holding her.

Doing things that required him to take his shirt off.

"Now! Call Daddy now!" Franz handed me my phone as I finished pulling on my socks, perched on the edge of the bed.

"Fine. Go get Anya. She's in the kitchen with Aunt Katie and Grandpa."

As Franz ran out of the bedroom, I tried FaceTiming Ronin—to my surprise he answered right away.

"Hey." I smiled. In spite of all that happened before we left, my chest felt warm and my stomach had butterflies just seeing his face. It had only been a few days, but I already missed him.

"Hey." He sat on the bed, propping his phone up on the nightstand while drying his hair with a towel. No shirt.

"Good timing. Looks like you just got out of the shower."

He nodded, hooking the towel around his neck. "I figured I'd get a call soon. Thought I'd at least shower for the occasion."

"You okay? Your words sound a little slurred and weak."

"Yeah." He ran a hand through his damp hair. "Just tired."

"I see you got a lot of snow."

He nodded, not making any sort of eye contact. It had been a long time since things were exactly "right" with Ronin, but that morning something felt especially wrong—completely off—about him.

"Daddy!" Franz hopped on the bed and looked over my shoulder at the phone screen while Anya climbed into my lap, poking her dark head into the shot.

"Hey, you guys are a sight for sore eyes." As he said those words, I noticed his eyes turning red, brimming with unshed tears. I rubbed my chest, trying to ease the ache. I wasn't sure I had ever seen him look so emotional-ly tortured.

"We're having waffles for breakfast. And Grandpa is cooking a turkey. Where's Mrs. Humphrey? I miss you, Daddy. Is it snowing there?"

Ronin chuckled, turning his head to wipe his eyes, but I saw it even if Franz and Anya missed it.

"Daddy kisses." Anya grabbed my phone and kissed the screen.

"Aw, muah to you too, baby girl. Here she is." Ronin angled his phone to show us Mrs. Humphrey on the bedroom floor chewing on an elk antler.

"We saw the Golden Bridge. It was not gold," Franz huffed.

"No? Well, that's too bad. Why name it the Golden Gate Bridge?"

"I don't know. I'm hungry. Bye, Daddy."

"Hey! Wait, buddy."

Franz grabbed my phone as Anya again poked her head into view. "What, Daddy?"

Ronin swallowed hard. "I love you guys. Okay. Don't ever forget that."

I quickly wiped the rebel tears from my cheeks.

"Okay. We won't." Franz handed me the phone and ran out of the room with Anya running to catch him.

Before I held the camera to my face again, I used my sleeve to completely dry my cheeks. Finding my long-lost friend, that mask I wore for so many years to hide all the pain and fear, I slipped it on and raised the camera to my face. "Wow. That was a heavy goodbye."

Biting his lips together, he averted his gaze to the side, maybe watching Mrs. Humphrey, and nodded. "Yeah. *Life* feels pretty heavy right now."

"Why?" I whispered.

He shook his head. "Don't worry about it. Everything

will be fine."

I didn't feel like everything would be fine. It felt like my world was ending and he just couldn't say the actual words. Before my mom died, she told my dad everything would be fine.

He wasn't fine.

I wasn't fine.

Nothing had been fine since she took her last breath.

"Do you have plans for today? Did Graham and Lila invite you to Thanksgiving dinner? Noah and Tami?"

"Work. Noah is covering for me. I didn't want to miss your call. But I'll be working the rest of the day."

"Well, I won't keep you, then."

I love you.

I almost said it. I felt like he needed it. But I refused to believe we were there. So I swallowed and smiled. "Be safe up there."

"Yeah." Just before he ended the call, he looked at the camera, reddened eyes fresh with tears.

I tried FaceTiming him back.

He didn't answer.

I tried calling him.

He didn't answer.

Something was wrong. Very, very wrong.

Lila hadn't answered my calls or messages in over a week. So I called Tami. She was closer anyway.

"Hey. Happy Thanksgiving."

"Tami, I need a favor. I know it's Thanksgiving, and I would never ask this if it weren't an emergency, but I need you to check on Ronin. I just talked with him, but he's not answering now, and I *know* something is wrong. I feel it in my gut. *Please*."

"Sure. Take it easy. Just don't panic. I'll go right now and call you as soon as I get there."

I wiped more tears. "Thank you."

"Evie, breakfast—hey, what's wrong?" Katie rushed to me, sitting on the bed and pulling me in for a hug. "Did something happen?"

"No. Yes. I have to go home." I pulled away and wiped my tears.

"You're scaring me. Did something happen to Ronin?"

"I can't explain it. Something's not right. He wasn't right. He … he …"

"Shh …" She pulled me back in for a hug. "Okay. Whatever you need. We've got the kids. Do you want me to call Lila and Graham?"

I shook my head. "N-no."

"Want me to see if I can get you a flight?"

"Yes." I pulled away again and wiped my face.

"What do you want me to tell Franz and Anya?"

"I … I don't know."

"What if I say Ronin has a really bad cold and you need to take care of him? Too scary?"

"It's … it's fine. Yes."

"I'll let them know and see what flights are available. You pack."

I already had flight information brought up on my phone. "There's a flight out in two hours. I'm not packing. Just take me there."

With a quick goodbye to the kids and a promise of giving their sick daddy hugs, kisses, and chicken noodle soup, Dad drove me to the airport while Katie and Tanner fed the kids.

"Is everything okay with your marriage?" Dad, a man of few words, finally asked less than five minutes from the terminal.

"I don't know," I whispered, temporarily out of tears as a general numbness settled over me. It wasn't a lie. I had no idea where my marriage stood.

"Want me to come with you."

"I … have to do this alone."

"Call me as soon as you get there? The weather's not great. I'm not sure you'll be able to get to Aspen."

"I'll get there. Eventually."

He hugged me goodbye. I ran to catch my flight only to have it delayed due to weather in Denver.

Two more hours. That brought a second round of tears.

Just as I finished drying my face again, Tami called.

"Tami!"

"Sorry it took me so long. He wasn't home. And when I called Noah, he wasn't there yet either. I called a few other people and even drove around town a bit, but Noah finally called me back and said he's at work. He said he seemed a little quiet, maybe a bit under the weather, but he's fine."

He wasn't fine.

"Thank you so much."

"Can I ask what had you so worried?"

"Just a feeling." I closed my swollen eyes and rubbed circles along my forehead.

"Well, thank God everything's okay. Hug the kids. Happy Thanksgiving."

"Happy Thanksgiving."

AFTER A SECOND delay, standing in line for a rental car, and navigating the snowy roads (which took six instead of three hours), I made it home by nine o'clock Thanksgiving night.

No lights illuminated the windows, and no smoke escaped from the chimney. Maybe Ronin didn't think starting a fire for one was worth it. Maybe he wasn't home. Maybe he was in bed already. Maybe he was with Lila.

A million maybe's.

I parked the rental SUV in the driveway and sent a quick text off to Katie to let her and Dad know I made it home safely.

When I eased open the front door, it was quiet, too quiet. And dark. Too dark. It was all these feelings of something being just a little *too* off that brought me all the way home on Thanksgiving, leaving my kids behind.

I slipped off my boots as I turned on the light. My whole body jolted with a gasp when I glanced up toward the kitchen table.

Jesus ... no ... no ...NO!

I froze, holding so still my lungs started to burn, begging me to take a breath. But … I couldn't breathe. I wasn't sure I'd ever breathe again.

Those same teary eyes, that triggered the chain of events that day, stared at me. Glassy and lifeless. His arms rested on the table. One hand cupped a glass of whiskey with a half empty bottle next to it, and his other hand rested on … a gun.

In a blink, nearly six years of marriage bled from my eyes, washing away my hopes and drowning my dreams.

The eerie silence carved a deep hole into my soul. Where was Mrs. Humphrey? Where were the squealing kids? The crackling embers. The buzzer going off to remind me to take the cookies out of the oven.

The giggles.

Monster dad chasing after his little ones while making roaring sounds.

The whispers … the promises of all the things he planned to do to me when the kids were in bed.

I couldn't hear my *life*.

Where did it go?

"I love you," he whispered.

CHAPTER THIRTY-THREE

Ronín

L ILA DIED.
        No one told me. I just knew. Around six p.m., I veered off the road on my way home from work.

My head.

My ribs.

My back.

My leg.

Then ... nothing.

No physical pain. And the world fell dead silent. No ringing in my ears. I couldn't feel her anymore.

Lila died.

I cheated on my wife with her best friend. And she ... died.

When I finally made it home, I realized the depression and desire to leave my problems behind—to leave this world—were no longer just Lila's. They were mine. I purchased the gun while feeling Lila's depression. I never imagined I'd use it without her influence over me. But that day in the library changed that. Her sins became mine and mine became hers. We would never be able to separate that. To make things right with Evelyn.

So …

I chose death over the truth.

I chose death over hurting my family.

I chose death over seeing that look in Evelyn's eyes.

I'd been on borrowed time for years. It was past my time to leave.

"NO!" She gritted her teeth as the first sob ripped from her chest. "You do NOT get to say that to me now!" Tears covered her cheeks as her body shook.

A last straw. A final breath. That was what we agreed upon. We'd say it when there was absolutely nothing else to say.

I hurt her.

I lied.

I cheated.

I could never make things right.

There was nothing left to say.

And I refused to say something as pathetic as sorry.

I gave her the truth. She deserved it.

"I touched Lila."

Her hand covered her mouth as if she could keep the pain captive. "What does that mean?" She choked on another sob.

The muscles in my face twitched, fraught with fear of hurting her. I had no choice. Nothing remained *except* hurt.

"We crossed a line."

Her gaze flitted to my hand clenching the gun, and

her hand slowly slid from her mouth. "You had sex."

I shook my head slowly. "Almost."

"W-why?" Her brow wrinkled as her head inched side to side.

On a hard swallow I blinked a new round of tears as my face contorted into as much pain and confusion as Evie's. "Because I felt her *feelings* for me. And it triggered something. Like a drug. Like driving under the influence."

Peeling the matted hair away from her face and tucking it behind her ears, she sniffled and hiccupped a ragged breath. "She let it happen too?" More emotion, more tears filled her eyes. "Why?" She choked out the word.

"I don't know."

Rubbing her quivering lips together, her eyes swept across the room, pausing on things like photos and Franz's books in a neat pile on the coffee table. "So …" She drew in another shaky breath, sliding her sad eyes to me. "You're leaving us."

"I … I …" Shaking my head, I searched for words to explain what she walked in on minutes earlier. Whiskey mingled in my veins, calming me, distorting reality. Taunting my judgment. "I think it's best."

I never imagined she'd be there, but I deserved to see her face—pure anger and complete disappointment. Once again, I had failed her. Being forced to face her felt like the proper reckoning—retribution for my sins.

"Then do it!" She clenched her jaw and fisted her hands at her sides. "But let's be clear—" One of her fisted hands moved to cover her mouth as her words broke into pieces. "Y-you don't love me. That…" she nodded toward the gun "…is n-not love. And I will spend the rest of my l-life knowing you didn't truly l-love me." Evie shoved her feet back into her boots and stood at the door with her back to me, her shoulders shaking as she held back more sobs. "And … you don't love Franz and Anya either." She drew in a shaky breath. "But … I do. I choose them." She ran out the door without a final glance at me.

Evelyn

I DROVE TO the shop and shut off my car lights, leaving the engine idling with the heat on. And I did the only thing I could do to keep from falling apart beyond repair. I called my mom.

"Can you keep a secret?" I whispered after the beep to leave a message—feeling numb like it wasn't real. Not my life. Not my husband. Not my reality.

I told her everything. How I lived in fear of my husband dying from some otherworldly phenomenon and how I knew he was cheating on me before he ever said the words. I told her everything … but I didn't tell her it was Lila. Nor did I mention I may have seen my husband for the last time in this life.

I think she knew.

"I love you, Mom. I miss you. And if you don't have any connections to help my situation, don't feel bad. I'll figure something out. Just the possibility that you're listening is enough. Today I miss you more..." the next round of emotions burned my eyes "...than I have in all the months you've been gone. Today I j-just really n-need my mom."

Shutting off the engine, I traipsed through the snow to my shop. The streetlight filtered through the front window. The many herbal scents filled me with the familiar.

My comfort zone.

My haven.

I locked the shop door behind me, leaving the lights off while I just ... stood in the middle of shelves and displays. How could I go back there?

How could he say that to me?

How could he take his own life in the middle of our home, where the kids could've seen their father's brains and blood scattered everywhere?

"I hate you," I whispered to his soul in case he already pulled the trigger.

"I hate you for offering me a chair in that fucking cafe!" I pushed over a display, sending products crashing to the floor. "I hate you for asking me to marry you!" Another display took the brunt of my wrath. "I hate your oatmeal."

Crash!

"I hate having coffee with you!"

Bang! Crash!

I shoved everything from two more shelves.

"I hate when you sing in the shower!"

Crash! Crash! Crash!

"I hate you for saving Lila and TOUCHING her!"

Bang! Crash!

With nothing left on any of the shelves, I fell to my knees and buried my face in my hands. And I just … cried. "I … hate … you …"

EVENTUALLY, I PICKED myself up off the ground and made it back to my car. I couldn't go home, so I made the insane decision to drive back to Denver. At that moment, sanity felt like an unreachable state of mine. After all, my husband was probably dead, slumped over our kitchen table—whiskey still clutched in his left hand.

Not my life. Not my husband.

I didn't remember the curves, the times my car nearly slid off the road, or the slew of snow plows I encountered on the long drive. By the time I arrived at nearly two in the morning, I just knew that I needed Lila to explain how we got there. How she could throw away a lifelong friendship to feel my husband touch her?

Being a permanent approved guest, the guard opened the gate as soon as he saw my face when I rolled down the window. I pounded on the front door over and over and incessantly pressed the doorbell. The light over the door turned on just as Graham opened the door, half asleep in his signature pajama bottoms but no shirt.

"Evelyn?" He squinted his eyes, scratching his head.

"Where's Lila?" I brushed past him.

"She's not here. What's wrong?"

Before I reached the stairs, I turned back to him as he shut the front door. "Where is she?"

"We had a fight. She left."

"What?" I shook my head. "Where did she go? What happened to your face?"

He rubbed the back of his neck as he shrugged. "Lila happened to my face."

"What? No. She wouldn't do that. Where is she, Graham? How can you not know? What was the fight about?"

I felt like ten cups of coffee at the end of a marathon. The chill of a cold shower when I needed ten hours of sleep. Nothing felt right.

Everything … *everything* was wrong.

Graham deflated on a long sigh and averted his gaze to the white and gray marble floor between us. "I found out she had an affair."

"With who?" I whispered.

One slow inch at a time, he lifted his gaze to meet mine. "I think you know that answer."

I swallowed that added dose of reality; it hurt going down that time almost as much as it did when Ronin confessed it. And it stirred up more emotions. "How did this happen?" I said on a tiny sob as my vision blurred behind more tears.

Graham closed the distance between us and hugged me, resting his cheek on my head. "I don't know. I just … don't know."

"I don't have anywhere to go."

"Not true." He kissed my forehead. "You can have your pick of bedrooms. Even mine. I promise to be on my best behavior."

I pulled away and shook my head. "I need to be alone."

"Of course. Come on." He took my hand and led me up the stairs. "You probably don't want to sleep in Lila's room. It's been cleaned, including the sheets. But you could grab something to wear from her closet."

"Night," I barely managed that one word.

As I started to pull away from him, he tightened his grip. I glanced down at his hand squeezing mine before meeting his gaze.

"We'll get through this. Together. I'm *always* here for you."

I tried to form a smile, but my face refused to cooperate. Widows didn't smile. After he released my hand, I headed toward Lila's room and Graham padded his bare feet in the other direction.

Turning on the light, I shut and locked Lila's bedroom door. Everything was in its place. The bedding crisp and void of a single wrinkle. Vacuum lines in the carpet like it had recently been cleaned. Even fresh flowers in a vase on her nightstand. It didn't look like the room of a woman who physically abused her husband and left without a word.

Too tired to look for something to sleep in, I tossed the three-deep layer of pillows from her bed and tugged down the comforter and sheets that the housekeeper tucked into each side military-style. As I started to climb into her bed, my gaze snagged on something barely peeking out from under the mattress. Lifting the edge of the mattress, I pulled out a black leather-bound book.

A journal.

I opened it and quickly flipped through the pages, not reading a single word. Lila loved journaling when we were younger. Organizing her thoughts helped her deal with so much grief. Setting it on the nightstand, I clicked the light remote and buried myself under the covers.

It took one … one single second for reality to hit.

It *was* real. It *was* my life. That man with the gun *was* my husband.

"Roe …" I whispered closing my eyes. "Why did you leave me?" My heart ached so much; I knew it would never beat the same way again.

Would Franz and Anya ever forgive me for not saving him? I hoped so. Maybe one day I would explain what happened to him, how he tried to be a superhero, and how he discovered he wasn't immortal. How I discovered I couldn't rescue him anymore because he was destroying me.

Franz and Anya. I thought only of them in the final seconds before I turned and left Ronin alone in the kitchen. They needed me. I saved the very best of my husband, the very best of me because I chose *them*.

After tossing and turning, rubbing my aching chest, and wiping tears all over the pillow, I sat up, unable to breathe well. Flipping on the light again, I crossed my legs and practiced slowing my breathing, taking in long breaths and letting them out slowly. Glancing over at the nightstand, I stared at the journal for a few seconds.

Yes. Reading her journal felt like a violation of her privacy. I never read her journals when we were younger. But she crossed a line with Ronin. Her privacy no longer meant that much to me.

Praises for her new husband filled the first part of her journal. I didn't care to read every word, every detail about their life—some details were about their sex life. I skipped ahead. She expressed frustration with her role as First Lady. I could have predicted that. Skipping ahead again, I read a few opening lines of another entry, but I didn't stop. I couldn't stop because I couldn't believe the words on the page.

I feel so stupid. So blind. So trapped.

He manipulates me. It's not rough sex. It's not a physical need. At least ... not anymore. I blindly fell for his excuses because he hurt me during sex. He justifies it. He makes me feel like my orgasm rights any sort of wrongs. It always leaves me confused because I love Graham. I love our intimacy, and sometimes I love the intensity, even when a little pain is the price to pay for pleasure. My desire to please him blinds me.

Today, everything changed. It's not a fetish or a preference. It's a sickness. Only a sick man breaks his wife's nose because she playfully grabbed his phone when he wouldn't give her his attention. I wanted him to notice me, my new white dress. Now, that white dress is in the trash, covered in blood.

"Oh my god ..." I whispered as my tears fell to the pages. It didn't stop. So much detail. I remembered her broken nose. It was shortly after I found out I was pregnant with Franz.

> *Ronin ... I feel so responsible. I should have died on that mountain. I wanted to die. Why did he try to save me? I didn't want to be saved. How am I still here? ...*

"Lila ..." I whispered. It wasn't an accident that day. She went in the wrong direction on purpose. My friend. How did I not see it?

> *The bruises are getting hard to hide ...*
> *Graham called me Evelyn during sex ...*
> *I thought about ending my life today, but I don't want to add to Evelyn's stress. Her mom is not well. She needs me ...*
> *My biggest dream became my worst night-mare when the pregnancy test came back positive ...*
> *I can't even breathe. I told Graham about the baby. He said I had to get rid of it. I said no. He got rid of the baby. The bleeding stopped two days ago, but I still have the bruises. He was right. We can't have children.*

It wasn't real. It *couldn't* be real. Ronin wasn't dead. And Graham didn't kill his own child. Things like that only happened in horror movies. Only fictional characters could be that monstrous.

It just ... wasn't real.

Pages. So many pages of awful, gruesome, heartbreaking detail.

> *Ronin hugged me and he said it made his pain go away. It made mine go away too ...*
>
> *I had to find an excuse for my bruises ... so now I have leukemia.*

"Jesus ..." My hand flew to my mouth. I could barely read the words through my tears. It wasn't real. I pleaded with any god who would listen to me, begging for it to not be real.

> *Evie told me Graham gave her the Clean Art building. He loves her. I wonder if he ever loved me ...*
>
> *Ronin needed me again today. It feels incredible to be needed. Evelyn is so lucky ...*
>
> *Graham has sex with me when I don't want it. That's rape. I think. I'm not sure. I don't think his sick mind understands what he's doing, and I don't know how to help him ...*
>
> *I just want to die ...*
>
> *I shaved my head to look the part of a leukemia patient. Graham hit me. He thinks I'm ugly now. How did this happen to me? ...*
>
> *Ronin made me feel beautiful today. I felt something for him I should not feel. I think it did something to him. He felt tortured when he felt my desire for him. I can't imagine what it must be like to feel two people at once. Nothing*

happened. We love Evelyn.

I sobbed thinking of what I always told Graham. *We love Lila more.*

The pages were never ending, the revelations dizzying.

I walked in on Graham masturbating to a video of him and Evie having sex. It shattered me. There are no real words to describe my level of brokenness. The complete desolate feeling of betrayal by the person I loved more than anyone in this world.

"What? No. No, no, no ..." My jaw hung in the air. Lies. What was wrong with her? It suddenly made me question everything I'd read up to that point.

He raped me again. I let him. I bit his face. His bitter blood tasted like a tiny bit of revenge. Then he nearly suffocated me with a pillow. Why did he stop? ...

I want to die ... We agreed I would die ...

Ronin needed me today. I needed him too. I wore a pretty dress with my best lingerie underneath it. I wonder what Evelyn wore to seduce Graham? I guess nothing lasts forever. Not even lifelong friends ...

I felt him at my back, turned on, begging me to stop. I couldn't stop. And if he'd known about Graham and his wife, he wouldn't have wanted me to stop. I take away his pain. All of it ...

His hand on my breast ...

Sliding between my legs …
He took off his shirt …
Kept on his pants …
I hated the material between us. I wanted to
feel him inside of me, but he couldn't go that
far …
We held each other for hours …
When I awoke he was gone …
We hurt Evelyn. And maybe she deserved it.
But it felt awful. I am awful …
I want to die …

Tossing the journal aside, I ran to the bathroom and heaved in the toilet, a cold sweat beading along my brow, my heart racing so fast it felt ready to explode through my chest.

After rinsing my mouth, I wobbled on unsteady legs back to the bed. Sitting on the edge, I stared at the journal, unsure if I could read another word.

But … I had to keep going. If Ronin took his life because of the words in that journal, I owed it to myself and to him to read every last word.

Graham beat me within an inch of my life.
I'm blind in one eye. My jaw is certainly bro-
ken. And I lost a tooth. But I don't even care
about my condition. He told me the woman in
the sex video was not Evelyn …
Not. Evelyn …
She will never forgive me. What I did was
unforgivable. I hate Graham for lying to me.
Still, I hate me more …

Today I will reunite with my mom and dad ...

"NO!" I covered my mouth quickly to hide my complete breakdown, dropping the journal on the floor. I grabbed a pillow and cried, sobbed, nearly died in that moment. What if? What if Lila and Ronin were both gone? How could I live in that kind of world? How could I be a good mom if the people who loved me the most in the world were gone?

I scooted off the bed onto my knees and picked up the journal with shaky hands and tiny sobs racking my whole body.

> *It's time ...*
>
> *A special note to my very best friend, my true other half, my sister, my family, my life— Evelyn. If you're reading this, I want you to know how deeply sorry I am for the accident, for Ronin, for not being what Graham needed me to be. I don't blame him for loving you. You are everything good about life. Please find it in your heart to forgive Ronin. Today ... I will set him free. He will truly be yours again in every way. I love you, Evie. I'll give your mom a hug, and we'll look forward to seeing you again someday. But take your time. This life of yours is nothing to be rushed. Live it. Love without regret. But please ... please ... forgive.*
>
> *Forever your favorite lesbian lover, Lila <3*

My body shook violently as I muffled my sobs with

my hand over my mouth. I let Graham into my life, and he destroyed *everything.*

Blank pages followed her final entry to me. Until … the very end. On the last two pages there was a list: Reasons for Bruises.

"Oh my god …" I cried more, blurring her long list of … lies. All the things she told people to explain her bruises. Some of them were crossed off, like tripping and dislocating her shoulder and fracturing her wrist. A tennis ball breaking her nose. A bookend falling on her face. Self-defense class injuries. *Leukemia …*

Before I could deal with my grief and sort it from my anger, Graham knocked on the door. "Are you okay? I thought I heard you yell just a minute ago."

I stood, fueled by pure rage. When I opened the door, Graham didn't get one word out before I smacked his face so hard I felt the burn clear up to my shoulder.

"What the fuck, Evelyn?" He covered his cheek as I stormed past him, hugging the journal to my chest.

He deserved to be arrested. To go to prison. I couldn't let him get away with it.

"Stop! Where are you going?" He chased me down the hallway and grabbed my arm, spinning me back around.

"LET GO OF ME!" I screamed, hoping his security people outside would hear me.

Graham instantly released me and held up his hand, confusion lining his forehead. "Okay. Okay. Just tell me what I did?"

"You killed Ronin! You murdered Lila! You killed

your own child! You raped her and beat her, you SICK FUCK!" I cried even through my anger.

"That's not what happened." He shook his head. "Ronin fucked her in my library. I can show you the tape. Then you'll know. We married the wrong people, Evelyn. It's you … it's always been you."

I started to speak, but I couldn't. When I turned to go down the stairs, to call the police, he grabbed my shoulders and forced me back around.

"Let me go!" I wriggled.

He tightened his grip. "Please calm down. I would never hurt you. I love you. I've always loved you. Don't you remember all the things I did for you? I sent you flowers and wrote you poems. I bought you everything. I saved your family. You owe me something, Evelyn." Anger escalated the emotion in his words. What started as a desperate plea ended in a very threatening tone.

I shoved him as hard as I could, dropping the journal to the ground. He came at me again. "You *will* love me." He narrowed his eyes—eyes so dark and unrecognizable.

I jumped to the side, but he fell forward, tripping on the journal or maybe the edge of the runner rug. Before I knew what was happening, he tumbled down the marble stairs. All the way to the bottom.

Not a word escaped my mouth. I didn't move for several seconds. My gaze stayed affixed to his limp body on the floor at the bottom of the stairs. A slow pool of blood oozed along the tile around his head.

No tears. Not for Graham.

No rushing to call 9-1-1. Not for Graham.

One breath.

Two breaths.

Three breaths.

Me. It was just my breath. Not his. Not Lila's. Not Ronin's.

Four friends, two lovers, one unimaginable tragedy.

I picked up the journal and smoothed the pages that were wrinkled. Then I hugged it to me and descended that long, hard, rigid staircase, being careful to not trip and fall. At the bottom, I stared at Graham's eyes—fixed, vacant, dead.

"You should have loved Lila more." I made my way to my purse that I'd dropped at the front door, and I called 9-1-1. "There's been an accident."

Completely numb from my heart's reluctance to keep beating, I waited for the police and ambulance to arrive. They carried Governor Graham Porter's body out in a black bag as an early morning media frenzy ensued around sunrise.

His parents.

Security.

People who worked close to him.

The house swarmed with people in shock, trying to figure out what happened. The location of his wife and my involvement. I gave my statement. Then I handed over the journal, knowing some very personal things about me and Ronin were in those pages. My only two requests: they find Lila (her body I feared) and they return the journal to me.

Too exhausted to drive home, I crossed town to my

parents' old house. The furnace had been turned way down, so I grabbed an extra blanket and slipped into their old bed, still unmade from my dad packing his single bag and moving to San Francisco. I chose my mom's side of the bed, closing my eyes and remembering the song she used to hum to me when I was a little girl—The Beatles "Blackbird." I hummed it softly until sleep found me.

Hours later, under sunny skies and improved roads, I drove to Aspen, taking note of buildings as I left Denver, their flags already at half-mast. The world knew.

I couldn't avoid my home forever. If there was a body in my kitchen, it had to be dealt with before I brought the kids home. Seeing him would haunt me for the rest of my life. But I had no other choice. Parking in the driveway, I climbed out of the vehicle and took slow steps toward the front door. Before I could open it, I forced myself to focus on Anya and Franz. They were always my grounding point, my source of courage, my truest reason for living. Whatever waited for me on the other side of the door—I could handle it.

My gloved hand reached for the doorknob. I held my breath as tears waited on standby, and my heart worked its way up my throat. My hand shook. My lips quivered, and my body began to fold in on itself as I fell to my knees. Pressing my hands and my cheek to the door, I cried. Everything was my fault. Lila marrying Graham. Lila on the mountain that fateful day. Ronin feeling like a failure as a husband. Me … it was all on me. And then I just left him with a bottle of whiskey in one hand and a gun in his other hand. Why did I leave my kids on

Thanksgiving if I wasn't going to save their dad?

"I'm sorry …" I whispered between sobs. "I'm s-so s-sorry …"

Ruff! Ruff, ruff, ruff!

Sucking in a quick breath, I slowly opened my eyes. I couldn't … fucking … move.

Not a blink.

Not a breath.

I wasn't even sure if I heard Mrs. Humphrey barking until she flew up the porch steps behind me and started licking my face.

Still, I couldn't move. Did he set her loose before I arrived the night before? Was she just now finding her way home?

Snow crunched behind me. Steps. Each one getting closer, louder. I turned one tiny inch at a time. Trudging his way through the snow, red jacket popping against the white background, black hat, and a stick in his hand was … my husband.

My living. Breathing. Husband.

A warm wave filled my chest, my skin tingled, and my eyes burned with tears, making my nose run as I gave Mrs. Humphrey a quick ruffle on her head. I tried to stand up, but I couldn't. On my knees I covered my whole face with my hands and sobbed.

When the footsteps stopped, I let my hands fall from my face as the tears continued.

"Lila's dead," Ronin whispered, standing at the bottom of the stairs.

I managed a single nod.

"I don't know how to make it—"

"I don't care." I shook my head over and over.

"Lila and I—"

"I don't care."

"Graham—"

"I don't care."

I really … didn't … care.

My heart had no room for grudges, no room for anger, no room for contempt. What would one give to have someone back … back from the dead? What would one give for that second chance?

Anything.

"You're alive," I whispered.

His gaze averted to his feet. Shame. Ronin felt shame. "It's unforgivable."

"You're alive," I whispered again.

"It's my fault."

"You're alive."

He shook his head repeatedly, face scrunched in pain. "I ruined us!" His gaze jerked up to meet mine. "It doesn't matter that I'm alive!"

"IT'S ALL THAT MATTERS!" That undying emotion, that sharp edge of reality brought me to my feet, to the bottom of the stairs, right in front of him with my hands framing his cold cheeks. A split second later, he blinked his red eyes, releasing so much grief as his hands covered mine. "It's … *all* that matters," I wrapped my arms around his neck, feeling his warm body, his heart beating, his breaths on my neck—*him.* I felt him.

WORDS … THEY were hard to find as we made our way into the house. We would be fine. I knew it. But I wasn't fine in that moment.

I was tired.

No … exhausted.

The bottle of whiskey and the empty glass remained on the table, but the gun was gone. I stared at the table.

Ronin grabbed the bottle and tossed it into the trash. Then he set the glass in the sink. I stared at the table.

He slipped off my coat. I stared at the table.

"Out back," he murmured while hanging up my coat.

I narrowed my eyes a bit but couldn't tear my gaze from the table.

"I wouldn't have done it in the house." He wrapped his arms around me, pressing his chest to my back.

When I didn't say anything, he kissed my cheek and released me along with a tiny sigh.

Again … I felt his guilt and his shame. I felt his fear that we would never get past this.

"Evie … please say something."

As Mrs. Humphrey settled onto the sofa, I turned around, leaving behind the images of Ronin at the kitchen table with a gun. There he was … in front of me, no gun, just … alive.

"I love you, Roe."

He lifted his gaze, disbelief etched into his face.

"Evelyn Alexander …" he took one step and wiped my cheeks, so much sadness still in his eyes. We lost our friends that day, and life would never be the same. "You're my favorite."

My smile grew, fighting its way past the grief. "Your favorite what?"

"Everything," he whispered, his voice breaking apart as he rested his forehead against mine.

My thumbs brushed along his tear-stained cheeks. My heart drummed, awakening those old butterflies that had been dormant in the pit of my stomach for way too long. "Are you going to kiss me?"

He grunted a tiny laugh, a sigh of relief as he smiled. "Probably."

EPILOGUE

Ronin

"I'M READY TO listen," I sat on the velvet pillow as Athelinda maneuvered her seemingly brittle self to sit on the pillow across from me. The same old nasty incense hung in the air.

Same tacky room.

Same creaky wood plank floors.

Same weathered book with the brown-stained cover and the words "I AM" on the front.

Different situation.

The day after my wife came back for me, they found Lila's body. She'd driven her car off a cliff. To anyone else, it looked like an accident on a treacherous snow-covered road. That was the story that made the papers.

The Porter family made the stories in Lila's journal disappear. Graham's death was ruled an accident. We stayed in Colorado long enough to bury our friends. Then we flew to San Francisco to get our babies.

Since San Francisco was only a twenty-minute drive to Berkeley, I felt the need to tie up some loose ends with my favorite parapsychologist.

"You're ready to listen or obey?" Athelinda grinned, showing me her gnarly smile. She hadn't aged a day since the last time I'd seen her. She still looked a century old.

"Obey." I returned a smile.

"Then that's easy. You don't need to see me if you understand the instructions. *Hinder not the soul's intended path unto the light … lest shards of darkness shed upon thee.* What's not to understand about that? Stop being a superhero. Boom! Problem solved."

"No catches? Caveats? Footnotes? Clauses? No giving the blood of my firstborn with two blackbirds wrapped in blue corn husks or anything like that?"

She laughed, but it turned into a cough. A cough she didn't cover up but rather spat in my face.

I cringed, using my sleeve to wipe the spittle.

"Don't bring back the dead, and God will be pleased with you."

"Why did my heart stop? When Lila coded a second time, my heart stopped."

"Yikes!" She cringed.

"Yikes? Your answer to why my heart stopped is yikes? I'm paying you for *yikes*?"

She thumbed through her book and scribbled an illegible note on one of the pages. "I'll look into this. I'll have to consult with …"

"God?" My eyebrows slid up my forehead.

"The Keeper."

"When do you talk to the Keeper?"

She shrugged. "When I die. My list of clarifications—

questions—is getting so long I fear my earthly heart won't restart if I dillydally too long." She tapped her pointy fingernail on her notes. "But this feels like an important one to clarify. My best guess is you were too close to this person. It's really a miracle you're still alive after she took her own life."

I nodded several times, not mentioning the gun and my intentions. "Find boring and embrace it if you like your life. Okay?"

"And if I die again, stay dead. Right?"

The woman of many lives gave me a wry grin. "Yes. A wise man would do that."

"You're not wise?"

She pulled her hair over her shoulder and began braiding it. "No. I'm weathered. You're showing wisdom."

I thought I preferred bravery. I thought I could prove to the world, to whatever god reigned over me, that I was worthy to decide who lived and who died. Maybe I even felt a bit of immortality having died and come back to life.

My time with Lila taught me just how fragile our existence was in the universe. I still didn't understand why my peers could save lives and not suffer consequences. Perhaps God was testing me. I failed that test ... or almost failed it. After all, had Evelyn not unexpectedly shown up Thanksgiving night, I would have taken that gun out back by the woodpile and pulled the trigger— given my life as a sacrifice for disobeying God, for letting Lila die, for hurting Evelyn deeply.

I stopped counting how many times she saved *my* life, but I realized my true indebtedness belonged to her. Every day I would live and love her and our perfectly imperfect life. I'd hang up my red ski patrol jacket and find a job where lives weren't in danger. What? I had no idea. And it didn't matter. We'd figure it out together.

Evelyn

Eight months later …

LOSING MY BEST friends and my mom in the same year nearly crippled me. It taught me the fragility of life. I learned I couldn't exist in this life by holding on to the past.

There were so many things in Lila's journal that I wanted to discuss with Ronin. Did he know she was being abused? Did he know her cancer wasn't real? Why did he keep it from me? What exactly happened in their moment of intimacy?

However, in the days we stayed in Denver after Thanksgiving, preparing to say goodbye to our friends, I never asked him those questions. Lila begged me to forgive him, so I imagined the worst. I imagined that he knew everything and that he kept it from me. Then I imagined the reasons for not telling me. I knew they were, at their core, born of love.

Ronin loved me.

And if I loved him, truly, in a million alternate universes loved him, then I would forgive him without demanding accountability and without apology.

I chose love. Always love.

"We're doing this." I grinned, breathless with excitement as we handed the keys to our house over to a realtor, the same realtor who sold the building where I had Clean Art. The money from those sales gave us a new freedom to go anywhere and start over. At first we considered Vancouver, but the memories of Lila and Graham were too raw to go there.

We chose Chamonix, France where Ronin grew up. A new beginning. I hated leaving my dad, Katie, and my niece, Ansley Madeline (not Porter) Reynolds, but they not only understood, they encouraged our relocation. My loyal intern, Soapy Sophie and her mom, Nanny Sue, inherited Clean Art—and they agreed to keep the generous ski patrol discount.

"We're doing this." Ronin wrapped his arms around me from behind and rested his chin on my shoulder as we took one last mental picture of our first home. I shed a few tears. It held so many memories of my life, even before Ronin.

"Daddy!" Franz yelled from the car with his typical impatience. "Let's go!" Mrs. Humphrey barked in agreement.

I turned in Ronin's arms. He wiped my face and smiled, knowing they were happy tears.

"Three lives."

He cocked his head, eyes narrowed.

I grinned. "You have my permission to save three lives

from this day forward. Your wife and your two children. You may *hinder our soul's intended path unto the light.*"

Ronin kissed my forehead. "Yes, because without you, *shards of darkness would shed upon thee*—me." He interlaced his fingers with mine and led me to the car. "But really, babe, you should have said four lives. Poor Mrs. Humphrey."

The End

If you enjoyed this story, please consider leaving a review. Thank you!

Check out an excerpt from Jewel E. Ann's bestseller, Transcend!

CHAPTER ONE

NEVAEH. IT'S HEAVEN spelled backwards and the name of the girl to my right with her finger five stories up her nose. I grimace while readjusting in my chair. It has nothing to do with her disgusting habit. One of the wings to my pad is stuck to my pubic hair. Mom worries about tampons and toxic shock syndrome. It can't be more painful than this.

The receptionist keeps glancing at us through her owlish glasses, tapping the end of her pen on her chin. "Nevaeh, do you need a tissue?" she asks.

My parents are not the weirdest parents in the world after all. Lucky me.

Roy.

Doris.

Cherish.

Wayne.

With over ten thousand baby names in the average name book, how does one settle on such horrible names?

Backwards Heaven glances over at me as if I have the answer to the receptionist's question. I'm not the tip of her finger. How am I supposed to know what it feels like up there? After inspecting her size—smaller than me—and her yellow hair in a hundred different lengths that looks like something my mom calls a DIY, I give the receptionist a small nod.

Without moving her finger, because it might be stuck, Nevaeh mimics my nod. The receptionist holds out a box of tissues. They both stare at me. When did I get put on booger duty?

"Swayze, do you need to go potty before we leave?" Mom asks, coming out of the office where I took my tests.

Swayze. That's me. Worst name ever—until five minutes ago when Nevaeh introduced herself and offered me a gluten-free, peanut-free, dairy-free, sugar-free, taste-free snack from her BPA-free backpack. My uncle thinks the millennials are going to ruin the world because they have no common sense, and all of their knowledge comes from the internet. He may be right, only time will tell, but then what's my parents' excuse? Or Nevaeh's parents' excuse? Common sense says you give your child a good solid name. Kids don't want to be unique. It's true. We just want to fit in.

I grab the box of tissues and toss it on my empty chair, turning before Nevaeh's finger slides out. Some things I don't need to know, like why it smells like cherry vomit in the waiting room, why there is a water dispenser but no cups, and what's up Nevaeh's right nostril.

"Restroom," I mumble, tracing the toe of my shoe over the red and white geometric patterns of the carpet.

"We can't hear you when you talk to your feet, Swayze," Dad says like he's said it a million times. Maybe he has.

I lift my head up. "No, I don't need to use the *restroom!* Or *potty*. Do I still look four to you?"

His blue eyes, which match mine, ping-pong around the room before landing on me. "Shh … you don't need to be so loud." He smooths his hand over the top of his mostly bald head, like I ruffled his feathers, what few he has left.

"Let's just go, dear." My mom reaches for my hand.

I jerk away.

"Swayze."

As if giving me such a stupid name wasn't enough, she has to draw it out. "Swaaayzee." Who wants a name that rhymes with lazy and crazy?

"Well, you said you can't hear me when I talk to my feet. Can you hear me now?!"

They hear me. The guy who tested me peeks his head out the door, squinting at me. He hears me too. I can't find my inside voice. Something has tripped my volume and it's stuck on playground voice.

"Potty is what toddlers do. I'm not a toddler! I'm eleven. And I know stuff that other eleven-year-olds don't know. So what? That doesn't mean something is wrong with me. You keep bringing me to places like this to take stupid tests and sit in stinky waiting rooms with weird kids who have crazy names and like to chant unsolvable riddles, pull their hair, and pick their noses!"

Balling my hands, I resist the rare urge to pull my own hair. My parents each take one of my arms and drag me out of the office. Just before we reach the door, I give Nevaeh a small grimace of apology. She slides her finger back into her nose.

"Am I a genius yet?" I ask in a much calmer voice as my parents rush me to the elevator and down fifteen stories like someone's trying to kill the president. Next to our blue hybrid car is a red convertible. Maybe it belongs to Nevaeh's parents. Then again, that car is a little too cool for people who would name their child Heaven backwards. Heaven in the opposite direction ... wouldn't that be Hell?

After checking my seatbelt, as if an eleven-year-old can't be trusted to listen for the click and give it a tug, my dad glares at me, jaw clenched. He's too mad to talk. That's fine. I'll know when he's ready to talk; his first demand will be an explanation. There really isn't anything more I can say. My words, although louder than necessary, were self-explanatory.

After long minutes of some self-imposed timeout on himself, my dad looks at my mom and nods.

"Swayze?" She glances over her shoulder at me, curling her dark hair behind her ear. I don't detect any anger in her voice. It's sweet and juicy like the Starburst candy I get at the movies.

I fear her words will feel like the cavities I get from eating too much sugar.

"How would you feel about trying a new school?"

Yep. She's drilling without numbing anything first. I've attended four different schools. Every educational psychologist and child development expert in a fifty-mile radius has evaluated me. They figured out I'm gifted, but not in a typical way. Smart. But not necessarily a genius.

My random recollections of historical events, that are

not at all noteworthy, are most puzzling. I'm not playing Chopin or speaking fluent Spanish. I enjoy talking with adults, but I fit in just fine with my peers as well. I can't name that many famous war generals. Even naming the presidents in order is a challenge. But random things that happened in Madison, Wisconsin, a few years before I was born seems to be my specialty.

"Move? Again?" I sigh as we pass the UW-Madison Arboretum, one of the places I like to go in the summer.

"We just want to find a good fit for you."

"I fit fine where I'm at."

"But they're not challenging you enough."

I shrug. "What does it matter? If I already know what they're telling me, then I don't have to do as much homework as my friends."

"It's wasted potential." Dad shoots me a quick look in the rearview mirror. He, too, has lost his fight over my outburst.

"Potential means—" Mom starts to explain.

"Possibilities, prospects, future success. I get it." I'm fairly certain other eleven-year-old kids in sixth grade have heard the word potential before. It's not exactly a word I'd see on my word of the day calendar.

"You know, Swayze, the Gibsons are sending Boomer to a private school only an hour from our house. If we send you there, you'd already have one friend."

Boomer. Another hideous name. Sounds like a Rott-weiler. Nice boy though. I like him, but not the way he likes me. At least I don't think so. He carries my backpack to the bus for me after school, but he also snaps my bra in class. The bra I don't need. My mom pressured me into getting one after several of my friends got them. I don't have breasts. Nope. Nothing there yet. Still, I wear it to feel like all of the other girls, and apparently Boomer's need to snap it during math every day means he likes me. At least that's the story my mom tries to sell.

Not buying it.

"I like my school." I twist my blond hair around my finger then slide it through my lips curled between my teeth.

Mom frowns. She has a thing about hair near the mouth. A hair in her food triggers her gag reflex to the point of vomiting, and then she can't eat that type of food for months. Dad always threatens to plant a hair in the ice cream she likes to sneak—his ice cream.

"You'll be in middle school next year. It's a good time for a change. The transition will be easier." Dad nods as if he only needs to convince himself and my mom.

"I like my friends."

"You'll make new friends," Mom says, shaking her head and scowling at the hair in my mouth.

I pull it out and flip it over my shoulder. "Why can't I just be normal and you be happy with that?"

"Swayze, if you just give this a try, I promise we won't ask you to switch schools again, even if it doesn't work out." Mom flinches like something's caught in her throat, probably bile from seeing hair in my mouth.

One last move. One last school. I'll do it. But I won't believe it's truly the last.

Read More

Acknowledgments

I'll start at the true beginning …

Thank you Jyl and Cleida for the best girls' getaway to Colorado where we plotted this fantastically complicated story.

Jenn Beach—keeper of my sanity—thank you for everything. It's hard to list all you do. We know you're the glue, and without glue there would be nothing holding me together most days.

YOU—my readers deserve a mountain of gratitude for willingly, or not so willingly, "going there" with me. You give my words so much purpose and continually make me a very happy author.

My amazing beta readers and editing team worked over the holidays—and quickly—to make it possible to publish these books two weeks apart. Leslie, Kambra, Maxann, Monique, Sian, Shauna, Shabby, Bethany, Sherri, and Amy … THANK YOU!

Instagrammers, bloggers, Jonesies—you killed it with this book! Ashely with Ashes & Vellichor, thank you for the beautiful trailers and graphics!

Kerry Ellis with Covered by Kerry, you nailed these covers. I can't wait to work with you on the rest of the books in this series. They are stunning!

Jenn, Sarah, and Shan with Social Butterfly PR, thank you for making things happen. I know I was a little high-maintenance with these books.

Paul with BB eBooks—as always, you're the best!

To Kate for Room 212. ;) Thank you for being my sounding board when my confidence crumbles.

Thank you to my favorite boys, Tim, Logan, Carter, and Asher. You are always my greatest love story.

Also by Jewel E. Ann

The Life Series
The Life That Mattered
The Life You Stole

Jack & Jill Series
End of Day
Middle of Knight
Dawn of Forever

Holding You Series
Holding You
Releasing Me

Transcend Series
Transcend
Epoch

Standalone Novels
Idle Bloom
Only Trick
Undeniably You
One
Scarlet Stone

When Life Happened
Look the Part
A Place Without You
Naked Love
Jersey Six
Perfectly Adequate

jeweleann.com

Receive a FREE book and stay informed of new releases, sales, and exclusive stories:
Monthly Mailing List
jeweleann.com/free-booksubscribe

About the Author

Jewel is a free-spirited romance junkie with a quirky sense of humor.

With 10 years of flossing lectures under her belt, she took early retirement from her dental hygiene career to stay home with her three awesome boys and manage the family business.

After her best friend of nearly 30 years suggested a few books from the Contemporary Romance genre, Jewel was hooked. Devouring two and three books a week but still craving more, she decided to practice sustainable reading, AKA writing.

When she's not donning her cape and saving the planet one tree at a time, she enjoys yoga with friends, good food with family, rock climbing with her kids, watching How I Met Your Mother reruns, and of course…heart-wrenching, tear-jerking, panty-scorching novels.